He dominated the little  laughing-eyed Robbie Bur other two, broadly built with short black hair, as black as her own, curling forward over his ears, and Barbara saw with surprise that the rest of it was tied back elegantly with a narrow ribbon.

She found herself at once repelled, yet attracted, by the lightness of his eyes, grey—even silver, glittering in that half-light now that the door of the Globe was shut again. As he stared up, a light flashed out from those strange eyes and seemed to pierce her, for all the world like a fork of silver lightning. Barbara shivered, and could not have told why she shivered, except that it was not from fear; more from a sort of challenge, a prick of excitement, as though she had been warned.

'Jack, Jack,' said his merry friend, his grin broadening. 'Are you struck dumb and incapable by wine or a bonnie face?'

The tall man was unsmiling as he turned to join his companions on their way along the High Street. But Barbara's ears were sharp enough to catch his retort.

'I'll have her yet, Robbie! Wait and see.'

Inga Dunbar was educated in Dumfriesshire, at the Academy and then at Edinburgh University and College of Education. She became a Head Teacher, living and working extensively throughout Scotland, from Edinburgh in the east to Ayrshire in the west, from Gretna in the south to the Shetland Isles in the far north. She now lives in Aberdeen. Upon her retirement in 1983 she turned to her life-long ambition—to write stories.

*The Rose of Redayre* is her first Masquerade Historical Romance.

# THE ROSE OF REDAYRE

## INGA DUNBAR

**MILLS & BOON LIMITED**
15–16 BROOK'S MEWS
LONDON W1A 1DR

Dedicated to the memory of Roy,
and for our daughter, Vhari.

*First published in Great Britain 1985
by Mills & Boon Limited*

© Inga Dunbar 1985

*Australian copyright 1985
Philippine copyright 1985
This edition 1985*

ISBN 0 263 75183 X

*Set in 10 on 10 pt Linotron Times
04–0985–72,700*

*Photoset by Rowland Phototypesetting Ltd
Bury St Edmunds, Suffolk
Made and printed in Great Britain by
Cox & Wyman Ltd, Reading*

# CHAPTER
ONE

SHE WOULD run away, Barbara Graham vowed passionately. It was not the first time the idea had crossed her mind, but it was the first time she could not dismiss it. Today was the worst day it had ever been, and something told her it would grow worse still before it was over.

Perhaps it was only the heat which was making her so edgy and nervous. But she knew very well it was not the heat. It was something far more intense even than that, to drive her into such a frenzy of revolt. She threw open the window of her stifling little room with a vicious thrust and gazed out over the Solway Firth in desperation.

Why did the sea never bring any good news, any adventure, such as a bold-eyed buccaneer to take her far away from all this? In her present mood she would go with him, and willingly—yes, even with a pirate. She would not have to love him, for it seemed that the feelings of a woman did not matter to a man. She would only have to obey his every command, as Mama had to obey Papa's.

But the blue waters of the Solway gave her no answer. They smiled at her calmly and emptily and mockingly. She found no salvation there, no pirate ship and no way of escape.

Barbara smiled back bitterly, and from out of nowhere a memory from her childhood flashed into her mind, a day when a very grand carriage had arrived at Starlochy. Uncle Robert and Aunt Elizabeth had come from Redayre, along with three of their children, to take them all to the Fair.

She could not recall where the Fair had been, but she

would never forget the merry-go-round, how she and her brother Sandy had climbed on to the painted wooden horses with their cousins and whirled round faster and faster in a ride that never seemed to stop.

How Jack had laughed! He was the oldest cousin, a tall boy with black hair, and his sister Margaret had clung on for dear life, the horse's mane clutched tight in her hand. And Sibylla—poor Sibylla, so small and so thin—said that she did not enjoy it. It was going so fast that everything was just a blur and she could not see.

When the merry-go-round slowed down and finally stopped, Barbara could not understand why the grown-ups were not out of breath, for in her infant mind she thought all the people had been running in the opposite direction. To her surprise, they had all been standing still. Nothing had changed. The fairground stalls were in the same places as before, and so were Mama and Papa, smiling and talking to her uncle and aunt.

Now it seemed to her that she was on a merry-go-round again, this time with wishes for horses. She could never find it in her heart to run away, anyway, and leave her mother to face the trouble at Starlochy Farm all by herself. She had thought about it over and over again, but always she came back full circle to the same answer. Nothing changed. Nothing ever would.

With a sigh, almost a sob, she flung away impatiently and sat down before her mirror with her head buried in her hands. She should be taking off her coarse sacking apron instead, brushing out her hair into its long black ringlets, and going down to the kitchen where Mama, the Mistress Grace, was waiting for her. But she was too dispirited to move.

The day was shining and hot, like each successive day that summer, with a high golden sun in a cloudless sky. In the long stone-flagged kitchen of Starlochy, the door set back on its hinges, the tiny window flung wide open in a desperate plea for the merest rush of air, the heat was suffocating.

Mistress Grace leaned her cheek against the cool stone wall beside the open window, wearied beyond measure, weary long past her thirty-nine years. The birds were astir again after their noonday silence, and noiseless butterflies danced and fluttered. Somewhere a drowsy bumble bee hummed in the warm air, winging its way up through the branches of trees thick with apple-blossom. A little breeze lifted a grey strand from her temple, a breeze salt-laden from the sea, and yet sweet from the shimmering hayfields between—and once again she was back in her dreams, back to her childhood, back at Redayre and the great sprawling house standing sentinel over the towering cliffs, their rumble of rocks below thrown so carelessly, so majestically, into the waters of the Bay.

There had been a night, with the round golden moon shrouded fitfully in racing clouds, when she had seized their cover to run away, to climb down the knotted ivy on the walls of the dreaming house, to fall into her lover's arms and ride away with him in a breathless elopement over hills and moors, following the curve of the Solway Moss, the ripples of the Firth black and glittering to the south.

She had been beautiful then. And young, and gay, and so much in love with the great powerful husk of a man, with his eyes as blue as the bluest summer sky, with the devils of merriment streaking out of them to turn her weak at the knees and set her heart on fire. But twenty years had passed—twenty years of endless toil on the farm, countless pregnancies mostly miscarried, strange fevers among their beasts and savage sicknesses in their crops to steal away her youth and trample her beauty into the grey earth—while he grew sullen, and his clear blue eyes red-veined with drinking too much brandy to drown his sorrows.

Brandy! The very word sent thrills of horror as hot as the spirit itself along her veins, so that she was roused from her reverie.

Startled and trembling already, although it was still only afternoon, she ran to the foot of the little half-stair at the other end of the kitchen and called up, 'Barbara! Barbie, are you coming?'

Her hands fretted amongst the billows of cloth on the white-scrubbed table, and she sank into a chair while she waited. Sandy, her first-born, had survived, cast in his father's mould. And then, barely a year later, came Barbara, who was the reincarnation of herself with her quicksilver ways, her clear-eyed courage and her fear of nobody and nothing.

Listening for Barbara's light foot on the staircase, Grace frowned and sighed, for she feared that anyone who tempted the devil as often as her daughter did could only inevitably land in trouble, one day. . . Why did she not come downstairs? Had anything happened to her?

'Barbara!' Her mother knocked softly on the door of the small bedchamber and came in to stand behind her. 'I have been calling you for the past five minutes.'

Barbara hastily choked back her tears, rubbing them off her cheeks with her roughened fingers, and swung round on the stool. Mama so rarely disturbed her in the privacy of this room. 'I am sorry, Mama. I did not hear you.'

'You have been crying, child. You cannot deny it, not to your own mother.' Mistress Grace took up the hair-brush as she spoke. 'And you still have not brushed out your hair. Turn round again to the mirror and I will do it.'

The long gentle strokes of the brush began to soothe her, even though now and again her mother found a tangle in the glossy black curls, and her nerves, already tense, jangled with the pain. But at last Mistress Grace was satisfied and began to curl the ringlets around the brush.

'The more you brush, the more the blue lights dance in your hair, my dear. You must remember always to take care of your hair. It is a woman's crowning glory.'

Barbara flinched at this reference to her new status of womanhood. That was part of the trouble. She did not want to be seventeen and of an age to be married, not after all she had seen and, worse still, understood more and more each day at Starlochy.

Mama seemed to know what she was thinking as

together they looked at their reflections in the mirror. For the first time Barbara saw for herself the startling resemblance, the same oval face, high forehead and wide-set eyes, her own brilliantly blue and Grace's soft grey beneath hair that had once been as black as her own.

'Even my nose is the same shape as yours, Mama.'

'Yes,' Mistress Grace said sadly, 'and that is only one thing to worry me. A gipsy told me once that a small tip-tilted nose denotes a sense of fun and adventure along with great determination. I followed my nose, Barbara. Make sure you have more sense.'

As they went downstairs, Barbara reflected that it was just like Mama not to pry into the reasons why she had been crying. She picked up the cloth and held it under her chin. 'How will it look, Mama? Is the colour too startling?'

Grace Graham smiled at her daughter affectionately and met the eyes of her lover in the pale oval of Barbara's face, a creamy canvas where each vivid expression chased the other, as one cloud had chased the last over that moon of long ago. But all she said was, 'Always choose this shade of blue, Barbie. It is exactly the same as your eyes.'

Was it only her imagination, part of this whole day's alarm and trepidation, that everything Mistress Grace said seemed to voice a premonition of parting? She was as gentle as ever, and yet they might have been back at their lessons again, when Mama never wasted a single minute of her daughter's schooling. Only, now, she seemed to want to teach her the lessons of life with the same urgency.

Barbara glanced down at the glowing sapphire wool her mother was pinning around her. On this soft afternoon in May it was so dreadfully hot and scratchy that it was making her itch and fidget uncontrollably when she would a thousand times rather have been as still as a statue for Mama.

Her mother made her two dresses every year, one for summer and one for winter. This was the winter dress she was starting now, and it was very important to get the correct fit, for it would take a long time to sew it all by hand. She made another tremendous effort to stand still, a pose quite foreign to her volatile nature.

And all the time, like a black thread running through her head, she knew it wasn't only the dress-fitting or even the irritation of the wool in the stuffy kitchen which made her so fretful. There was something in the air, in the wind, something hanging over the whole farm, a feeling of imminent evil so strong that she could reach out and touch it. Yet nobody spoke of it, and eyes avoided eyes, as if there were some great sin, some terrible depravity, they all knew they would share. Barbara shivered, trembling at the thought of it.

'Oh!' Mistress Grace jumped at the movement, wincing as one of the pins jumped out of the springy wool and pricked her finger.

'Mama!' Barbara grasped the thin hand, pressing the tiny spot of blood firmly under her handkerchief, concern flooding her heart. Her mother's hands used to be so white and soft, as graceful as two little butterflies.

'Can't you feel that something is going to happen, Mama? Can't you feel it?'

'No!' Her mother shook her head in violent denial, and as Barbara gazed down anxiously she detected a shadow of fear, an expression of dread in Mistress Grace's eyes, dulled now in her careworn face. 'We will not do any more today, dear.' Her mother's calm voice was betrayed by the agitated manner in which she got to her feet. One corner of her mouth was twitching pitifully. 'Take your bonnet, Barbara, and go and find some shade in the fresh air. Heaven knows there is little enough pleasure for a young girl in this Godforsaken place.'

So. Her mother felt it too, then, and this realisation of shared foreboding increased her tension, stretched out her nerves and senses until they were fine tuned like the strings on a violin. Barbara walked quickly over the grass to the shelter of the trees, and perched thoughtfully on the seat of the swing. It was then that the grim truth that she had been trying so hard all day to avoid burst upon her. *The Lingtowmen were coming*. She could almost smell them.

The very blades of grass, young and lush and green, quivered in sinister apprehension. Barbara's senses sharpened with every rhythmic movement to and fro in the creaking old swing. It had hung since childhood days from the great gnarled apple tree, the oldest in the orchard. Encased in their old, worn slippers, her toes trailed through the dust. Not so long ago they had dangled six inches off the ground.

They had been happy, in those days. Her father, a giant of a man, had played and sported with them as though they were a litter of young puppies. Her earliest memory was of being tossed up above his head and gazing down into those blue, blue eyes dancing up at her. Her mother had been pretty and dainty, and so much in love with him. The farm was filled with love and laughter in those days. But that was before Alexander Graham had taken up with the Lingtowmen. After that, everything had changed.

Now, even the dust she was kicking up seemed to quiver and twitch before it fell back uneasily. Barbara's small nose sniffed the delicate breeze from the southwest. Over and above it she sensed excitement and danger in the soft Solway air, and she felt the hairs rise on the back of her neck. She could not continue to live like this in terror of the unknown, she told herself. She would not.

This time she intended to find out the business at the farmhouse. Once again she would be packed off to bed early, to close her ears, her mouth, her eyes, and to sleep. But not this time, not Barbara Graham. She could not confide in Mama, it was out of the question. And as for Sandy—Barbara's brow darkened as she thought of her brother. She now hated him almost as much as she hated her father. Her swinging became faster, more agitated. Besides, he was in on it, too, this shadowy business with the Lingtowmen. Her last brush with

Sandy had been in the barn, a month ago, one warm evening.

Curious to find out what all the scuffling was about, she had climbed the ladder to the hayloft, up the rungs just far enough to peep over the hay. What she saw there made the blood rush to her head, and her heart hammer in her chest, as a cold sweat broke out all over her.

Her brother had young Jessie imprisoned, as was clear from her wide terrified eyes, which was all Barbara could see of her face. The rest was obscured by Sandy's red coarse hand clamped over the little scullery-maid's mouth. With the other he was attempting to push her wriggling, struggling little body back on the hay. It was too much.

'Sandy Graham!' she lashed out. 'Get down from there. The devil take you, Sandy, for a great bully!' The venom with which she delivered this had the effect of a pail of cold water over him. He turned his head, his mouth slack as if he had been boxed on the ear.

'Come down!' Barbara commanded, as he shambled to his feet. 'Jessie, we will go and speak to Mama about this,' and she grasped the girl's hand and fled before her brother could gather his wits again. 'Don't go near him again, Jessie,' she said when they were out of his ear-shot.

But she hadn't told Mama, after all. She was too frail and broken already to have another burden thrust upon her. So Barbara had said nothing, and confined herself to glaring furiously at Sandy at every opportunity, appalled at his increasingly coarse brutality. It had all begun gradually, with furtive little men coming about the farm, pedlars or gipsies, perhaps. They came from all directions, but nothing was sold, and nothing bought. They came with messages for her father, she was sure of that; for every time, a few nights afterwards, the smugglers came.

She would have shrugged her shoulders at smuggling alone. There had always been smugglers, their caves and bolt-holes like rabbit warrens along the Solway shore. It was not the smugglers who terrified her half so much as

the Lingtowmen, the desperate men, hard cruel murder-
ing men, the runners who beat through the desolate hills
to Edinburgh or Glasgow with the illicit goods. Her
father's downfall and Sandy's depravity had something
to do with the Lingtowmen, and tonight she was going to
find out exactly what that was.

The feeling of uneasiness persisted throughout their
evening meal of fresh bread and home made cheese, and
was reflected in the jerky, clumsy movements of their
mother's hands as she served them.

'What the devil do you think you're doing?' Alexander Graham was on his feet, his arm upraised as he
roared at his wife after one particularly convulsive
movement swept pitcher and milk crashing to the floor.

'And you, miss,' turning on Barbara, whose eyes had
shot an accusing glare at him, 'you're too sharp by half!
You're so sharp that you'll cut yourself one day!'

Sandy guffawed at this witticism, and thus mollified,
their father subsided on to his chair again, and the meal
continued, while the two men exchanged knowing
glances throughout. Barbara kept her eyes fixed on her
plate until it was over. Then, as soon as the chores were
done for the day, she went to bed.

Up in her room, she leaned out of the casement,
where the air was soft and warm, and away to the west
the sun flung great patterns across the sky. Now was the
time for going forth alone. Flinging her long dark
hooded cloak around her, she flitted out of the house
like a small shadow, down the creaking wooden steps
outside her window. Then over the cobbles and through
the midden mire, moving silently from hedge to hedge,
tree to tree and boulder to boulder, she crossed the fields
and climbed the Pink Hill. Here they had played as
children among the rosy sandstone outcrops which gave
the hill its name. There was no moon, and in the
gloaming she had to rely heavily on memory to find the
little natural staircases which led up to the curious
bowl-shaped top.

And here in the bowl was the tiny lochan by whose
shores Grace and Alexander had loved and laughed in

those early days of their marriage. Barbara knew the story well enough. How, if you looked in the middle of the loch on a clear night, the North Star was always reflected. And so her parents had named the farm 'Starlochy' in a romantic moment which had long ago withered and died.

She turned to look down on the house where she had been born and lived all her eighteen years. Well, almost eighteen years. In two months, in July it would be her birthday, a day she silently cursed. She would never get married, only to wither like a leaf, like Grace. Never!

But now her eyes were scanning the outhouses around the farm. All seemed to be quiet. Yet the prickling feeling was unremitting on the nape of her neck. She shivered, and drew her cloak closer round her as she turned to survey the foreshore and the quiet silver waters of the Solway beyond. A lapwing rose from the turf below and beat across the dunes, its mournful cry echoing in her heart. The small round tussocks of grass in the sands were green in the daytime. They had been the hiding-places and the stepping-stones in the playground of her childhood. But now the night confused her, for they seemed thicker and darker than she remembered, each one silver-circled in shining water. Soon waves would lap round them, like tiny licking tongues. The tide was coming in.

Then, from out of nowhere, a massive black shape moved swiftly over the flowing waters, the black shape of a lugger well down in the sea. It must be heavy laden, she thought, and waiting for the tide to get inshore—this ship from nowhere, from out of a nightmare. At the same time, many of the dark tussocks unfolded themselves and stood upright. So that was what her mind had registered, yet could not reconcile in the darkness. The tussocks had been the Lingtowmen, and they were moving out now, along the sands.

Whirling round, she was in time to see the strings of horses accompanied by shadowy figures converging on the farmyard barns. Filled with utter terror, she scrambled down the Pink Hill, and knowing that her life, and more, depended on it, crept back towards the house.

"Sandy! Sandy! God's teeth, boy, get out here!" It was an explosion of sound from the huge dark shape of her father outlined in a blast of light as the farmhouse door crashed open.

Barbara crouched back into a hawthorn bush, its hidden spurs piercing her clothes and finding her flesh. In agony, she dared not move one way or the other. If she tried to enter the house, she would only run into her brother. To her relief, her father was not going into the stable which faced the kitchen, but was making for the cowshed behind it. With an excruciating tug and an ominous tearing sound she freed herself. Foot by cautious foot she crossed the midden stones until she reached the haven of the stable and disappeared into the hayloft which lay above it and extended over the cowshed beyond.

She crawled into a corner by the central beam and buried herself in the warm pungent depths, hay tickling her face and her legs. So this was why the cows had all been driven back out to the fields, night upon night after milking. She peered down to see the cowshed full of small wiry ponies, herded in by the dark figures she had seen from the hill. When her father appeared in the doorway, those same figures rushed towards him, unwrapping their plaids, shouting and laughing.

Barbara saw with astonishment that they were women. And women of the commonest kind, to judge by their long matted hair and their bawdy comments. Her father seemed to revel in them, she saw with disgust, as the door burst open again to admit Sandy. The women went wild, dancing around them both and singing raucously. They had a leader, tall and gaunt with a blotched face and wild red hair, and she was the rowdiest of them all.

The sound of men's voices outside put a halt to it temporarily, as father and son flung wide the cowshed doors to admit twenty or so ruffianly-looking men, each burdened with kegs or bales on his back. These they deposited in the middle of the shed before setting off again, this time with the Starlochy men.

Left alone, the women, shouting and cursing, began to rope the bundles across the ponies' backs. Their fingers were strong and expert as they knotted the thick tow. Before long the men were back with another load, heavier even than before, and set about opening one of the kegs, while the women continued the roping.

Soon the job was done and every pony loaded up, evenly weighted on either side. Then the women, too, began to drink. Barbara could smell the brandy-fumes even in the depths of the hay.

'Which way do you take, Billy?' her father asked the leader.

'What business is that of yours, Alexander Graham?' countered the big fierce-looking man bedecked with coloured scarves.

'God's blood, ease yourself, man. I know where the gaugers are, if you want to jink them. You want to jink them, eh?' And Barbara's father threw the half-empty keg at the man. 'You want to dodge the excisemen?'

'Ay, do I. We go by Glen Trool and the Dalveen Pass to Edinburgh.'

'Well, look sharp about Kirkcowan then, you old fox.'

During this exchange Barbara heard rustlings in the hay not far away from her. She shut her eyes and crept further down into its depths. A moment later she thanked God she had done so. Feet walked over the hay on top of her, and she waited a long time before she cautiously poked out a peephole. The loft was filled with the Lingtowmen and their bawds, and the brandy-keg was passing from hand to hand amid roars of laughter.

Trembling with fear and shock, she crouched lower into the depths of her hiding-place. She must have slept, how long she did not know, before she became aware of the thick silence around her, broken only by stertorous breathing and heavy snores. She must get back to the house before the men did. Inch by inch she edged towards the ladder until she could descend it, her

bare feet making no sound. She stepped from the
bottom rung among the patient ponies, heavy-laden
and waiting.

They eyed her nervously as she stole like a wraith
between them, only the last one whinnying as she
pushed him towards the others to open the door wide
enough to allow her to escape. To her dismay, it disturbed all the others, and as she fled into the farmhouse
she could hear them clattering and neighing behind her
in the cowshed. The noise must have wakened the
drunken sleepers aloft, for her father's voice could be
heard roaring at the others.

'Get out of here, Billy Marshall, and take your tribe
with you,' he was shouting, still half-drunk. 'It's long
past midnight! You'll have to take the short cut up
Brandy Loaning. Do you want us all to be taken by the
excisemen?'

Barbara fell into the kitchen, her cloak covered in
hayseeds.

'God's mercy, child!' Her mother fell back at the sight
of her from her seat at the fireside. Barbara judged she
must have been sitting there, a small drab figure, silently
crying and praying all through this evening's work.
'Where have you been?' And then, not waiting for an
answer, and perhaps too frightened to hear it, 'Get
upstairs, Barbie, before they come back.'

Barbara did as she was told, and not a moment too
soon. Peering round the crook of the little wooden
staircase, she saw her father entering the kitchen, his
clothes askew and a brandy-keg in either hand. At the
sight of his wife, a string of oaths flowed from his lips,
and his face changed to a terrifying shade of purple.

Grace Graham cowered back, and Barbara saw with a
stab that cut her to her very bone how her once beautiful
mother, now shrivelled and grey-haired although she
was not yet forty, flung up her bony arms to protect her
head. Alexander lunged towards her and then seemed,
in the same second, to turn to stone. Barbara's eyes
widened in horror, and her mother peered out from her
up-raised arms, as the two kegs dropped heavily to the

ground and rolled backwards and forwards, backwards and forwards, before steadying themselves in the nightmare silence.

The massive frame of Alexander Graham writhed and twisted, and his eyes bulged as a curious sound, half choking, half rattling, came from his throat. And then, after a violent convulsion, he crashed face down on the flagged floor and lay still.

After a long moment of shocked silence, Barbara rushed back downstairs. 'Mama!' she cried.

'Hush, child,' Grace said quietly. 'Your Father is dead. Thank God for that. Now I have only one to contend with, and I'll make short work of him.' Barbara saw with astonishment how her mother's painfully thin back seemed to straighten as though a great load had been lifted from it, and her head lift as a look of patient triumph illuminated her face.

There was no sound in the kitchen until the door opened violently and Sandy stood swaying in its opening. One glance at the scene inside seemed to sober him fast.

'Your Father is dead,' Grace told him in such a tone of icy bitterness that Barbara could not believe her ears, or her eyes, as she watched her mother rise to her feet, all the dignity and command in the world seemingly centred in that small frame.

"He is gone, and now I want you gone, too. You must have thought this farm would come to you, or you would not have abused your mother and your sister so. Oh, yes,' and she held up her hand to stay his hot retort, 'I know all about it. That and everything else that has been happening here these past few years. But Starlochy is mine. It was always mine, gifted to me by my brother, Robert Jardine of Redayre, and in my name alone. Thank God for that. *You* could not manage it.' Her tone was of such utter contempt that Sandy seemed to wither before her.

'Look at you! You are a disgrace, a wastrel, a beautiful young man gone to Hell and the Devil.'

Barbara saw her brother with fresh eyes as he stood

there under the whiplash of his mother's words, his mouth slack, unable to believe what he was seeing and hearing. His magnificent frame was pure animal, she saw with dismay. Fair and ruddy like his father, he just missed good looks. Suddenly Barbara knew why. He was stupid: his small blue eyes, so very blue, so very bloodshot, lacked intelligence; his whole face was brutish and coarse.

'Go, now,' Grace continued. 'Go with the friends you have preferred to us. You can escape from the farm at last,' she added with obvious cunning, at which the small eyes lit up.

'You can go with the Lingtowmen. They are going to Edinburgh. But when you are gone, there will be changes here.' Her voice was ominous and threatening. 'So, remember, if you choose to leave now, you can never return.'

Without a word or a backward glance, Sandy crashed out of the farmhouse door, and the two women were left to contemplate the dead figure on the floor, the fate of the two small boys asleep upstairs, heirs now to the devastated farm of Starlochy, and a future which seemed full of uncertainties for them all.

It was a nightmare which was to last three more days and nights, while her father lay icy cold in the darkened parlour, his face gradually changing to the unmarked face of a young man, as though death erased those years of calamity and sin, those years that were cursed. As it was happening, her mother's face changed to a living mask, closed up, her thoughts hidden. In the night Barbara would wake to hear the dreadful sobbing from her chamber, but she did not rise and go to her. Intuitively she understood the tears that washed away the bitterness of these last years, and some instinct warned her not to intrude upon her mother's farewell to the young lover whose shell she never left during those days, the sweetheart she had run away with, so long ago.

Then on Saturday, out over the sea, what little wind there was must have veered easterly, to polish the hard bowl of the sky so shiny and blue. Barbara went to dress her small brothers in their dark suits and fasten the diminutive silver buckles on their black shoes. The children hailed her with delight, then subsided again, their looks timid and afraid.

'Where are we going, Barbie?' Jamie, the more hopeful of the two, asked her.

Barbara hugged him close, and with her other arm drew in Robbie, a replica of his twin, but smaller and thinner.

'We are going for a walk, darlings. We are all going, Mama too. To the church, to say goodbye to Papa.'

'I don't want to,' Robbie wailed immediately, his eyes filling with tears.

'We won't see him,' Barbara rushed to reassure him. 'He has gone to Heaven. But the minister must say prayers for Papa, and we must say them, too.'

Gently persuading, she brought the boys downstairs. Six fishermen from the Powfoot cottages carried the coffin, and behind them walked Grace, leaning heavily on the arm of James Aitken, the farm grieve. It was hot again in the sunshine as the little procession set off, and the road wound grey and dusty between the hedgerows, with here and there a round grass tussock between the cow-spattered ruts.

Barbara followed with the twins clinging close to her skirt, their faces hidden in its folds. She wondered that her mother had not sent for any of the menfolk from her own side of the family. Was it because they lived so far away, miles along the shore, in Galloway? Her mother's brother lived there, she knew—only he wasn't really her brother, but a distant kinsman whose family had adopted Grace, an orphaned infant. Her uncle had some daughters, and one son at least. and he was very rich. She was surprised that none of them had come.

Mistress Grace had been a Jardine before she ran away to marry beneath her, brought up in a fine house with many servants. She had been a lady then, and so beautiful with her black ringlets and wide grey eyes. Barbara could remember how beautiful, with the help of the miniature of her mother, delicately painted by some famous artist. But of course that was gone now, sold along with all the rest of her jewellery and valuables to keep them all in food, while Alexander drank any profits from the farm.

The six fishermen kept glancing sideways at each other, toiling along the road, hitching their heavy burden back up on their shoulders from time to time. When they arrived, they exchanged stealthy, secret glances with the minister at the church. Then Barbara understood. They were all in it—fishermen, the Lingtowmen, her father and brother, and even the minister. The whole district was corrupt, degraded. Some people said the ministers were the worst of all, because their stipend was so meagre, and one had been found out not far away with the casks of brandy under the very pulpit from which he was preaching the word of God.

Starlochy was a quiet place in the days that followed, chilly in spite of the sunny summer days, stunned with shock rather than grief. The days struggled wearily by until imperceptibly a different, lighter feeling began to take its place, a feeling tinged with expectancy and hope. The five-year-old twins were beginning to play without constantly looking over their shoulders. James Aitken began the uphill struggle to restore the farm, with the help of two newly hired men.

'You'll not be bothered again, ma'am,' was all he ever said to his mistress on the subject of the Lingtowmen. Peace was descending, at last.

Mistress Grace took down the invisible shutters, which had masked her face and her thoughts, as soon as a letter arrived at the farmhouse, and called her daughter to her side again.

'This is what we have all been waiting for, these past three weeks and more,' Barbara thought.

'You must know how depressed this farm has become in recent years, my dear, but at last I have here a letter with the seal of Redayre upon it. It will be in reply to my own, sent at the time of your Father's death.'

Her mother burst open the seal, and a paper fluttered to the ground. Barbara could tell, even upside down,

when she picked it up and handed it to her mother, that
the handwriting was both firm and flowing, and the
signature slanted upwards a little, with a flourish. It
seemed to her the mark of a young man, bold and
dashing, in those few seconds while she held it.

'Oh, but this is not my brother's hand!' Mistress Grace
said at once. 'What can this be?' She was faltering in a
voice broken with sobs before she had scarcely begun to
read it aloud.

Redayre, June 16th, 1792

To my Aunt Grace Jardine or Graham
Dear Madam,

I am only this day favoured with your long letter to
my father, and only half answered by him, which I
have found among his papers.

I am, Madam, deeply grieved to acquaint you of
very bad tidings, which with your own present sorrow
you will find it even harder to endure, that my father,
Sir Robert Jardine, Lord of Redayre, and my mother,
the Lady Elizabeth, having been thrown from their
carriage, were outright killed ten days since.

It was his wish that your daughter Barbara should
join his household, and it is my wish to carry out his
instructions. My sisters are also desirous that she
should present herself upon the Whitesands of
Dumfries on the afternoon of June 25th, where my
carriage will uplift her.

I remain, Madam, your respectful nephew,

John Jardine,<br/>Lord of Redayre

'Everything goes in threes,' Barbara was thinking,
'and there have been three deaths now.'

'Of course I shall not go,' she said. 'I cannot leave you,
dearest Mama.'

Mistress Grace dried her eyes, gasping and coughing.
'I'm afraid you must, my Barbara. We are far worse off
than I have ever told you, and near to bankrupt. For the

sakes of Jamie and Robbie this farm must be revived. It is their proper inheritance. And indeed I could not even contemplate such an undertaking had I not such an excellent grieve.' She straightened her thin back. 'No, dear, you will go to Redayre, to my old home, and to a better life than I can ever give you.'

She had not supposed her mother could prove so stubborn and determined, but there was a steely glint about her grey eyes for the next few days which brooked no further argument.

'It need not be for ever, Barbara. But at least you must go and try. There is Jardine blood in your veins, too, remember. You are your mother's daughter,' she said with a haughtiness which was all the more surprising in the way it flashed between them, like a blade of steel. It was as if her mother were back at Redayre, and one of its great ladies again.

Barbara could see that there was no way out of it. There could be none, for everything Mistress Grace had said was reasonable, logical, and could not have been arrived at without a great deal of heart-searching. She studied her mother's face anxiously, and the pain she saw in it ended the argument. She never wanted to see that pinched, haunted look there again.

'Well, then, Mama, you must tell me all about it. Who shall I meet at Redayre?''

'Whom, dear,' Mistress Grace said gently. 'Well, there's John—Sir John now, of course—the head of the house. You must try not to offend him, Barbara. He will be responsible for you.'

'What is he like, this Sir John?'

'Not the sort to stand any nonsense, as you can see from his letter.'

'Who else?' Barbara cast around, determined to find a brighter spot on her horizon than Sir John, who must be Jack, the tall dark boy who had laughed on the merry-go-round so many years ago.

'You have seen them all before, although I could hardly expect you to remember. You were only four when they came one day and we all went to the Fair.

That was the first day of their holiday with us.'

'But I do remember! Little bits of it, at least.'

'Do you remember Margaret, then? She is the youngest at Redayre now, of course.' A sadness flitted over Mistress Grace's face. 'She is a superb housewife already, although she is not much older than you. She was taught by her mother, and you could learn a lot from her.'

Learn about cooking and polishes and receipts? Barbara looked doubtful.

'And then there is Sibylla, dear Sibylla. Only a year older than Margaret, but her eyesight has become so poor recently that she has taken to wearing spectacles.'

'But many short-sighted people wear them! I do not mind about the spectacles.'

'Nobody does, for she is very pretty, and what is more important, she is as kind as she is pretty. It was Sibylla who chose the story-books for you from her father's library when he was sending the others, so that I could teach you your lessons.'

There had never been a tutor at Starlochy; Mama could not have afforded one. Instead she had done her best to teach her children herself, remembering her own schooling from her days at Redayre. When one box of books had arrived at Starlochy, Mistress Grace always had the last one ready to go back with the same courier. And oh, the excitement, when the new books came! Barbara loved every word and every picture in them. There was always one novel in the box, books about times long ago, and places far away, and books about plants and wild animals, even about animals in the jungle, which she would never, ever see.

They had opened her eyes to the world of butterflies, their names and their exquisite colourings. Otherwise she could never have rushed in one day excitedly and told Mama, 'I have seen her! The Painted Lady!' It was such a flamboyant little fluttering creature, with its orange-red wings dotted with black and white spots! It was just so sad that such gorgeous living creatures lasted for so brief a spell on the summer breeze.

It was such a pity that Sandy had never learned about the butterflies, or about anything out of the books. Barbara doubted if he could read, even yet, or write anything else except his own name.

She sighed as she gathered together her small mementoes of home to take away with her, and prepared her few garments. There did not seem much, when they were all spread out on top of her bed, ready to pack. Only her gowns, her petticoats, a nightgown to change with and her tortoiseshell brush and comb which really belonged to Mama. She washed and dried them scrupulously, and came back to her bedchamber to check her cupboards for the last time. Tomorrow she must go, and the nearer it came, the heavier grew her heart.

It was only then that she discovered the thin little book, just a pamphlet, wedged in at the back of the top drawer of the chest. She had not been sufficiently thorough when she was supposed to be cleaning, she thought guiltily as she drew it out. She would have to confess.

'See what I have found, stuck tight in my drawer, Mama.'

'Oh, Barbara, if only you were not so careless! If only you did not rush about so! You are too quick, too impetuous, my dear. I see it is the first volume of *The Scots Musical Museum*. Have you read it?'

'Read it? Of course I have read it! There are so many of Robert Burns's love-songs in it, and I loved it so. Once I could understand the Scots tongue written down, that is. It is so hard to understand.'

'But you hear it all around you, Barbara, in the dialect.'

'It is still difficult,' Barbara said, skimming the pages, 'although it was my favourite book.'

'Well, you can take it back to Redayre with you. Sibylla will forgive you, I am sure, if you say you are truly sorry.'

'Yes, Mama.'

'You may even meet Robert Burns himself. He is a

great friend of Jack's—Sir John's—I believe. But . . .'
Mistress Grace hesitated delicately.

'But what, Mama?'

'I have met Robert Burns. He is a man no woman
could easily forget, no matter what her age. It is the eyes
. . . He has such glowing, merry, man's eyes. He has a
way of looking at you . . . I cannot explain what I mean.
But I have his likeness, which I have kept over the years
since I saw him. I will go and fetch it.'

In a few minutes she came back, dusting off the
picture and smiling. 'Do you see what I mean?'

'I could not fail to see,' Barbara said as she looked at
the handsome young man in the picture, into his ardent
and flirtatious eyes. 'But he is only a young man in this
likeness. How long is it since you got it?'

'Five years, perhaps. No, he is not yet thirty there.
Even now he can only be thirty-three at the most.'

> 'Robin was a rovin' Boy,
> Rantin' rovin', rantin' rovin';
> Robin was a rovin' Boy,
> Rantin' rovin' Robin.'

Barbara laughed. 'He wrote that about himself, didn't
he? I do see what you mean about his eyes. He has
roving eyes.'

But her mother did not smile. She said seriously, with
a warning in her voice, 'You are very pretty, Barbara.
Men will look at you, and in a strange way.'

Barbara had not met many men outside Starlochy, but
she knew what her mother was meaning. She remembered Sandy's hot eyes that day he was trying to push
poor Jessie down on the hay. She had seen the way he
sometimes looked at her, his own sister, although not for
the world would she have told Mama about it.

She understood that her mother was trying to warn
her of the dangers of the outside world, about men in
particular, but she was much too gentle and too refined
to speak about it openly.

'Robert Burns loves the lassies, my dear. It is his great

weakness. Or his greatness—who can tell? How else could he have the genius to pierce our hearts as he does in his love poems?'

'Yes, I understand that he must have been deeply in love to be able to write them. But the name of the lady he writes them to changes so often.'

'I met him shortly after he was married, at a function in Dumfries,' her mother replied a little primly. 'He married Jean Armour, the real love of his life. Her father did not approve of the marriage.'

'Why was that?'

'Well . . .' Mistress Grace hesitated, then rushed on. 'He was very poor at the time, for one thing. And there had been scandals . . . He started life as a ploughboy, and went on to be a farmer in Ayrshire. He told me at the function that his life had been very hard, with scarcely time to lift his head from the fields. One day when he did so, it was only as far as to see a little field-mouse. That was when he wrote his famous lines, "To a mouse".'

'Yes, I had noticed he writes about the fields and the hills, and all the creatures living there, including human beings; he writes very little about the sea. So he is a farmer still?'

'A failed farmer, I'm afraid, Barbara. He gave up his farm at Mossgiel, bankrupt.'

'And the scandals, which his father-in-law so disapproved of?'

Mistress Grace sighed. 'It grieves me to tell you, but about that same time, before they were married, Jean Armour gave birth to twins. In the Kirk he had to stand and receive his public humiliation for the sin of fornication. Do you understand what that means, child?'

'Not exactly, Mama.'

'Before I let you go, you must understand that it is a heinous crime in the eyes of the Kirk to love a man before you are married. It can lead to an illegitimate child.'

'You have explained to me how a child is born. And I know that one unfortunate enough to be born out of wedlock has a hard life, through no fault of its own.'

'Yes. This is the Church's way of seeing that it happens as rarely as possible in Scotland. You have never seen a public castigation of that sort in our own Kirk, for which I thank God. It is not pleasant.'

'Barbaric and cruel,' Barbara agreed, shuddering. She could imagine that it was very far from pleasant.

'Then,' her mother went on, 'Robbie Burns went to Edinburgh, where at last he was recognised, and after a Grand Tour of the Highlands, writing more poetry, he made enough money to buy another farm but it, too, failed. As far as I know he lives in Dumfries now, but for these past few years I have been so sadly out of touch.'

'I know, Mama.'

'But Sibylla or Jack will tell you more about him. They know him and his works much better than I do. Only be very careful; that is all I am trying to say to you, and do not give your heart too easily to any man.'

Barbara wound her arms around her mother's neck, and the tears sprang in her eyes. Poor Grace, in another way, had been so cruelly deceived in love.

'I love you, dearest Mama. I do not want to leave you in the morning. But I will not forget all that you have taught me. You can trust me, I promise.'

'God be with you, my darling,' Grace Graham said. 'And remember, when you are away, it need not be for ever. If you are dreadfully unhappy in your new home, you must let your Mama know, and I will send James Aitken to come and fetch you back. But I am sure you will find nothing but happiness in Redayre, that beautiful place, or I would never send you.'

And so, on a glorious morning in June, Barbara left Starlochy, riding out on Snowy behind James Aitken who led the way on the big black stallion which had been her father's. He had saddled Negro with a large pannier on either side containing her best clothes and her few belongings.

Once out of the farm gates, and down the same grey uneven road as they had last travelled for Alexander Graham's funeral, they rode through the village of Powfoot and past the churchyard where he lay buried.

Every Sunday since that sad day, Mama had led them out from Starlochy by the little path through the orchard. In that way they could enter the Kirk by the other door, the one furthest away from the graveyard. It was as though she did not want to look at Papa's grave. Perhaps it was too painful, or perhaps with him she wanted to bury the past. Whichever way it was, it was a bitter ending to the romance of Starlochy, Barbara reflected. There had been no fairy-tale ending there.

They rode on in silence past the row of fishermen's cottages, so low and so white, strung out round the bay in a perfect semicircle, and started up the rough track of the Brandy Loaning. It was well named, for many times in the dusk of evening she had watched barrels of contraband liquor rolled up here into some secret hiding-place known only to the local men. Once again she stared at the little houses on either side of the Brandy Loaning, and once again they stared back blankly, and gave her no clue.

The day was already turning hot under a high sun when she began the debate with herself she wished she had had with her mother before she left. Where did the fault lie? Was it because her mother and father were not of the same background, the same upbringing? She could not decide, and the only conclusion she came to was that if she herself ever married, which seemed unlikely, it could only be a marriage of two minds, as well as two bodies, otherwise there could be no happiness for her, let alone any freedom within it.

By midday they had travelled west to Bankend, keeping the waters of the Solway on their left. Barbara wore the riding-habit her mother had run away in, so many years ago, but it had been made for the winter, and was thick and hot.

'Oh, Mr Aitken, may we not remove our coats?' Barbara asked him, gazing down with dismay at her long dusty skirt.

'We will rest here at the Lochar Water,' he replied. 'You may remove your coat while we eat, but not your hat. Young ladies of breeding do not remove their hats,' he pronounced, spreading a checked kerchief containing slices of cold beef and buttered scones before them. Grateful of the cool respite in the shade of a tree, Barbara shook out her skirt and splashed her face in the stream.

'The water is pure,' Mr Aitken said. 'We can drink it.'

While they ate and rested, Barbara talked to him, asking his plans for the restoration of the farm, and listening intently as he answered. It would be slow, he said, and the going would be hard for at least five years. While he outlined how he intended to set about it, she was fascinated to listen to an expert who really knew his job, and best of all to hear of his clear intention to stay at Starlochy and support her mother. She felt immensely reassured. Mr Aitken's craggy face was kind and fatherly, and impulsively she laid her hand in his.

'Thank you for looking after my dear Mama,' she said gently.

'She deserves to be looked after,' James Aitken replied, looking straight into her eyes. 'Don't fret, child. I'll never leave her, or the bairns.'

The slow journey continued, the horses strung out one behind the other along the bridle-paths of the Lochar Moss under the blazing sun. Barbara's eyes were on James Aitken's black coat, immaculate and smoothly fitting over his broad back. It was strange that she had never before thought seriously about him. A widower, who had tended his late wife to the end, refusing all offers of help, he would have made a good father, she thought. And there was no doubt of his devotion to her mother.

Now the sun was well down in the sky in front of them, positioning itself in the place where it would set. As they climbed a steep hill, she felt the first cool breeze of the day.

'We will dismount here for a moment,' said Mr Aitken. 'We have reached Noblehill. Put on your coat, Miss Barbara, for soon we ride into Dumfries. There it is below.'

Stretched out before them lay the burgh of Dumfries,

with its fine red sandstone buildings, encircled by the winding River Nith. The road into the town was hilly, but after the last rise they went past St Michael's Kirk, which Mr Aitken pointed out to her, now that they were almost down at the riverside. Then he turned off and led her into the High Street, which seemed very imposing. All the houses in it were of the same red sandstone, tall and narrow, and close together, and the street between was littered with little heaps of dirt and refuse. Mr Aitken did not seem to be put out at this. He led the way, steering a path among it all for Barbara.

'Over there is my sister's house,' he pointed. 'That is where we will spend the rest of this day, and the night. She is expecting us. In fact, it is a great wonder to me that she is not out upon the road looking for us, for I warned her when we were likely to arrive.'

'It is a big house,' Barbara observed. 'Does she have a large family?'

'No, none at all. And she has lately been widowed. Even if she were to marry again, she could not have children now. She is ten years older than I am, you see.'

'So she lives there all by herself?'

'So much is the pity, as she will tell you, for she loves company, especially that of young people.'

By now Barbara was feeling very weary, stiff and sore, and very happy to hear that they would travel no more that day. Their horses clattered up to the door of the house Mr Aitken had pointed out, and at once it was opened and a lady came out to greet them.

'James! I have been out a hundred times to see if I could see you! How are you, dear brother?' Then, without waiting to find out, 'And this is Miss Barbara?'

'My sister, Mistress Flora Cowan, Barbara,' James Aitken laughed. 'I told you what to expect!'

'Come awa', my bairnie. You must be fair worn out,' Mistress Flora greeted her, enveloping her with plump motherly tenderness. 'I'll tak' you up the stair to your room, and you can have a wash and a wee tidy up while I mak' the supper.'

Barbara was only too glad to do her bidding. Changed into her cool sprigged white dress, with her hair brushed out with cold water, she began to recover. The bedroom she was in was as comfortable as a sitting-room, with a small grate and easy chairs before it. She wondered if it had once been the room where Mistress Flora and her husband had sat in those chairs and warmed their toes and talked before they went to bed.

There was a padded seat under the wide, squat window. She would have loved to sit and stare at the people going by, but now there was no time. From downstairs there came an appetising smell, and she could hear Mr Aitken's voice booming as he talked to his sister while she went to and fro.

She followed her nose and found that the supper was ready, and they were waiting for her. Mistress Flora had prepared a splendid meal of shrimp paste on strips of toasted bread, followed by broth—Scotch broth—and a leg of mutton. Barbara was surprised at how hungry she was. She even managed to eat the egg custard, which was as light as a feather.

But it was not long before the meal and the long day's ride in the fresh air began to take effect, and she begged to be excused to retire to her bedchamber. Tired or not, she could not resist crossing to the window, attracted by the noise and the bustle outside. It was soon evident where the noise was coming from, for directly opposite was a hostelry doing a roaring trade, and she saw by its sign that it was the Globe Inn.

As she watched, a dainty figure in her low-cut gown, her blue-black hair curling around her cheeks and tumbling over her shoulders, a strange couple were running past the light streaming out of the open door of the Globe as if they did not want to be seen. They scuttled away together, and she caught a glimpse of wild red hair spilling down the woman's back, and something flared and startled in her memory, tying her stomach into a knot of fear. She frowned down, trying to remember, and saw that the man tried to look taller than he was under the long dark cape, and that a wide-brimmed hat was pulled down over his head—almost as though he were in disguise, she thought—when her attention was diverted to a party of revellers leaving the Globe.

The first man out had his arm about a voluptuous young girl, so plump around her waist, in fact, that Barbara wondered at her being in such an establishment in so delicate a condition. She was fair-haired and well-shod, and dressed in pale green with a small lace square around her shoulders, the points tucked into her sash. The man's attention was so devoted to kissing her that Barbara felt free to absorb every detail of the scene. It came as a shock to recognise Robert Burns from the likeness Mama had shown her.

'Why must you tempt me so, Anna Park? And me a married man?' he groaned into the little pointed face turned up to his adoringly.

But he must have felt Barbara's close scrutiny, for he glanced up, and she met the almost physical impact of his large glowing brown eyes. No, this was not a man to stand on ceremony with the ladies, as Mama had tried to warn her, she thought, when his upward gaze attracted the others to do the same.

The girl, Anna, followed his gaze first with a ready smile. There was not more than eight feet of distance between Barbara and her, since they had halted right under her window, and she could see the clear blue of her friendly eyes, her dimpled cheeks and her fair curls peeping out from under her flat lace cap. Barbara smiled back warmly.

And now that she had recovered from the excitement of actually seeing the famous poet, she found to her acute embarrassment that his male companion, the third person, was appraising her as searchingly as she had been inspecting them. He dominated the little party, even the roguish laughing-eyed Robbie Burns, for he towered above the other two, broadly built with short black hair, as black as her own, curling forward over his ears, and she saw with surprise that the rest of it was tied back elegantly with a narrow ribbon.

He wore buff-coloured breeches tight to his legs under

the most beautiful leather knee-boots she had ever seen. His coat was darker, and the daringly short cream waistcoat was straight cut across, above his hips.

She found herself at once repelled, yet attracted, by the lightness of his eyes, grey—even silver, glittering in that half-light now that the door of the Globe was shut again. As he stared up, a light flashed out from those strange eyes and seemed to pierce her, for all the world like a fork of silver lightning. Barbara shivered, and could not have told why she shivered, except that it was not from fear; more from a sort of challenge, a prick of excitement, as though she had been warned.

'Jack, Jack,' said his merry friend, his grin broadening. 'Are you struck dumb and incapable by wine or a bonnie face?'

The tall man was unsmiling as he turned to join his companions on their way along the High Street. But Barbara's ears were sharp enough to catch his retort.

'I'll have her yet, Robbie! Wait and see.'

Cheeks aflame, Barbara withdrew and undressed in the dark, before she crawled into the big soft bed, and once the racing of her heart subsided, her eyes closed in spite of her desire to relive and unravel that past half-hour.

It was in the heart of the night, when once she almost woke, that the last one she would have bidden to share her dreams came back from her memory and into her consciousness. The woman with the long red hair who had come out of the Globe Inn with her mysterious companion was none other than the leader of the pack of gipsy women who went with the Lingtowmen.

# CHAPTER
# TWO

'Come awa', my lassie! It's past ten o'clock, and I've let you lie as long as I could,' Mistress Flora woke her next morning.

Barbara saw that it was another fine day.

'You've had a caller already,' her hostess went on. 'A man by the name of John Jardine, a proper gentleman he was, called to tell you to be on the Whitesands by one o'clock. My brother James will escort you to Mr Jardine's carriage. Just take your time, and dress bonny. We'll have a bite to eat when you're ready.'

Barbara stretched out, her muscles aching after the long ride of yesterday, and her first thought was for the young men of last night. Then, flinging back the bed-clothes, she told herself she'd seen enough of drink, and what fools it made of men.

'Forget them, Barbara Graham,' she scolded herself briskly as she dressed.

After breakfast, accompanied by Mr Aitken, she picked her way down the narrow Vennel until they came opposite the old bridge with its six arches, and with a leap of her heart she saw her horse, Snowy, already tied behind one of the carriages drawn up at the riverside.

When they got nearer, the coachman nodded to a tall dark man whose back was to them as he leaned over the parapet to watch the waters of the Nith dancing past. He turned to greet them, and Barbara found herself gazing up, this time, into the silver eyes she had found at once so attractive, and yet so disquieting, last night.

'Jack Jardine, cousin,' he announced himself.

She collected herself sufficiently to curtsy politely, and at the same time lowered her gaze, in the earnest hope that this manoeuvre would hide her burning cheeks.

By this time Mr Aitken had strapped her baskets to the back step of the carriage, and bustled forward to settle his charge safely into her seat. Then he stepped back with the look of a man who could admire his work, a job well done.

The coachman took up the reins, the horses' hooves clattered on the cobbles, and Jack Jardine sprang in beside her. Barbara put her hands on the open window of the coach, and looked down at Mr Aitken as if imploring him not to leave her to journey alone with this rather frightening man, cousin or no cousin.

'I wish you could come all the way with me, dear Mr Aitken,' she said. 'Thank you for looking after me so well. Give my love to Mama and the boys!' Then they were off.

As she waved farewell to James Aitken, standing there four-square and solid on the Whitesands, Barbara was overwhelmed with waves of homesickness and dread, uneasy with her travelling companion and very apprehensive of her new life ahead. She wondered if this was how a ship felt when the security of harbour was left behind. No vessel could feel more desolate than she did, not even if the wind thundered in the rigging and the sea washed her decks, on this beautiful soft day with Dumfries receding ever further behind them, and the coast road before them, leading to the unknown.

'And how am I to address a young lady who leans out of her window at night to watch the big bad world go by?'

His voice, filled with mockery, instantly replaced her melancholy with a guarded wariness, and remembering his words to his friend last night, brought another flush to her cheeks and struck terror to her heart.

'Barbara Graham, sir.' She tried to sound firm, although she was sure he would detect the quiver lurking at the back of her voice.

'It is an agreeable enough name,' he observed, 'and yet I believe I prefer the one your Mama calls you by. Barbie, isn't it?'

'When I am in her good books, it is true.'

'Ah, then you are not always so sedate as you appear now. I thought as much.'

'And on what do you base that conclusion, sir?'

'I am under no obligation to tell you,' he smiled coolly. 'But I have already observed your preoccupations of the night, and I see that by day you ride horses that are too spirited for a beautiful young lady, like the white one behind us. Why do you do it?'

'Oh, Snowy,' she replied, stung to recklessness. 'Because of his speed, of course. Because of the danger. Because I may fall off.'

His eyes narrowed. 'Spoken like a true Jardine, my dear. A lady of spirit. Or a lively little filly. But I prefer to regard you as a young and innocent rose, its petals just unfolding, and that is how I propose to keep you, in my care.'

A rose, indeed! Barbara glared at him.

'Well, very young, anyway,' he laughed. 'How old are you, Barbara Graham?' His face was turned sideways, and she studied his profile with covert interest. She could not deny the fascination exerted by his austere features, however much she deplored his remarks.

'Nearly eighteen, sir.'

'Call me Jack. And I will call you Barbie—when you are good!'

Barbara said nothing. In any case, there was nothing to say. He seemed to know a great deal about her already, and she wondered uneasily what her mother had written in the long letter to her uncle. She supposed that there was a great deal Mistress Grace could have said, while she studied the toes of her slippers and considered one of her more recent escapades, fat Mr Hogg, the old white bull, and . . .

'We are entering New Abbey,' Jack informed her, interrupting this unhappy train of thought.

Small cottages crowded along both sides of the narrow road, which turned suddenly in an acute bend to bring them face to face with a great crumbling red sandstone church, a very large church in Barbara's eyes. One wall left intact contained a perfect round window, petalled like a rose, and she realised that it must once have been a very beautiful building.

'They call it Sweetheart Abbey,' he said. 'Founded five centuries ago by Lady Devorgilla, who was so devoted to her husband that when he died she had his heart cut out, so that she could carry it around in an ivory casket. Then, when she herself died, she was buried with it, here.'

Barbara hesitated. 'That is very romantic,' she said, doubtfully.

'That is not what you really think.' He smiled accusingly into her eyes, and once again she was pierced by shining steel.

'No,' she agreed. 'I cannot believe that a man's spirit remains in his heart, or his liver, or any other organ, come to that. I only know I could not have my husband's body mutilated for such a whim. If I ever had a husband, that is to say.'

'Oh, you will have a husband, Barbie, never fear,' he said softly, with such a wealth of meaning that its implicit threat struck her coldly, with a little thrill of fear.

She crept back further into the blue leather upholstery of the carriage and stared out of the window. She was too outspoken—Mama had always said so. 'It will get you into terrible trouble one day,' she had warned. And now here she was with a total stranger in a swaying carriage, with the conversation somehow at a provocative turn.

But he wasn't a stranger, she reminded herself, although he wasn't a cousin either, strictly speaking. She was forced to admit, with a little shock, that he was now virtually her guardian, and she was far from sure that she liked the idea.

However, the long silence was not uncomfortable. He seemed entirely preoccupied with his own thoughts, as the miles of coastline passed slowly by, with glimpses of the sea through the thick trees bordering it. The coach rocked gently, rumbling along where in places the road narrowed unevenly. The scenery was entrancing, and she was almost sorry when the journey came to an end, with the carriage sweeping through a wide gateway, up a curving drive through ornamental parklands, and coming to a halt at the steps of a large sprawling house set in gardens where the shrubs and flowers glowed like jewels against velvet lawns.

'This is Redayre,' Jack said.

Barbara recollected her manners. 'Thank you for bringing me here, Sir John,' she said stiffly, as he jumped down and held out his hands to help her.

'Jack,' he corrected her, his grasp warm and firm.

'Very well, then—Jack.' She smiled up at him, and lifted her skirt a few inches to mount the steps.

It would be better to appear to agree with this man—in small things, of course.

A woman appeared in the doorway, tall and slim. Her eyes seemed enormous behind her eye-glasses, which made her softly curling eyelashes seem even thicker than they already were. 'Welcome home, darling,' she said.

'This is Sibylla,' Jack said in her ear.

But she didn't need to be told that, as she reached up to kiss Sibylla's cheeks. Mama had told her all about Sibylla, at least. How those lovely blue-grey eyes were so short-sighted as to be almost blind, and how everyone who knew her loved her for her gentle ways.

The coachman brought up Barbara's baskets and laid them on the step.

'I will show you directly to your bedchamber,' Sibylla said, and to a little serving-girl who appeared. 'Follow us, Nessie dear, with Miss Barbara's luggage.'

They walked on into the great panelled hall of the house, scented petals spilling from their vases onto the dark oak of the tables, and up a wide staircase lined with paintings, leading to the gallery above.

'Redayre is built in the shape of the letter E,' Sibylla explained, 'although the wings are short. You and I will occupy the west wing. Margaret likes to be in the main part of the house, over her beloved kitchens. Jack is in the centre too, of course. We keep the east wing for guests.

'But, Sibylla, is this not your own room?' Barbara

protested when she was ushered in to her bedchamber.
'It must be the largest room in this wing.'

One long narrow window looked southwards, directly
over Redayre Bay. On the wall at right-angles to it was
another window of similar size and shape, which looked
west along the coast.

'I prefer the view from the back of the house, into the
trees. I find them soothing, and I do not always care for
the sea. But come along, my dear, and let me show you
the other rooms so that you may get your bearings, and
then I must leave you to rest for a while. Travelling in the
coach is so tiring.'

Sibylla led her along the passage, opening the doors of
all the other rooms as she went. She had said the wings
were quite short, but Barbara became quickly confused,
noticing only that the rooms all seemed to be lit by small
skylights in the roof, and the passage itself was dim, even
on this afternoon in summer. Then, round a corner, they
came to a little archway, and Sibylla flung open one of
the low twin doors set under it.

'This is my sitting-room,' she said, and Barbara
gasped with pleasure at the cool, calm vista from the
windows, the soft greenness of the trees breaking the
harsh contours of the hills beyond. At each side of the
fireplace there were shelves of books, and more books
lay in piles by the warm chimney-seats, and a low fire
burned in the hearth. 'Just lately I have been feeling the
cold dreadfully. I keep having attacks of the shivers.'

Then Sibylla led her into the room next door, cool and
green, a bedroom with a gentle, wistful air. Barbara had
noticed before how rooms took on the characters of
those who lived in them.

'Now, dear,' Sibylla said, as they went back to the
front of the house, 'you should lie down for a little while.
I will come and fetch you when it is time to go down for
dinner.'

Left alone, Barbara felt too excited and too strange to
do anything of the sort. Only yesterday morning she had
left her own little bedchamber at Starlochy, with one
small window, the top half of the door which opened out

onto the outside staircase leading down to the midden mire. Yet it had never seemed inadequate, with her narrow little bed, her chest of drawers and the large wooden trunk where all her dresses were kept, folded up, and most of them outgrown.

Neither had the impression of the room Mistress Flora had given her last night in Dumfries left her. It had been larger, with a carpet on the floor and many chests and cupboards, and the wide window-seat she could have sat on for hours, looking down on the High Street, and never been bored. But even Mistress Flora's room was only a comfortable bedchamber, she realised, in comparison with this room in Redayre House. In her eyes it took on the proportions almost of a ballroom, with its shining floorboards scattered with carpets and rugs, and its four-poster bed, the like of which she had never seen before. She drew the heavy brocaded curtain, made of the same material as the casement curtains, forwards and backwards on its rings to see if it really worked, and then tied it up again with its loops. It was so very elegant.

There was not only one wardrobe, made of some wood so dark as to be almost black, and inlaid with narrow strips of mother-of-pearl, but two. The second, smaller one was fitted down one side with shelves and little drawers, labelled 'Hats', 'Gloves', 'Handkerchiefs', 'Ribbons'; and the graceful dressing-table angled between the two windows so that the light should always be reflected from its oval mirrors had a top drawer compartmented and lined with velvet—for jewellery, she supposed.

The area round the marble fireplace was furnished like part of a sitting-room, with its chaise-longue and padded chairs and little side-tables decorated with vases of flowers. Barbara could not decide if the room dwarfed her, or did it in some way add to her stature. She only knew she felt at home in it at once. It gave her the same impression as she had received as soon as she had stepped over the threshold of the front door of Redayre House, a benign and happy feeling, that it was a place of music, and yet there was no music playing.

She went to lean her elbows on the window-sill and stared out into the sunlit gold of the late afternoon, over the glittering sea, over the treetops' rustle, and over the parklands surrounding the house. She was so glad that Sibylla preferred the back of the house. Here it was bright and alive, and full of movement.

She watched as the carriage rumbled off round the corner of the house to the stables at the back, with Snowy still following obediently behind. Just as she was turning away, a whirl of darkest green caught her eye, the whirl of a man's cape, long and full, around a figure walking along to the steps of the front door at Jack's side. The man wore a wide-brimmed hat, unlike any hat she had seen before. The brim was so floppy! It could be pulled any way, up or down, although now it was straight and flat. There was a little jog in Barbara's memory, a tiny pricking. She had indeed seen *one* hat like that before, and quite recently, and a cape so long, like this one, that it swept the ground. It had not made the man inside appear any taller on that occasion either, although perhaps that was one of its purposes.

Was it one of the latest fashions for gentlemen, unlikely to be seen in a tiny backwater like Powfoot? Dumfries was the largest town she had ever been in. Yes, of course—*that* was where she had seen such a cape, worn by the companion of the red-haired woman as they had scuttled past the lights of the Globe Inn, only last night, the man with the strange flat hat, with its wide brim to hide his face from view. Here was the same man, she was sure of it.

She was even more interested in Jack's figure, how tall, how elegant by comparison, as the two men stepped side by side, a little apart. Barbara received a fleeting impression that some uneasiness walked between them, but Jack stood aside, immaculately polite, to allow the other man to climb the steps to the front door first, a sardonic smile playing about his lips. It was then that her cousin looked up, and round, and once again into Barbara's eyes.

She retreated hastily from the window, and heard a

little tap upon her door. When she went to open it, a girl
waited outside with her hands folded.

'Please, miss, I am Fanny, Miss Sibylla's maid. She
has sent me to help you.'

'Come in, then, Fanny,' Barbara said. 'I suppose I
should have unpacked my baskets by now. But, as you
see, I have not begun. I was looking out of the window,
and watching Sir John and a gentleman in a long cape
and a flat hat.'

'That was the minister, Miss Barbara,' Fanny sniffed,
with such disapproval that Barbara could not tell if it was
directed at her or the minister, and decided to change
the subject.

'Just put my things wherever you think best, Fanny,'
she said vaguely. 'I will watch, and talk to you at the
same time. What do you do here?'

'I look after Miss Sibylla, miss. Her eyesight is so
weak, and being a great scholar, she is also rather
forgetful at times, with her head stuffed full of poems
and such-like. She says to tell you that you may borrow
me until your own maid arrives.'

'My own maid? Am I to have a maid, then, Fanny? All
to myself?'

'Miss Sibylla has sent to the village for a girl, one who
is a seamstress as well. All the ladies in this house have a
maid.' Fanny eyed Barbara's meagre belongings
emptied now out of the second basket. 'Is this all, miss?'

'I'm afraid it is, Fanny,' Barbara said, 'I did not bring
much. There was not much to bring, you see.'

Fanny smiled back reassuringly. 'All that will change
here, Miss Barbara. Now I'll go and fetch some water,
and then you can wash and change your gown for
dinner.'

She was a good maid, Barbara decided, when half an
hour later Fanny was making short work of her tousled
ringlets, threading them up neatly with a white ribbon to
match her last year's dress of white muslin.

'Don't you worry, Miss Barbara. When the new girl
comes, I am to train her,' Fanny told her proudly while
her capable hands worked busily. 'I have young sisters of

my own, so I shall know how to deal with her. I'll see to it she looks after you properly. Now, don't you move—it's only a carriage arriving with guests.'

'Guests? For dinner?'

'In your honour, Miss Barbara.'

Feeling fresh, and a great deal more polished than usual after Fanny's ministrations, Barbara descended the staircase at Sibylla's side, taking her cousin's arm when she realised how difficult it was for her to see the edge of each tread, and so they entered the dining-room together. At once Barbara felt overpowered by its opulence, the dark richness of its panelled walls, and the long gleaming table set out in silver and fine glass. A little knot of people stood about the wide fireplace at the other end where an old lady was seated, each holding a glass of wine.

'Ah, here she is!' Jack detached himself and came forward to meet them, as though they had been speaking about her. 'Mistress Marchbanks, and Squire George Marchbanks, allow me to present our young cousin to you, Miss Barbara Graham.'

Dressed so plainly in her shabby white gown, Barbara felt awkward, no longer an elegant young lady, but a child, put in her place like a child by Jack Jardine. But Mistress Marchbanks was smiling kindly at her, when she raised her head from her curtsy.

'A sweet child,' she observed. 'How old are you, Barbara, my dear?'

'Nearly eighteen, ma'am,' Barbara replied, curtsying in turn to the Squire.

'Eighteen, and going to be a beauty, if I am any judge,' said the old man admiringly. 'You're going to break a few hearts before long, I'll warrant. What d'you say, eh?' and he dug Jack in the ribs.

Jack smiled a little grimly. 'Indeed, I have promised her Mama, the Mistress Grace, that she will be every inch as much a lady as her mother. She has the looks and the breeding, certainly.'

'Just what I was thinking myself, damme!' the old man wheezed. 'A lovely little filly.'

'Really, George,' his wife reproached him. 'He thinks of nothing but horses, my dear,' she said to Barbara. 'But we knew your Mama, long ago. We must have a long chat, very soon.'

'Do you ride?' the Squire pursued.

'She does,' Jack cut in. 'A white gelding, full of spirit, at that. I should be obliged if you would allow her to ride on your flat parks, Squire. There are too many hills hereabouts.'

'Come eastwards then, dear child. I have the estate bordering Redayre,' the old Squire told her. 'You must come at any time.'

'And the Reverend Mr Faulks has also come to meet you, Barbara,' Jack said, and she found her hand in the grasp of a man with red-brown hair, and her eyes gazing into those of the minister, as green and as deep as mountain lochs.

'I am delighted to make your acquaintance, Miss Graham,' he said in his quiet voice.

How could she have thought his eyes to be green? For she saw now, as he turned his head towards the light, that they burned with a deeper glow, changing colour as the waters of a tarn, to brown and then to bronze, as if some animal within rose up to the surface, ready to leap out in all its strength and glory, to run and play with her.

'The family here have always been pleased to call me by my Christian name,' he went on softly, and even as he said it, Barbara felt some little current of rebuke directed at no one in particular. 'It is Browne.'

And very appropriate, Barbara thought, pulling a little as Jack took her arm and swept her past the minister.

'Ah,' he said, 'here is Margaret at last, your other cousin, my younger sister. She has been busy in the kitchen. It is her great delight.'

'Dear Barbara,' said the large plump girl, enveloping Barbara in a motherly embrace. 'Welcome to Redayre! You must tell me all your favourite dishes just as soon as you can.'

Jack grasped Barbara with one hand and Sibylla with

the other while they were all still laughing. 'Let us sit down,' he said, 'and find out what you have concocted for us this evening.'

Seated at Jack's left side, Barbara found herself diagonally opposite Mr Faulks, who sat further down the long table beside Margaret. He was not as old as she had at first supposed; in fact only about Jack's own age, she saw with some surprise. His thick-set figure and darkly ruddy complexion had made him seem ten years older, forty at least, at first glance.

'And do you think you will be happy at Redayre?' He smiled softly up the table at her, catching her eye.

'It's all a little strange as yet, sir,' she replied demurely.

'Oh come, Barbara!' Jack's voice was low and mocking in her ear. 'To anyone as inquisitive as you are, it will not be strange for long. I saw you up to your old tricks, hanging out of windows again.'

'How long I shall feel strange will depend on how I am to be treated,' she retorted. 'As a child, or as a woman.'

'And that will depend on how you deport yourself.' He smiled down at her, his eyes silver ice.

Barbara thought swiftly. 'It is true I have plenty of energy,' she said, 'but I suppose there are many interests to engage upon at Redayre?'

She felt rather pleased at the way she had worded this observation. It would force her cousin to define her status here, and what would be expected of her.

'Interests?' snorted Jack. 'What other interests occupy the female brain save dresses and new bonnets, may I ask? They seem to spend a deal of time sewing and stitching, and perhaps gathering a few flowers now and then in order even to paint them. Sibylla with her books, and Margaret with her recipes, are two exceptions to the rule.'

'You will find that I am another exception, greater even than they, for I am afraid that any such pastimes may be too gentle for me, sir. I prefer to walk my dogs, or ride my horse, or sail my boat. We always had a boat at Starlochy.'

'Yes. I had heard that you were something of a tomboy,' Jack said coolly, as the soup plates were cleared and the large oval platters for the roast beef were set before them. 'But that was when you were at Starlochy, when you were a child. But now you have come to live at Redayre, and I am going to change all that.'

'What do you mean?'

'I made one promise to the Mistress Grace, and another to Robert Burns, a friend of mine. I intend to keep them both, and that long within the year, Barbara. Vowed it, in fact.'

'And how is your dear Mama?' asked the Squire on her other side, overhearing her name. 'At your age she, too, was a great beauty, you know. Long black hair, I remember, and a waist so tiny a man's fingers could meet around it.'

'She is recovering, sir,' Barbara answered, turning to the old man in relief, while the hot flush on her face at Jack's words slowly cooled. Her cousin seemed to possess a perfect gift for making her feel like a shy and awkward child, tongue-tied with nervousness. She shivered with embarrassment.

'You are cold?' asked Mr Faulks with solicitude, smiling a smile of great sweetness, his small white teeth gleaming in the tan of his face. 'May I fetch you a wrap?'

What a very nice man he was, she thought, and answered politely, 'No, thank you, sir. It was only my blood running cold for an instant.'

'Well, one day soon, some lucky fellow will make it run hot, damned if he won't,' said the Squire, laughing. 'Begging your pardon, minister.'

'We must not stay long, dear,' Mistress Marchbanks said to Sibylla when the ladies withdrew to the sitting-room after the brandy was brought in to the table. 'Or else my poor George will soon be under the table altogether. He does not have the head for it nowadays. You must ride over and see us, child,' she added, turning to Barbara, 'although there are no young people in our house, I'm afraid. We were not blessed with children.

Still, there are plenty of friends for Barbara to make around here, are there not, my dears?'

The conversation turned to people of the district, and before long Mistress Marchbanks was calling for her cloak, and her husband, and their carriage. With their departure, the little dinner-party broke up and Mr Faulks took his departure soon after.

'I will see you in my congregation on Sunday?' he asked Barbara, bowing farewell.

'It will be a pleasure, sir,' she replied warmly, and as she went upstairs with Margaret and Sibylla, she looked forward to the end of her first week at Redayre, when she would see him again.

'What do you think of our minister?' Sibylla asked, on the first tread.

'Oh, so pleasant, and so kind and handsome. I felt how much I could trust him, immediately.'

By this time they had reached the little gallery, and some instinct made her turn round quickly and look behind her. Then she saw it was hardly an instinct, it was rather the splinters of ice in her back from Jack's glittering eyes which had caused the shiver up her spine. He was still standing in the hall watching them, and his mouth was set in a hard line before he turned away.

What on earth was wrong with him? Why was he so angry? Was it something she had done? She did not think so. Then was it something she had said? He had just heard the conversation between her and Sibylla. For the life of her she could not think of anything out of place, and as she went into her beautiful room she began to go over every word.

Long afterwards, when she looked out at the quiet moon over the Solway, the cold, lonely moon riding high over its silvery path reflected in the water below, the only answer she could find was that Jack perhaps did not like Mr Faulks. But that was ridiculous. Everyone respected the minister of any parish. Nevertheless, she did think that her introduction to him by Jack had been as brief as good manners decently allowed.

That night she went to bed more tired out by this

feeling of uneasiness than by the events of the whole day since she had left James Aitken on the Whitesands of Dumfries. She had so longed to make a good impression for Mama's sake, and she could not overcome her disappointment that in some way she had let her down—in Jack's eyes at least. She fell asleep, determined that from now on she would be very quiet, listen more, and say a great deal less.

Next morning, Fanny woke her out of an exhausted sleep and helped her to wash and dress. The whole procedure was calm, unruffled and soothing, and Barbara realised how easy it would be to fall into this new way of living. Already she felt cared for, pampered, even.

'Wash your own petticoats, Miss Barbara?' Fanny looked utterly scandalised. 'Of course you will not. I shall attend to all that, after I have taken you down to the dining-room. Not that there is anyone there,' she added.

It was true. The table was set, but the room was deserted.

'Where is everybody, Fanny?' Barbara was asking, when Margaret opened the door.

'I thought I heard you,' she said. 'Would you rather eat breakfast alone and in peace today, or come into the kitchen with me?'

'Oh, please, Margaret, let me come with you!'

'Jack has gone out already, and I have sent something up to Sibylla on a tray. What shall I take through for you? Eggs scrambled, or kedgeree, perhaps? I can recommend it.'

She was lifting the lids of the chafing dishes on the sideboard as she spoke, and the delicious smell of the kedgeree whetted Barbara's appetite.

'A little, then, please. But what is wrong with Sibylla? Is she ill?'

'Oh no,' Margaret replied on the way through to the kitchen. She waved Barbara into a chair at the table. 'This has been going on since the deaths of our dear Papa and Mama. Sibylla is just so tender-hearted. Of course, she will become ill if she cannot overcome it.'

Barbara had never tasted kedgeree before. 'This is very tasty, Margaret.'

'It is a new recipe I have discovered,' Margaret beamed, 'and so economical. We have plenty of fish here, and a family which specialises in smoking it. And the eggs are plentiful, of course, from the home farm. So there is just the rice to buy. Everyone seems to like it.'

Barbara continued her breakfast in the large homely kitchen. In some smaller one beyond she could hear Nessie and Jean, the two little maids she had seen yesterday, clattering about and talking to each other as they worked. But from the house itself there was no sound.

'You are very quiet here at Redayre, Margaret?'

'We have been, since the funerals. But Redayre was always so full of life, before.'

'What was it like then?'

'Well, Papa and Jack were always so busy about their business on the estate, constantly seeking new ways to develop it, to give the people work. Also they wished to encourage the fishing industry, and all that led to an endless amount of entertaining their friends and colleagues on the ventures. And Mama's interest in the children of the district led to the setting up of the first parish school here, which Sibylla was so interested in. Every afternoon Mama had ladies in the drawing-room in discussion about these matters. It led to a wide social life, and quite a lot of political work, too.'

'So your Papa and Jack took part in politics?'

'Indirectly. They supported the Hanovarian succession and the Whig supremacy, whereas most other landholders, especially to the north, are Tories, with Jacobite sympathies, even yet.'

'Will Jack pursue these interests, now that his Papa is dead?'

Margaret smiled. 'Jack and I are marking time just now, Barbara, waiting to see if Sibylla can manage to come back to this world again. Besides, I think Jack has some other problem on his mind, one that I know nothing about, so far. He is not usually so much away from home as he has been lately.'

Everything in the kitchen was spick and span, Barbara noticed, as she looked around. Margaret caught her look. 'Would you like to see round the kitchens?'

Leaving the table and the dishes to the maids, they began their leisurely tour, Margaret leading the way, full of enthusiasm. Barbara was shown the small cold kitchens, one for the meat and the fish, one for dairy products only, and one for the storage and preparation of the fruit and vegetables. Beyond that she saw the two washing sculleries, one for dishes and the other for linen, and then outside in the courtyard the huge spit along one side, and opposite the stables and barns.

'Ah, it is still only ten o'clock,' Margaret said with satisfaction, and they looked up as the clock above the stables rang out its ten tinny chimes. 'There is plenty of time to show you the store-cupboards.'

The shelves and presses in the pantries were neatly stacked with provisions of every sort, from pulses to dried herbs, all in neat rows, precisely labelled, and the shelves themselves were covered with scalloped muslin, with little tassels hanging down.

'Oh, it is all so neat, and clean, and beautiful,' Barbara sighed, thinking back to the half-bare cupboards of Starlochy, grim and austere by comparison.

'Then you must come and see the linen,' Margaret said, leading the way to a small room lined with cupboards which, when their fine oak doors were unlocked, revealed deep drawers and shelves, all lined with fine paper, enclosing the sheets and linens of Redayre embroidered with a little crest.

They arrived through a doorway in the great hall, with the little gallery above.

'My rooms are directly above,' Margaret said. 'It is very convenient, for I like to be up and about very early, and in that way I do not disturb the rest of the household.'

Barbara looked into her bright blue sparkling eyes and decided that she liked her very much, with her

cheerful manner and her kind ways. Nothing would be
too much trouble for Margaret.

'And will Sibylla come down soon?'

'Oh no, dear. She came down out of her rooms
yesterday only in your honour.'

'Then may I go and visit her?'

'She would like that very much, Barbara. Shall I take
you?'

'I know the way, Margaret. And thank you for your
lovely breakfast—and for being so kind.'

Barbara ran all the way to her own room first and took
up the pamphlet from the low table beside her bed. With
it in her hand, she knocked at Sibylla's sitting-room
door. To her great relief, there was an answer. Sibylla
was lying fully dressed on the long sofa before the fire,
looking tired and drawn. Barbara decided to entertain
her, to try to take her out of herself.

Half an hour later she believed she was succeeding.
Already Sibylla was sitting up, and chatting about the
books she so clearly adored. Barbara led the conversation first to this one, and then to that one, which Sibylla
had lent to Mama.

'Oh, I do enjoy talking to you, Sibylla! And some day
soon I hope you will tell me so much more, especially
about Robert Burns, for now I have a personal interest
in him. I saw him in Dumfries.'

'Oh, my dear!' Sibylla was now bolt upright on the
sofa. 'How interesting! When will you come back and
see me?'

Barbara looked away. She did not know quite how to
put what she knew she must say next. 'I will wait,
Sibylla,' she said gently, 'along with Jack and Margaret,
for you to come back downstairs and see us. Perhaps you
will come outdoors and show me Redayre some day. I
fear Jack and Margaret are too busy. Perhaps it will put
the roses back in your cheeks, as Mama used to say.'

Suddenly she felt her eyes fill with tears, to have
spoken about Mama like that, as if she were already
dead.

'You are lonely, Barbara, and a little homesick, I

think. Only I am still mourning, you see.' Sibylla sighed and looked down at her black dress. 'I cannot believe it, even yet. It is as if any day I may go and speak to Papa in the library, and I find myself so often with my hand on Mama's sitting-room door. None of us can understand how it ever happened at all, out of a clear blue sky.'

A clear blue sky. A bolt from the blue. The words whirled through Barbara's head as she wandered out to the stables. The morning was sultry and heavy, and there was an uneasy quivering in the blue of the sky as it deepened lividly almost above her head.

'Oh, Snowy,' she murmured, stroking her horse's velvet nose. 'How hot it is! Too hot for a gallop today. Would you like to come for a little stroll—up into the hills, perhaps, for some air?'

'As you have already observed, Barbara, it is too hot.'

Jack's head appeared above the next stall. She saw with surprise that he had been grooming his own horse, and was in his shirt-sleeves. It was the first time she had seen him without a jacket on, and with his shirt-buttons undone she was confronted by his bare chest, covered with thick dark hair. Added to the shock of that, his eyes appeared almost dark as he looked at her in that 'strange' way, as Mama would say. Barbara blushed uncontrollably.

'You are looking very cool and beautiful this morning, Barbara, in spite of the heat. I am surprised that your creamy skin can take on such a becoming flush.'

'Nevertheless, sir, I am very hot,' Barbara flashed at him, her good intentions blown to the winds. 'And I am surprised that you can stand there and smile at me this morning, after frowning at me so much when I went to bed last night.'

There; it was out! And she was glad it was out, after spending so much time in her bedchamber worrying about Jack Jardine and his frowns!

'But you lost no sleep over it, I can see.' He smiled maddeningly, and began to button up his shirt.

'I did not like it,' she glared at him.

'I was not frowning at you, Barbara. I was frowning at some very uncomfortable thoughts.'

'Did they include the minister?'

'Now, Barbara, what gave you that idea?'

'I do not think you like him.'

Jack's eyes hardened, and when he had put on his jacket again, he was once more the Lord of Redayre. That conversation, she could see, was at an end.

'I am riding over in the direction of Squire Marchbanks's house. It is all flat ground, and much more suitable as you say, "for a little stroll" than up in the hills. I shall accompany you.' His tone allowed no further argument.

Above all, Barbara detested riding side-saddle. At Starlochy she could kilt up her skirts and ride around the farm with perfect freedom. But now, in the company of Jack Jardine, she was forced to behave with decorum. Wondering rebelliously if this was forever to be her lot, she sighed gloomily as they walked their horses out along the drive and headed east.

'Come now,' Jack said, with a note of cheerful reasonableness in his voice. 'It's not so bad after all, is it? We are out in what fresh air there is, and you are on your way to make your first call in the district as one of the ladies of Redayre.'

Barbara smiled a little tremulously. To tell the truth, her head was aching a little in this oppressive heat. It would have been folly indeed to be scrambling up a hill, instead.

'Perhaps I should have told Sibylla or Margaret where I was going,' she said.

'Margaret knows. She saw us from the kitchen. She knows you are with me, that I would not allow you to go alone.'

'Allow me?' Barbara asked, bitterly.

'Yes, allow you,' he said, suddenly stern. 'You are in my charge, Barbara, and I am the master here. It would be as well to remember it.'

Snowy fidgeted uncomfortably, as though he sensed his mistress's discomfiture, diverting Barbara's attention from her companion. She looped the rein more firmly through her fingers and turned her horse about.

'And it would be as well to remember that it is a young lady and not a little girl you have in your charge, sir,' she said tartly. 'Young ladies wear hats when they go on visits. That much my Mama did teach me. And so it is better that I return to Redayre. I will not go further with you today.'

Jack laughed coolly. 'You learn faster than I thought. I will see you tomorrow, Barbara. My business in Dumfries will detain me late into the night.'

He wheeled sharply, and galloped away into the skyline. Barbara tossed her head, and returned her gaze to the road before her, and Redayre. By the time she crossed the courtyard she knew she could have ridden no further, not in this heat. She slid down from Snowy's back on trembling legs and went into the kitchen.

'You are too flushed,' Margaret said at the sight of her. 'I will mix you one of my herbals and a cool drink. You will feel much better, quite quickly, see if you don't.'

In the space of half an hour, she had recovered sufficiently to don a bonnet and follow Margaret out into the kitchen-garden.

'I grow herbs for flavourings in my cooking,' her cousin said, 'for my teas, wines and cordials, for my ointments, cough syrups and other remedies, as well as for the pomanders and the scent bags.'

Barbara had hardly heard her, for she had plucked a sprig of rosemary, and 'There's rosemary, that's for remembrance; pray, love, remember' came winging into her mind. How could she be so moonish and so silly, she wondered? Words like that were only for people in love, and she was not in love—with anyone. It was the thunder. She was always moody with thunder in the air.

That night she lay in a hot uneasy sleep until an ear-splitting clatter jerked her bolt upright in her bed, her heart racing wildly, and she looked about her dazedly. Then there was another deafening crash, followed by a brilliant flickering light. She stole out of bed and pattered across the shining floorboards to the wide-flung casements, so heavily overhung by the eaves that no air stirred within the stifling room.

But, by the same token, none of the torrential rain which was pelting down could splash in. She stood at the embrasure all through the thunderstorm, each clap hammering home the pounding in her head, watching the vivid green flashes of the lightning streaking and zig-zagging over the Solway Firth. Then at last it was over, and it receded southwards to hover over the Cumbrian shore, leaving the air cooler and refreshed.

Barbara felt a little lift of invigoration, her head clearing, and filled with a great desire to be outside in the dripping gardens now that the downpour had stopped as abruptly as it had begun, she saw that daylight was beginning to marble the darkness and dispel the blackness of the sky. She flung on her muslin gown and crept out of Redayre barefoot, across the lawns trembling with raindrops, leaving a grey trail through the dark green velvet where her feet had trod, and then she was on the dunes and sands of her beloved Solway. Without another thought, she threw her gown down on the grass and walked naked over the scalloped sand. The tiny ridges felt cool and damp under her feet, and it was as though she floated, drifted, into the tranquil waters, all alone in all the world.

But she was not alone in the swirling mists of dawn. As she splashed and played in the silky water, her back was to the bank where two watchers stood transfixed, the one in front drinking in the childish feminine back tapering sharply at her waist and rounding over her buttocks. As she turned to throw up handfuls of water at the rising sun, his eyes burned like red coals to see that it was no girl he was watching, but a woman in the first flush of her maturity, her small tip-tilted breasts rosy in the morning glow. Barbara did not see how the man behind the watcher waited only long enough for him to turn and slink back into the bushes before he, too, retreated, his eyes slitted into silver ice.

Unaware, she walked straight and proud back up the beach and over to her right, where the little freshwater stream flowed between its high banks into the sea, to rinse her hair and splash the salt from her body. Then she put her dress on again, and began her leisurely climb back up to Redayre, refreshed in mind and body.

It seemed a long time since the drive in the carriage with Jack had brought her here to this beautiful bay. She looked back on the magnificent sweep of it, the cliffs towering at either tip, running down to the smooth plateau at the crook, where the house commanded its panoramic view. Behind Redayre the Galloway hills rose sharply, clothed in every shade of green.

The days seemed to have drifted by one after the other like puffs of thistledown floating along, ever since she had come here, and she was taking a long time to become accustomed to their gentle rhythm. She supposed this was what a holiday must be like, but she had never had a holiday in her life, to know.

Redayre House was too tranquil and too old a place to be at all put about by another addition to the Jardine family. It was as though it had opened one eye when she came and said, 'Welcome, my dear,' and then closed it again, to slumber on in peace.

And its occupants, too, were in no hurry. They did not live at a great pace. Sometimes Margaret was invited out. She would go away in a carriage sent for her especially on some evenings, and when that happened there was always a Cold Collation for dinner, and Jack and Sibylla would raise their eyebrows at each other, and smile.

Sibylla kept a great deal to her rooms, but more than once Barbara had seen Fanny showing some ladies, clearly on business bent, up to her sitting-room in the afternoons, and then there would be a rushing about with trays, and silver kettles and teapots, and cakestands daintily set out.

So far, Barbara had not been invited to any of these meetings, or on any excursions, but she was not disappointed. She still felt too new and too raw to have to meet any more new people just yet, when she was only just acquainted with her cousins.

It seemed a long time since yesterday when she had last spoken to Jack, she admitted to herself, for Barbara was nothing if not painfully honest, especially with her own thoughts. What was this work he did, she wondered? So far, she had only seen him riding about, in immaculate fashion, a gentleman travelling the countryside as he did yesterday. He was on his way to Dumfries, he had told her. What sort of interests would he have there? Perhaps social ones along with all the rest, she thought, with a surprising little drop of her heart. Perhaps a lady waited for him there. It was not to be wondered at, for he was so very handsome, and so very distinguished. Indeed, it would be far more amazing if there were not.

It was none of her concern . . . Here at Redayre she had the run of the house and the grounds, pleasant and easy in the carefree sun—at least, so far—and so very different from the grinding worry of the life at Starlochy.

She was sure that Margaret would place no restraints on her. As to Sibylla, Barbara was not so sure at all. She had a little feeling that once Sibylla was her normal self again, she would take her young cousin in hand. Quite clearly, she adored her brother Jack, and would aid and abet him in every way she could.

To tell the truth, she sighed, she was already becoming a little bored. When Jack came back she looked forward to the cut and thrust of his conversation, to give back as good as she got. The gleam in her eye as she turned this thought over in her mind would have agitated her Mama more than words can say.

Idly, she speculated on the variety of the three Jardine personalities, differing so much in appearance and character, which Sir Robert and Lady Elizabeth had produced, and it glanced sharply and uncomfortably through her mind that she had thought there to be more children than that. What had made her think so? She concentrated on Margaret, the youngest of the three.

Barbara calculated her age at about twenty-three, with Sibylla a year or two older, and Jack nearly thirty.

Margaret was large in every way. Enveloped in her white pinafores as she invariably was while bustling about the kitchens, she resembled a stately ship in full sail. Barbara had seen no servant engaged in cooking at Redayre. It seemed that none was needed, for cooking was Margaret's main reason for living. Her cousin was not so much a cook as a culinary artist, Barbara mused as she reached the lawns which fanned out from the house.

It was in the kitchen that she found her, as she entered the house from the rear. The sun was full up now, with the promise of another lovely day. Yet Margaret had the fire blazing already, and heat poured out from the open doors and the windows flung wide to the walls.

'Will you take breakfast, Barbara?' she asked, with a majestic sideways swoop from the fire, fork in hand. How comfortable she was, with her apple cheeks and large capable hands! The smell of kidneys and mushrooms sizzling in the pan behind her was very tempting. 'Jack's been looking for you. He has asked if you will go to the library as soon as you are ready.'

Barbara's erstwhile bravado deserted her as completely as her appetite as she tried to digest this disquieting news. 'Why? It sounds like a summons.'

'He didn't say, dear.' Margaret was calm and smiling. 'But he will wait, and your breakfast will not. Whatever it is, it will sit better on a full stomach,' and she pushed Barbara down firmly on a chair and set her plate before her.

What could Jack want? she asked the mirror in her chamber. She tugged at her rebellious curls, her unseeing eyes blind to the blue metallic sheen dancing on the black hair reflected in the glass, and the golden glow her skin had taken on.

'Devil take it,' she cursed, throwing down the brush and giving up the battle. Impatiently she ruffled through her ribbon-box until she found the blue-flowered one to match her dress, and hastily tied back her ringlets. She stepped into her blue slippers and ran downstairs, pausing at the last tread to school herself into a more demure step, and stopped at the low wide doorway of the library, hesitant and nervous, for much as she had strangely missed him during the short time he had been away, this man who wished only to rule her and subdue her, her heart was in a perfect flutter, and it felt like a flutter of alarm.

# CHAPTER
# THREE

JACK TOOK no notice of her entrance, and continued instead with his writing at the polished table. She watched him secretly, aware of a sudden shyness, and hating herself for it—she, Barbara Graham who was never shy. She wondered how long he would keep her standing there. It was rude and unmannerly, and yet she knew she could not be the first to speak.

He went on writing, and Barbara went on standing there at the door. How detached he was, how intent, like someone hard at study. He had not even bothered to lift his head when she came into his presence. What could he be scribbling that was so important, anyway? She ventured a step nearer and saw that he was not writing at all, but drawing—sketching a little animal with great care. Perhaps he was angry that she had taken so long to answer his summons, but she saw that he would not stop until he had put the finishing touches to his work, finely separating every hair on the animal's great bushy tail. She could almost smell the fox's fetid stench.

'You must not bathe alone, Barbara,' he said at last, without looking up. Immediately she was stung to anger. How would he know, unless he had been spying on her? And then, behind that, came the sickening realisation that he must have seen her naked, if that were so. She felt the hot colour starting at her toes and spreading over her entire body before it settled, a scarlet stain, on her cheeks. But even if he had seen her, the tide was so far out over the sand that she could only have been a blur, she comforted herself, and the blush receded.

'I had not thought you to be such an early riser,' she retorted tartly. His head came up at that, and she thought his look was veiled, secretly amused.

'Indeed?' His remark had an icy undertone. 'And, pray, why not?'

'I am sorry if I have offended you.' Barbara managed to convey a complete indifference as to whether she had offended him or not, in this off-hand apology. 'But it does not seem worth while, perhaps, to get up in the mornings, when there is so little to do.'

To her vexation, he threw back his head and roared with laughter. 'All may not be as it seems, little cousin,' he said. 'For instance, I was not the only one to see you from the shore at dawn this morning.'

'No?' she asked coldly. 'Who else was there?'

'This fellow,' he answered, pointing to his drawing.

Barbara heaved an inward sigh of relief. *That* was all right, then, if it was only a fox.

'It can be very dangerous, alone on the Solway Firth,' he said quietly. 'Not only because of the foxes of this world, Barbara.'

'You mean the sands?' she said swiftly. 'The shifting sands. Yes, I do know. I'm sorry; it will not happen again.'

He glanced up again, as if surprised at this sudden capitulation. 'You fear the sands more than you would a fox?'

'I have been brought up on the Solway,' she reminded him.

'Good. Now to pleasanter things.' He indicated the massive desk behind him. 'I am working through my father's affairs, and I have come across another letter, in reply to one of his own. It seems he had engaged the services of a Mr Garbutt, a dancing master.'

'A dancing master?' Barbara had known that wealthy families were accustomed to employ tutors of all kinds for the general education of their children, to teach drawing and music, and the study of literature. But she had never heard of a dancing master.

'He has been at Redayre before,' Jack told her. 'But some time ago. Mr Garbutt will arrive on the 15th of July for two weeks. This house has been in mourning now for more than six weeks, and I fear for Sibylla. She does not improve, and indeed nothing so far has lifted her apathy. Perhaps having to make all the arrangements will speed her recovery.'

'The arrangements?'

'Yes, the arrangements for our friends to come and stay here and join us for the lessons. It has meant a great deal of work in the past, sending out the invitations, preparing the guest-rooms, and so on. I shall remind her of that, and also that it has become a sort of tradition, especially the Ball at the end. Everyone would be so disappointed if these happy occasions were to come to an end.'

So he did have a heart, Barbara thought. She felt a sudden rush of sympathy for this man who found himself in charge of a vast estate prematurely, and three dependent women, none of them even his own wife. But perhaps there was a prospective bride somewhere she had not seen as yet.

The sarcasm of his next remark quickly dispelled all such compassion. 'And it will be something to occupy us all, in our idleness, will it not?' he asked with the same slow mocking smile she had come to expect. 'So get out your dancing shoes, Barbara,' he added as she left the room.

She felt a little surge of excitement, although whether it was because of the dancing lessons or because of the gleam in his eyes when he passed his last remark, she could not have told, and went out on the lawns in front of the house.

The gardeners had been up early and done their work, for the grass was fresh trimmed and the formal hedges clipped. Somewhere, from an open window in another part of the house, she could hear Margaret's voice calling for Nessie or Jean to fetch water, and then she walked away to the stables, round behind Redayre. It would be wonderful to break free, to have an adventure, to scour those hills back there, shadowed and cool and brown where the bracken grew, since the shore was prohibited.

She whispered in Snowy's ear, and soon they were galloping across the moors, wilder than she had supposed they were, rolling like an immense desert from east to west with tracks here and there across the surface. They followed one of them, and it was slowly now, for they had reached the lower slopes of the nearest hill. Snowy picked his way delicately among the fallen boulders, and as they climbed the stones were bigger, sometimes great slabs of rock scattered by a giant hand.

Barbara slid down and tethered her horse under a shady tree, for she felt within her bones that in the dips and hollows where the bright green tufts grew it would be marshland, dangerous for Snowy, and fit only to skirt round on her own feet. She climbed up round the next hump of the hill's shoulder, and far below her, on the sea's edge, stood Redayre, its massiveness reduced to the proportions of a doll's house in the distance. A deeply wooded gully ran along here, containing the freshwater stream that ran out into the bay, the one she had washed in this morning. Half-way along the gully, up on a clearing, stood a small church, a graveyard behind it, the whole enclosed by neat stone dykes into a perfect rectangle.

'That must be the Redayre Kirk,' she thought with a surge of excitement, 'where we will go on Sunday.'

But there was no manse near by for Mr Faulks, as far as she could see. Then she noticed a house almost perpendicularly below her, with its back hard up against the hillside in a small wood. Only the smoke spiralling up lazily from one of its tall chimneys through the branches of trees betrayed it. Who lived there, hidden away so completely?

She scrambled down the hillside to the fern-filled grass surrounding the house, and paused uncertainly. It was so quiet, not a sound, until a snap behind her made her whirl about, perhaps only the sound of a twig snapping underfoot, but in that silence like the report of a gun. She saw with relief that the man who came up out of the deep bracken carried only a long gnarled stick he had found, perhaps in the undergrowth.

'Oh, it is you, sir!' Barbara smiled at Mr Faulks.

'I'm so sorry. Did I startle you?' he asked in his gentle, reassuring voice.

'No—that is, yes,' she stuttered. 'You see, I saw this house from the hill, and never dreamt it could be the manse. It is so far from the church. I grew curious to see it.'

'Then see it you shall, Miss Graham. Yes, it is my home. The North House, it is called.'

'I must beg your pardon, Mr Faulks,' Barbara said, wondering what on earth her Mama would say if she knew of her daughter's casual invasion of the minister's privacy. Or, worse still, what would Jack say, if he knew? 'I'm afraid I am intruding.'

'On the contrary, it is delightful to be favoured with your visit,' he assured her. 'You will stay and drink a dish of tea with me, Miss Graham?' Then, when she hesitated, 'Do stay. Please, I insist. No gentleman would allow a lady to leave unrefreshed after so strenuous an exercise to come and visit him.'

Barbara considered the matter, realising that indeed her throat was very dry, and she was feeling quite hot and dusty. She smiled gratefully. 'Tea would be most acceptable, Mr Faulks.'

'Then it is settled, my dear, and we will drink it out here in the cool shade of the summerhouse.'

He led her round to the other side of the house and settled her in one of the long wooden benches which ran right round the central stalk of the small four-sided stone house, a column at each corner, and with no walls. How clever it was, open to the sun and yet protected from the wind whichever way it blew!

While Barbara waited for Mr Faulks to give his housekeeper directions, she admired the long vistas in every direction, all over the district.

'What wonderful views you have from here!' she exclaimed when he returned.

'Ah, yes,' he agreed. 'Especially the coastline, I

always think. I can watch the temper of the Solway to east and to west, and yet be well out of its reach.'

'And Redayre itself,' Barbara observed, 'and all its comings and goings.'

'Indeed, although my duties do not often permit it. But the view I enjoy most is straight ahead down Willow Walk,' and he indicated the path leading from the summerhouse down through an avenue lined with trees.

She thought she had never seen anything so lovely as the way the branches arched up to meet overhead, creating a little private world of cool greenness, a long green tunnel where the shape, even the shadow, of a man or an animal could be seen at once from this look-out.

'I often sit here,' he said, 'when I am troubled, or have a great deal to think out.'

She felt astonished that he could be troubled, or have to plan out anything, in this beautiful place.

'When you make up your sermons, you mean?' Understanding crept into her voice.

He laughed softly, a strange little laugh. 'My sermons,' he said. 'Yes indeed, my sermons.'

He got to his feet at the approach of a woman bearing a large round tray, and Barbara scolded herself for allowing a tiny cloud to dim her delight on this happy occasion.

For there was no doubt that he really was quite short and perhaps a little thick around the middle, giving him the rather stocky appearance which his dark clothes did little to disguise. Of course, she had become accustomed to tall men. Indeed, she had had little else to look at except a certain tall lean figure of undeniable elegance, although she would have to avoid its owner now after this escapade.

But her first glimpse of Mistress Sadie Caldwell chased any other thought quite out of her head. She had not imagined this quiet, gentle man to need such a dragon of a housekeeper. Big and bold, she darted her blackly inquisitive eyes over their visitor before setting down the tray and folding her hands over an apron which, to Barbara's fastidious taste, was far from white. She did not like Mistress Caldwell's hard looks or her slatternly appearance. In short, she did not like her at all; and as usual, Barbara's mobile face betrayed her thoughts, for the woman's eyes narrowed as she turned to the minister.

'Will that be all, sir?' And there was just a small inflection on the 'sir'.

Barbara frowned at this undeniable insolence, tiny though it was, and she would have been more surprised if Mr Faulks's voice had not had the edge to it that it had, when he replied, 'That will be all, Sadie. You may go.'

Mistress Caldwell's lips pursed in a grim line, and she stalked away, her big shoulders held back in that swaggering way.

'She is a little familiar, perhaps?' Barbara remarked, as she poured out the tea, regretting the words almost before they were out of her mouth.

'I have known Mistress Caldwell for many years. She is very useful to me.' His voice held a note of sad reproof.

She changed the subject quickly. 'That is your church I saw from the hill?'

'Yes, the Kirk of Redayre. It is part of the Jardines' estate, of course, as are all the lands here as far as the eye can see.'

'Oh,' Barbara said, 'I had not known it was so large.'

'Would you like to walk back that way?'

'I have left my horse tethered half-way down the hill,' she answered regretfully.

He stood up to look in the direction she showed him. 'Then that is not a problem, Miss Graham. There is a bridle-path from the church leading that way. I will show you when the time comes for you to leave.'

Barbara set down her cup in the saucer, thanking him for the refreshment, although she had not much enjoyed the tea. 'Tinkers' tea', Mama would have called it, thick and brown and sweet. They walked down the Willow Walk until a high wall could be seen to its left.

'What is this?' she asked, her bearings quite lost.

'This is the graveyard. Come, I will show you round.'

'Who is it for, besides the family?'

'The villagers of the estate also lie here. There are four small villages scattered through it, you see. But here is the family ground.'

'Frances Jardine aged 14, Marjory Jardine aged 12, Thomas Jardine aged 10,' Barbara read out, aghast that she could have forgotten the scourge of the smallpox epidemic her mother had told her of, years ago, when the three children had died all within one year.

'There were three more children, who survive, as you know. I have been tutor to most of them, and in fact that was my first appointment,' he told her, and choked a little as he added, 'and to be appointed minister here when the living became vacant is my second.'

They went on to inspect the recently erected headstones above Sir Robert and Lady Elizabeth Jardine.

'It is a great wonder that they are not all very bitter people,' said Barbara, still shocked, as they were leaving the graveyard.

'They have the comfort of their faith,' the minister said smoothly. 'But it is certainly true that the Jardines seem doomed to an early grave.'

She was even more shocked and dismayed at this chilling observation, worse still by its deliverance in such silken tones. When her senses came back to her she realised he was speaking about the possible—no, the probable—untimely deaths of dear Sibylla and Margaret. Even Jack.

'And this is the family crest,' he pointed out as they were passing the church. He looked up at it with an odd expression, in its place above the chapel door. 'Two coats of arms entwined, the Jardines' and the Gilmours'. Lady Elizabeth, my aunt, was a Gilmour, you see. Indeed my name is Browne Gilmour Faulks, and while my aunt lived I was always known as the Reverend Mr Browne. But now the family have reverted to a more formal address,' he added quietly.

'How stupid of me not to realise that you are related to the Jardine family!' Barbara exclaimed.

'How could you know? We were introduced in a rather off-hand manner, were we not? But I am one of the poor relations, I'm afraid,' he replied, and she felt his hand upon her foot, placing it in the stirrup, and looking down on him she saw the gleam of his eyes in the clear light: bronze eyes, turned red now, the same colour as his red hair. She was reminded of someone, or something, but it eluded her in the warmth of their farewell. Some animal, perhaps as so often some people remind one of an animal? She took up the reins, smiling and happy to have found such a friend, one whom she felt instinctively she could trust, and began the slow, careful descent back to Redayre.

But even in that bright sunshine, the boulders assumed grotesque and frightening shapes, the marshes seemed more brightly green, pretty in their deadly invitation, and there were shadows in the valleys now that she had not seen before. She would not like to come here alone in the dark, and a shiver passed over her, for the North Hill was a place of mystery, perhaps even of danger.

Jack was waiting as she and Snowy clattered over the cobbled paving to the stables, and she saw at a glance that he was ashen-faced, white with rage, his eyes silver-hard and blazing, raking her from head to foot like shafts of steel. 'Get down, Barbara,' he commanded, his voice harsh.

Her heart sank, staring down into his hard face, and she hesitated before she swung from the saddle and felt his hands encircle her waist when he helped her. She turned to face him, lifting her chin proudly, and when he met her challenging look there was no hint of pity in his eyes.

'I had not taken you for a fool, cousin,' he said. 'That was very unwise, to ride out unescorted on these hills.'

Barbara's eyes flashed with anger. 'I cannot see what harm there was in it! Snowy is very sure-footed, and on this lovely day we could see for miles.'

'I believe I have told you before, that you must not

take things at face value. All may not be as it seems. But I see you have come to no obvious *physical* harm,' Jack said, his voice expressionless. 'I take it you met nobody, then?'

Stung to anger by his tone, Barbara's eyes sparkled dangerously. 'On the contrary,' she said proudly. 'I have made a new friend. His name is the Reverend Browne Gilmour Faulks, and he is your cousin, is he not? I wish someone had informed me.' 'Surely,' she thought triumphantly, 'nothing could be more circumspect than *that*! Not even Jack Jardine could take exception to it.'

But he could, it transpired, for his face hardened to granite. 'Indeed?' he asked icily. 'And where, pray, was this?' ignoring completely her allusion to the relationship.

'At the North House,' she flashed at him defiantly. 'I took tea with him there.'

'That was not ladylike, without an invitation, as I am aware.'

Barbara glared at him, struggling to conceal her nervousness, uncomfortable in the knowledge that this grim-faced man was absolutely right and she had been wrong, as if she were not a properly brought up young lady.

'*He* did not make me feel awkward, anyway. He was very kind to me.'

'And I am not, Barbara?' his voice was mocking again. 'But then I should have insisted on escorting you home again, had I been in Mr Faulks's shoes, and a little minx turned up on my doorstep quite unannounced from out of nowhere.'

It was true, she thought unhappily. Any gentleman would have done as he described, and the descent from the North Hill had not been pleasant at all.

'I believe you would, sir,' she replied through tight lips. 'Which makes it the second time today that I must tell you that I am sorry for the vexation I have caused you. But perhaps you would prefer that I should ask for your permission every time I go out of the door?'

'Now what the devil do you mean by that ridiculous question, Barbara?' he asked irritably. 'But I will have you obey me in this, that you will not go abroad alone where you may meet with danger. As your guardian, I insist on it.'

She bowed her head. 'Very well,' she agreed, with a lingering trace of bitterness in her voice. 'I will obey you from now on.'

'Then that is one of the three promises I had intended to extract from you, settled straight away.'

'Three?' Barbara stared at him suspiciously. Why had his eyes deepened to that strange shade again? And if she had not known better, she might even have said that they danced.

'The next most important one, in ascending order, is that you should respect me. "Honour", I believe, is the appropriate word.'

'Ah, that will depend. I have not known you long enough yet to promise to honour you,' Barbara said truthfully, her gaze blue and clear.

'But you respect and honour Sibylla, for example?'

'Oh, yes. But, then, that is quite different.'

'Why is it different, Barbara? You have known us both for the same length of time.'

'But she is a woman.'

'Ah!'

'And I have not known many men—certainly very few who were honourable. Perhaps that has influenced me not to trust any of them.'

'Then I must work hard for the second promise, I can see.'

'And what is the third?'

'We shall speak of the third, once we have achieved the second,' Jack laughed. 'If I can wait so long.'

They began to go round the house to the front, and as they walked it came to Barbara what words he had been quoting to her. 'You have been teasing me, Jack. To love, honour and obey, indeed! But I am not your wife. I am only your cousin.'

'And my friend, I hope? That would be a beginning.'

'Of course. So long as you do not tease too much, Jack Jardine.'

His smile disarmed her, his eyes soft, and at such close range she saw that they were pale grey and thickly ringed with very black eyelashes.

'Then let us go and eat,' he said, taking her arm. 'And I am your best friend in the world, Barbie. Don't forget that.'

Barbara wondered why she felt a strange longing all of a sudden to rest her cheek against the smooth silk of her cousin's coat. Perhaps she was a little tired. Her legs, certainly, had turned quite weak at the knees.

It was high noon now, hazy with an east wind, and the scents from the flower-beds made her heart sing, as she walked along at Jack's side. She felt absurdly happy as they took their seats, smiling, in the dining-room. The shutters outside the long lattice windows were half closed, so that the air inside was dim and cool, and the meal Margaret had prepared smelled inviting, delicious with herbs.

Sibylla arrived at the same time, no longer wearing black, but in a grey silk gown, very plain with lace about the neck and wrists. How young she looked!

'You look much better, Sibylla, my dear. That gown is very becoming,' said Jack with relief in his voice.

'Thank you, Jack,' she said gravely. 'Since it was Papa's desire to have the dancing lessons, then the time has come to try to shake off the grief and the black of mourning. Indeed, we must all attend to our dress, and appear happy, for his sake.'

'Papa would be the first to agree with that, dear,' Margaret said, a world of reassurance in her deep voice. 'He would want us to carry on the good life he made for us here. Shall we sit down, before the soup grows cold?'

She explained her recipe for the clear light soup with enthusiasm, and then served everyone with a little Partan Pie in its own crab-shell, along with the heart of a lettuce, crisp and green and sprinkled with garlic. She waited, beaming, until it was time to ring her little silver bell again, and then the young serving-girls came through from the kitchens bearing a great bowl of junket, and another of the first wild strawberries of the season.

'There will be guests to invite, and menus to prepare,' Margaret said happily, 'with plenty to do between now and then.'

'I must make out a list of invitations,' Sibylla nodded, frowning thoughtfully. 'Jack, whom shall we ask?'

He smiled encouragingly at his sister. 'As many young people as you can think of, my dear. Since we all know the steps already, the lessons are merely an excuse for social intercourse, which was always our father's purpose for inviting Mr Garbutt.'

'Well then, Margaret—you will wish to invite John Reid and William?' Sibylla asked.

Margaret nodded, a broad beam lighting up her face. 'Perhaps I shall tell him this evening.'

'John Reid is a farmer up Castle Douglas way,' Jack explained, a gleam of amusement in his eyes. 'Very well-to-do and, besides that, a man of great discernment, since he has asked Margaret to marry him—three times now, isn't it?'

'Twice,' she said. 'And will no doubt do so again, for the third time.'

'And will you accept him?' Barbara asked, over the laughter.

Margaret's plump bosom heaved with the joke. 'I dare say I shall'—she wiped her eyes—'in the end.'

'John Reid likes his food, you see, Barbara,' Sibylla explained, 'and Margaret's cooking. She has accused him of liking it better than her. So she is making him wait and want, to prove himself.'

'And there you have it,' said Jack. 'Women were ever the deadlier of the species.'

'I told him last time that I would consider myself thoroughly proficient, and therefore ready to marry, once I had catered for a wedding or some other grand occasion,' Margaret said. 'But the trouble is that nobody else seems in a marrying mood.'

'Ah,' thought Barbara, 'then Jack does have no sweetheart.'

'So I may have to eat my own words, instead,' Margaret sighed.

'And serve you right,' Sibylla said reprovingly. 'It is quite cruel of you, Margaret, when you know he follows you about like a worshipping dog. So that is settled. John Reid and his young brother William. William will be a splendid partner for you, Barbara; he's about your own age. And then there are the Beatties and the Scotts,' she went on, 'and our cousins from Dumfries.'

'To say nothing of our old friends the Favenels,' Jack put in slyly.

'Ah yes, indeed, the Favenels,' said Sibylla, ignoring the innuendo Barbara was sure was in Jack's words. 'Yes, they are very pleasant, Barbara, although unfortunately in recent years we have not seen as much of Philip and Louise Favenel as we would have liked.'

'Especially Philip.' Margaret winked in Barbara's direction. She realised that both Margaret and Jack were telling her that Sibylla was very fond of Philip.

'Philip was ordained not long ago in London,' Sibylla explained, 'and he has been spending a lot of time there. Indeed, he is still in the city. But we have heard that Louise is in their Dumfries house at present, so I shall send an invitation for them both.' She lowered her voice and looked slightly embarrassed. 'Louise is being an actress, at present.'

'An actress?' Barbara did not mean to sound so taken aback. How scandalous!

'Only for this year—so far, at least—my dear. Next year she may be trying to be a nurse.'

'Or even open a Salon,' Margaret smiled.

'She is really rather unpredictable,' Sibylla agreed with a sigh. 'Very restless, and I am afraid a little too modern in her ideas, which she has so much money to indulge. Philip tries constantly to curb her.'

'She is delightful,' Jack smiled, and Barbara took an instant and violent dislike to Miss Louise Favenel. 'And she can, as Sibylla says, afford to be as shocking as she pleases. Delightfully so. Their father is a wealthy French Count who married a lady from Dumfries. We have known Louise for years, and we excuse her little peccadilloes.'

'She has turned out to be a brilliant actress, by all accounts,' said Margaret.

'Yes. Which is unfortunate in some ways, Philip says, for at the very time when she will be appearing on the stage in Dumfries, he has been asked to preach in Greyfriars Church. And that reminds me, Jack. We shall have to invite Mr Faulks?'

'Oh yes, Browne,' Jack said. 'To be sure, we must not forget Browne.' Something in his tone made Barbara glance at him. His eyes were almost closed, mere silver slits, and the secret sardonic look was back on his face again, she saw unhappily, all gentleness gone, and the light-hearted banter.

'And what of you, Barbara dear?' Sibylla asked. 'We must look out gowns for you this afternoon.'

'In a suitably frivolous style, of course.' Jack's smile was entirely cynical as he rose to his feet. 'She is of the opinion that frivolity is of supreme importance at Redayre.'

'You will have to forgive him,' Sibylla put a soothing hand on her arm, as Barbara glared at his retreating back. 'Jack has always loved to tease. We will look in the cupboards upstairs, and see what we can find.'

Barbara followed up the staircase, her mind preoccupied with the lunchtime conversation. She was not going to have young William Reid for her partner, that much was certain, she told herself loftily. Not now that she had changed so much lately. Now she much preferred the conversation and the company of older men, Mr Faulks, for example, with his mature opinions and his courteous solicitude. It cheered her considerably to think of him.

'I spoke to Mr Faulks this morning, Sibylla.'

'How nice, dear. Where did you see him?'

Barbara related her adventures of the morning on the North Hill, finishing with her unhappy interview with Jack.

'I'm afraid it is all my fault, Barbara. I should have been taking you about with me, and introducing our friends and acquaintances to you,' Sibylla sighed. 'I have been very remiss. But that is over now, and as Jack says, life must go on.' Then, after a pause, 'We will pay a formal visit one day soon to Mr Faulks, with the invitation to the dancing lessons.'

'I would like to meet him again,' Barbara admitted. 'He is very attractive.'

'Yes,' Sibylla laughed. 'He preaches a good sermon, too, when he doesn't shout too much. Tell me, what colour do you favour?' she asked, holding up a yellow gown.

'Blue,' Barbara said absent-mindedly. 'Or pink.'

Sibylla rummaged in the large wicker hamper inside the door of the closet, turning out gowns, their colours spilling over the shining floorboards on the landing.

'I always wondered about this door,' Barbara said, 'and where it led to, tucked away in the corner like this.'

'There is a secret attached to this closet. A little staircase runs down from it and out through a small door in the ivy. There is another closet in the east wing, exactly the same. We used to play out and in, and up and down, when we were children. But they're locked up now, of course, and overgrown with ivy, I expect.'

'Where?' asked Barbara, excitement pricking, as she delved inside.

'At the back. Yes, just round that corner, which, as you see, is a false wall, only a partition. From outside here that opening is invisible.'

'Oh, Sibylla, I've found it! Let me go down. Oh, please, Sibylla!'

'Of course you may, my dear. But it will be dirty.'

Barbara descended the small spiral of steps into darkness, putting each foot down cautiously under her until she reached the flatness of a floor, a tiny chink of light in front of her eyes. She prodded the wall around it, and daylight streamed in. She had found the door, and it opened noiselessly into the strings of ivy stems, pulled away and dangling free. The stone floor she was standing on was clean, and the narrow winding steps behind her bore no cobwebs. It had all been recently swept. She closed the little door again and climbed back up into the closet, deciding she would not tell Sibylla what she had discovered. Not yet, anyway.

'How quaint, Sibylla! Why were they built in there, in the first place?'

'Oh, for escape routes long ago, I expect,' Sibylla answered vaguely, her arms full of silken billows, sleeves and ribbons dangling. 'Shall we try on some of these dresses? If any of the ones you like can be altered to fit you, I shall put them aside for your new maid to sew.'

The long hours of the afternoon passed drowsily among the lavender-scented drifts of muslin, silk and lace, Sibylla peering short-sightedly at the pins as she tucked in waistbands and smoothed out the materials over Barbara's slender hips.

'The blue suits you, and the lilac, and the pale green, my dear. They can be altered for practice dresses. But the rose satin is beautiful on you. It shall be your ball-gown, I think,' she said, standing back to admire it.

'So Jack was not teasing? There really is to be a Ball?'

'There always is, dear, on the last evening of Mr Garbutt's stay.'

Then it was tea-time under the mulberry tree, and so round to early evening once again, and a ceasing of the wind while the sun set, the sky glowed and the first stars shone. And Barbara was possessed again of the same wild desire that had seized her at Starlochy, to go out in the still night, to seek adventure and find out the secret stirrings in the trees and on the hills around Redayre.

But it would not do, to escape from the restrictions Jack had placed upon her, and which she regarded as no less than prison bars—not tonight, at any rate, not the very minute that Sibylla had shown her the way out. Filled with an unaccustomed prudence, she hugged her secret to her heart, and stood leaning and dreaming out of her casement window until it was time to climb into her bed and fall asleep.

By Sunday morning, Sibylla had come back from that

other world where she had sojourned so long with her
father and mother, and returned firmly to the land of the
living. That Jack had delegated her to the business of
Barbara's surveillance, as well as arranging for the
prolonged stay of guests, soon became obvious. But not
painfully so, for Sibylla proved to be the most gentle, if
conscientious, of chaperons.

'Yes,' she said, as she inspected Barbara's appearance
before they went down to join the others waiting in the
hall. 'How Fanny achieves it, I do not know, but any lady
she dresses takes on a crispness of turnout as though
straight from a bandbox. Let us hope she will soon have
Betsy trained. She starts tomorrow.'

The little procession left Redayre, winding their way
over a well-trodden path to the church. Jack led the way,
with Sibylla on his arm, and Barbara followed with
Margaret. Fanny, looking stern and quite unlike herself
in her black bonnet, brought up the rear.

'Do the other servants attend the Kirk?' Barbara
asked.

'Indeed,' Margaret told her. 'They have all been
already, at the early morning service, and we allow them
another opportunity later today, at six o'clock, for the
short evening service. But now, at eleven, it is the most
important ceremony on Sundays, for Mr Faulks
preaches his full sermon, and makes all the announce-
ments for the parish, as well as dealing with any
miscreants.'

'Then it is much the same as at home,' Barbara said,
'except for the miscreants. How does the minister deal
with them?'

'There are none today, that I know of,' Margaret
replied, and then, heaving a sigh, 'I hope you will never
have to witness any of that, Barbara, for it is far from
pleasant for any of us.'

The Jardine family filed into the pew almost directly
under the pulpit, at right-angles to the rest of the congregation. Jack entered last, and locked its little door,
on which was outlined the Jardine crest, and sat down at
Barbara's side. Squire Marchbanks and his wife were

there already in the pew behind, smiling and nodding, and Barbara became aware that many eyes were upon her, a stranger in their midst, an object to be stared at and appraised during the tedium of the long service. She felt exposed, vulnerable, as she glanced around. There was not an empty seat in the church, and right at the back, at the door, sat Fanny with other girls wearing black hats. What nonsense it all is, Barbara thought, glancing up at Jack's face, but his eyes were fixed on a point straight ahead, and his face was set rock-hard.

Mr Faulks was clearing his throat in the pulpit, and smiling down at them, and delivering the opening prayer, and then they were on their feet to sing the first psalm from the note of the tuning-fork. For there was no organ here, not at the Kirk of Redayre.

An hour later, cramp setting into her every muscle, Barbara wondered how she could ever have considered the minister's voice to be soft and silken-toned, as it roared and thundered majestically around the rafters, and he berated the sinners, the sinners of his congregation, the sinners of all the earth, especially those, it seemed, who dwelt in high places. For Mr Faulks had taken his text from the Gospel according to St Matthew, chapter five, verse five, 'Blessed are the meek: for they shall inherit the earth.'

Barbara stole a look at Jack's profile, where a sardonic little smile played about his lips. At last it was all over, and she felt she had escaped, out into the fresh air, out from the pits of Hell and damnation, and that that had only been by the skin of her teeth, far more by good luck than by good judgment.

'Well, Barbara,' said Jack, taking her arm once all the pleasantries had been observed: the shaking of the minister's hand, the rather raised and excited look from his eyes, and the chatting at the church door with friends. 'What did you think of that? Mr Faulks is a great orator, is he not?' Something in his tone made her pause. Something cynical and derisive. She turned round, to see that Margaret was accompanying Sibylla on the walk back to Redayre, while she cast around for an appropriate comment.

'He possesses a very loud voice, certainly,' she replied. 'I had not thought so before.'

Jack laughed, 'You are learning diplomacy, as well as deportment, I see. But you must never be afraid to speak your mind. It is part of your charm.'

He was teasing her again, she thought, and changed the subject.

'Do you go often away,' she asked, 'on business to Dumfries, as you did the other day?'

'Dumfries, Castle Douglas, Wigtown, and sometimes even further afield. I carry on my father's business, Barbara, which is to give employment to as many of our tenants as is possible, in our trading affairs.'

'I did not know that my uncle was a trader.'

'That was only one of his roles. He was trying to build up the fishing, even to establishing links abroad for the dried fish from hereabouts, and the woollen garments from our sheep. Then he supplied all the necessities of fishing, including boats and gear, providing meal during shortages, and securing a proper share of proceeds from the numerous wrecks on this coastline.'

'I can see that it is very different here from the long flat sands of Powfoot. There were no wrecks there, only boats and men disappearing without trace beneath the shifting sands.'

'At present, these never-ending wrecks are my main concern,' Jack told her. 'We are finding too many already picked clean before we ever get to them, or the excisemen either. I fear there is some conspiracy going on, some unholy alliance, and I intend to find it out.'

It was the first time that he had spoken to her as an equal, disclosing the thoughts in his mind. He had never told her anything of himself before: his problems, all the worries that he had inherited, simply by being born the son of the Jardines. Glancing towards the vicious rocks around Redayre Bay, Barbara felt a little chill of fear for her cousin, a sudden feeling of protectiveness, that she should be helping him instead of placing yet another burden upon his shoulders in his adoption of her.

Impulsive as ever, she half turned to look up into his pale eyes. 'I will find a way, I swear it, to help you, Jack!'

He laughed and flicked her lightly under her chin. 'Will you, Barbie? I wonder.'

# CHAPTER
# FOUR

THAT EVENING the weather changed. They felt it first like a playful little draught, a current of air rippling in through the open windows of the sitting-room. The Jardine family sat round the hearth, where a fire had been lit, reading and yawning, and watching the embers die away to grey ashes.

Jack raised his head sharply and rose to look out, frowning a moment, and turning his cheek to find the little breeze.

'What is it?' Sibylla asked.

He waited a second or two before replying, still sniffing the air like an animal for scent. 'The wind has backed to the south-west.'

'And that will bring the sea rushing up the Solway Firth,' Barbara thought. The fishermen at home had never liked too much wind from the south-west.

The candles had burned low, but there were three that remained burning still, the grease dripping on the floor, and the light they gave was yellow and queer. The clock in the stable yard struck the hour. They heard its thin high notes like the echo of a bell as Jack snapped shut the windows. Another candle went out, and only two stayed now to flicker and dance upon the wall.

'That was ten o'clock ringing,' said Sibylla. 'Time for bed, anyway. Come, Barbara, we will go up.'

They climbed the darkened staircase, one hand upon the railing, their candles making grotesque shadows along the gallery and the passages beyond until Sibylla whispered good night, and Barbara closed the door of her bedchamber and undressed. Her thin nightgown felt cool and shivery when she made her accustomed pilgrimage, barefoot, to gaze out over the sea before she lay down.

Away to the west where the jagged rocks were foamed with seas, there was a little dancing light, a will-o'-the-wisp light, flickering, flaring, and finally disappearing into the black night. Surely that had been the beacon, which should never go out? With a little shiver she withdrew and fastened the window catch, and the first moan of wind rushed up from the west, out of nowhere, and a swift hard spatter of rain beat across the diamond panes. A sudden draught blew out her candle and Barbara huddled down under the bedclothes uneasily. Summer storms came fast and fierce on the Solway, and shifted the deceitful, treacherous sands.

'There has been a shipwreck round by Yawkins' Hole,' Margaret told her next morning in the kitchen. The rain was not so heavy now, and the air much cooler. 'We will know by midday if the weather has broken, or it was only a passing storm, the same as two nights ago.'

'Was anyone drowned?' Barbara asked, shivering. She could not shake off the sudden chill she felt.

'Come and drink your tea here by the fire,' Margaret commanded. 'Have you caught a cold?'

'No. It was only a goose walking over my grave. Tell me what happened?'

'I'm afraid some lives were lost,' Margaret admitted. 'But Jack is down there. That is one of his duties, to examine the wreck. He is the custodian of the coastline, now that Papa has gone.' Her eyes filled with tears. 'No, I am all right, Barbara—it is just that now and then something brings it all back. Papa was called out so often, as the receiver of wrecks.'

'What does that mean?'

'It meant that Papa had to mount a guard over the wreck until the excisemen came and calculated the duties payable on it. Until then, he could not claim it, nor distribute any part of it.'

'And so Jack has to do that now?'

'Yes. It is not a pleasant task. You will find that it

depresses him. It puts a gloom over all Redayre, in fact, for inevitably there are poor drowned bodies which have to be dealt with.'

'Do you mean that there have been many wrecks around Redayre Bay?' Barbara asked.

'Very many, especially these past two years. Smuggling, too. The excisemen make constant raids along here, and then we are plagued by them for a bed or a meal.'

The comings and goings at the far end of the bay went on for most of the morning, while the rain turned first to a drizzle, then hung in an iridescent curtain of mist before vanishing in the burning sun, and the birds began to sing once more. The grass was wet after the rain, and there was a silver sheen on it, and a damp warm smell in the air like an autumn mist. Barbara watched the trees dripping, then drying, and then the leaves, clean and sparkling again, beginning to dance and shimmer in the light warm air.

She went on watching until at last Jack's tall figure came nearer and nearer as he walked wearily around the bay, his head bent, and up the steep incline towards Redayre. She was waiting silently for him with Margaret and Sibylla in the hall, where there was an air of sadness now—the roses drooped, the petals all dropped off and withered—when he came back.

'It is the same as before. And before, and before that again,' he said heavily. 'The ship smashed to pieces into driftwood, the crew lost or drowned, and no trace of any cargo. I must go to Dumfries. Immediately, and I shall be gone for some days.'

Margaret swept the brown rose-petals into her apron and shouted, 'Jean! Nessie!' Then, when they appeared, 'Go up and attend Sir John. He leaves at once. And when you come back, we will have this hall dusted and polished until it shines.'

'Come, Barbara,' Sibylla said with a small sigh. 'We may as well make a start to the invitations. Jack will not be using the library now. But first I must speak to Alan Kerr.'

'Nessie,' she called out as the little serving-girl rushed past in the direction of the kitchen. 'See if young Joe is in the stables. Tell him to send Alan Kerr in here to me.'

'We will make out two lists, Barbara,' she said, sitting behind the great desk Jack had been sketching on when she had stood before him like an erring child. 'One for the ladies and another for the gentlemen, for we must be careful of our numbers, so that everyone has a partner for the dances. Come in,' she added, raising her voice as a knock came to the door.

'Make Sir John's horse ready, Alan, and then I want you to go to the North House, and inform Mr Faulks that I shall be visiting him this afternoon with Miss Barbara.'

He nodded his curly fair head. 'I'll see to that at once, Miss Sibylla.' He left Barbara and Sibylla to work.

They had scarcely got half down the lists when another knock came to the door. 'This will be Fanny,' Sibylla said, 'with Betsy Proudfoot, the new maid. If you do not take to her, Barbara, you must let me know, for remember, she will be very close to you, by day and even by night, should you need her.'

'I will tap once on the table for no, twice for yes,' said Barbara.

'Very well, dear. Come in, Fanny,' Sibylla called.

Fanny came in, pushing the new girl before her, and then stood quietly back, as Sibylla and Barbara sat behind the large desk and regarded her. Betsy surveyed them calmly out of quiet dark blue eyes.

'I know your Mama, dear,' Sibylla said kindly. 'Did she explain to you what your duties may be here?'

'Yes. To look after the new young lady—with Fanny's direction—and to be seamstress, Miss Sibylla.'

Betsy half-turned when she said this, to smile and include Fanny in their interview. The older maid's eyes blinked, but she made no other sign.

'This girl is kind, she knows her place, and she has a sense of humour,' Barbara thought. 'Besides that, she is intelligent.'

'And your sewing?' Sibylla asked.

'Everything I am wearing, I sewed,' Betsy replied.

'That is beautiful work,' Sibylla said, peering at the smocking on the bodice of Betsy's dress. 'Come here, child. Let me see.'

The girl moved nearer to them while they admired the stitching, and Sibylla put her head on one side, scrutinising the workmanship on the dress, and glancing up at Fanny, who nodded a little nod. Barbara's eyes met those of Betsy Proudfoot, and in them she beheld frankness and sincerity, but more than that, the courage of an independent mind.

'Perhaps Miss Barbara has some questions she would like to ask you,' Sibylla said, and sat back.

'Just one,' Barbara smiled. 'Do you think you would be happy with me, Betsy?'

'Very happy, Miss Barbara.'

Two taps on the table concluded the interview.

'When can you start?' Sibylla asked. 'Fanny will show you everything.'

'Now,' said Betsy, and the two maids left, leaving the slow work of the invitations to proceed.

'Perhaps we will manage to finish the rest this evening,' Sibylla said later that afternoon when they set off walking. 'We shall not be able to deliver any more by hand, anyway, except for this one to the minister. The rest we must send.'

'Which way do you take to the North House?' Barbara asked.

'We will go by the shore. It will be refreshing in the sea-breezes, and the mauve thrift is so pretty just now.'

'How long will Jack be gone, do you think?'

Sibylla shook her head. 'Days, weeks sometimes, we never know.'

'Now,' thought Barbara, 'I am as free as a bird, to come and go as I please.'

They walked along the squelching turf, its grass short and dark green, and saw the waving flowers of the sea-pinks, listened to the startled cry of a moorhen as it paddled away into the reeds and hid itself, until they came to a bank of high shingle which separated them from the sea. From the top, the sky had all the clarity and radiance of midsummer, and the sea murmured and sighed on the beach. Now and then a tremor on the waves would bear a ripple upon its glassy surface, where it would shiver for an instant and then wash away into the quivering reeds.

Barbara turned round to look back on Redayre, its sloping lawns, its tall chimneys and the west wing where she and Sibylla had their rooms.

'Mine is the only window looking west up the shore,' she remarked. 'All the rest on the upper storey are skylights.'

'That is true,' her cousin answered, 'and that is why I do not care for it. When the winds howl up the Solway Firth and the rain lashes at that window, it seems as though the very sea would hurl itself inside. I do hope it has no such effect on you, dear.'

Barbara laughed. 'I love the sea, Sibylla, and I love the room.'

The high shingle bank had a twin on the other side of the freshwater stream running down from the North Hill. Barbara discreetly forbore to mention that she had seen it before, and Sibylla struck out for the path which disappeared into the trees. When they looked up to the North House, its whole approach was sheltered by the trees growing right down to the shore, with the gully acting like a moat.

'It is well concealed,' Barbara commented, and they walked up the gentle incline in the cool of the Willow Walk.

Mr Faulks stood up from his seat in the summerhouse, where he had been watching for them, and taking an arm each, walked with them into the house, and showed them into a room at the front. He went away, murmuring quietly that he would see about some tea, and Barbara took stock of her surroundings with a lively interest. The room was quietly impersonal, as though it were some drawing-room visited unexpectedly by night. It had no personality that Barbara could trace, and she wondered when it had last been used. In fact the whole house seemed strangely peaceful, like the house in the fairy-tale that had slept for a hundred years.

The minister came back in, carrying the same round silver tray himself, and waited upon them quietly and with so little show that it seemed a natural everyday occurrence. While his hands were busy, Barbara looked about her, accepting without question the lack of the usual biblical pictures on the walls, even the lack of books themselves, not even a bible, opened at a selected text.

Sibylla handed him an invitation card. He nodded his acceptance, smiling, and once again Barbara admired his strange colouring, the curling red hair, golden where a shaft of sun glinted it, and the slanting eyes of bronze.

'I will look forward to it, Sibylla,' he said, and there was no mistaking the sincerity in his voice. 'Although my duties may prevent me from attending every day, I hope to have the pleasure of partnering each of you as often as I can.' His brown eyes rested on Barbara as he said this, lingering on her face, so that she felt a little thrill of pleasure, mingled with a self-consciousness quite new to her.

'What is that sound?' she asked, as they walked out of the long window onto the lawns again, to cover her sudden shyness.

'The doves in the dovecote.' And then, turning to Sibylla, he said, 'All noble families build a dovecote, do they not, somewhere on their estates? It is another mark of the gentry.'

Was there a jarring note in that smooth voice? Barbara wondered briefly.

But Sibylla smiled and answered, 'Oh yes, the dovecote has always been here, all my life.'

He led them round to the side of the house, and there towards the back, in a small courtyard, stood the little house, where the doves whirred in and out, or sat at their tiny doorways.

Last night's rain had left mud in its wake, and Barbara wondered at so many hoofprints before the minister hurried them away. Her eyes followed some of the trails, her glance lifting sharply to a sudden movement at one of the windows. She was sure that it was Mistress Sadie Caldwell who dodged out of sight, and just for an instant she caught a glimpse of another figure behind her, the figure of a tall woman, half remembered, and she had long hair, but the colour of it she had not time to see.

'Come, it is this way,' said Mr Faulks's soft voice in her ear, and his hand on her arm dug into her flesh a little painfully as he turned her firmly aside.

Then they walked slowly home again, glad to reach the shade of the Willow Walk, for the afternoon had turned out very hot.

Over the next few days excitement rose steadily in Redayre House, and was brought to fever pitch by a note from Philip Favenel to Sibylla, to tell her that he had arrived home from London, and would be delighted to accept her invitation to come with Louise.

The carriages came one after the other on Saturday, and the guests were disposed among the rooms in the East wing, and settled in. Margaret was entrenched in the kitchens, preparing all the extra meals with a zeal and an expertise which proved that she was far from stretched to her limit, even yet.

In the afternoon Barbara began to worry over Sibylla. Scarcely over her convalescence, she was looking very tired. The physical effort required to attend to the arrangements for the swelling household was proving too much.

'Do go and lie down for an hour, Sibylla,' she pleaded, 'or else you will not be able to speak to Mr Favenel when he gets here. I will meet all the other guests this afternoon. I know where to put them.'

And so she was the one to welcome the coach bearing Miss Louise and Mr Philip Favenel to Redayre.

'Oh,' said Louise, descending in her delicately pointed slippers the little steps the coachman had unfolded. 'I had expected Jack to meet me, or at the very least, dear Sibylla! How very disappointing! And who may you be, child?'

Barbara took an instant and passionate dislike to this apparition of sophisticated beauty, and for a moment was quite unable to look at anything else except Louise's golden high-heeled slippers. It was as though her eyes were glued to them. She had never seen anything so feminine and beguiling before, in the way of enhancement of the female form. At once she ranged herself for battle, but in that long look downwards she had prepared her defence.

'Barbara Graham, Miss Favenel,' she said steadily, and even managed to smile. 'A distant cousin of Sir John's.'

She did not know what instinct made her disclaim any intimacy with him. It came from somewhere deep within herself, age-old, female against female, and she looked away from Louise to her brother Philip. He regarded her with apologetic, if slightly amused, eyes.

'I am honoured to welcome you both here, Mr Favenel,' she said, curtsying prettily. 'Sibylla is lying down for a little while in her bedchamber. She felt a little fatigued, but begged me to tell you how much she is looking forward to meeting you both later this evening. Now, if you would follow me, I will show you to your rooms.'

'But where *is* Jack?' Louise said, a peevish note now in her voice. 'I thought he would be here.'

'Sir John is away on business, I'm afraid.' Barbara hoped Louise did not hear the relish with which she said this. 'But he hopes to be back for the Ball.'

'Oh, how boring,' Louise said. 'It was Jack I came all this way to see. Still,' and she laughed, a little tinkling laugh, 'it will give me a chance to speak to some of the other gentlemen of the district, I suppose.'

'To flirt with them, you mean,' said her brother.

Louise waved a languid hand. 'That, too, perhaps. *Are* there any other handsome gentlemen here, child?'

'Some very nice ladies and gentlemen have arrived here today,' Barbara said primly. 'This is your room, Miss Favenel, and Sibylla thought you might like to be next door to your sister, Mr Favenel.'

'Oh, do call us Louise and Philip,' Louise said impatiently. 'And what did you say your name was?'

'Barbara.'

'Very pretty,' Philip said. 'It suits you.'

Barbara had no sooner arranged them in their rooms before the next carriage could be heard arriving, and she was kept busy all that day. On Sunday Mr Garbutt himself arrived, a dapper little man wearing pointed slippers with silk rosettes on the toes in the very latest fashion, carrying his fiddle-case in his hand.

The lessons began on Monday afternoon in the Long Drawing-room, specially cleared for the occasion, its carpets rolled up and stored away, revealing its springing floorboards. During that first week Barbara found her attention quite taken up in the acquaintance of so many new friends, and in admiring yet another of Margaret's talents, her graceful dancing. Light as a feather she floated over the dance floor with John Reid—John, who was even bigger and stouter than his prospective bride.

'It is always the same with roly-polys,' young William Reid lamented as he stumbled, all knees and elbows, on to the floor and tripping over Barbara's slippers for the hundredth time. William would never be a dancer, Barbara sighed. 'They can dance.'

It was true. John, when he could spare the time to come for an occasional hour to the lessons, put all the other gentlemen to shame. He kept his broad back so straight, his shoulders so square, and his arm encircling his partner did more than gently guide her direction, it almost lifted her and set her feet into the steps. He must be immensely strong, Barbara thought one afternoon as he whirled her round. She looked up at his rosy face shining like a beacon, heard his deep voice humming along with the fiddle and could not help but like him as much as she admired the music in his soul. He was a happy man.

And he never looked so happy, or so comfortable, as when he was with Margaret. Barbara could visualise it now, the home they would share at John Reid's farm, where no one would ever be refused shelter, she was sure of that. There would be a smile, a friendly hand and a bed, always, for anyone who ever asked.

And all that week she managed to avoid the Favenels, which turned out to be quite easy. Philip and Sibylla would much rather be alone in each other's company, with their beloved books and their long discussions, as everyone could see. And Louise was concentrating her energies on the gentlemen instead. There was no doubt that she made a deep impression on them, for they clamoured to be her partner for every practice. She was the centre of attention in her unusual and often bizarre dresses. She was centre stage. Clearly, it was her true and rightful position in life.

And still Jack had not come back.

By the second week, the household had settled down to its new routine. Every afternoon was spent under the supervision of Mr Garbutt, who pounded away on his fiddle, sometimes stopping to correct a fault, or place a foot just so.

It was during one of these pauses that Barbara's partner did not loosen his hold on her. 'Shall we go out into the garden?' Mr Faulks asked her.

Barbara nodded. Perhaps he was too hot, which would account for the dampness of his hands and the tiny beads of perspiration on his face. She had seen many of the young couples going outside in the intervals for some air. But there was nobody else in the garden that she could see, and the white-painted seats scattered around the lawns were all empty. However, Mr Faulks was not making for any of them, but headed Barbara straight for the shrubbery. 'Of course,' she thought. 'It will be cool in there.'

From somewhere further away, she heard a muffled giggle and then a little scream. So they were not alone, where the heavy green foliage of midsummer made a roof over their heads, and the branches of the low-growing trees made little private walls around them.

The minister put his arm round her, to guide her, she thought; but his grasp swiftly became closer, tauter, and infinitely more unseemly even than the way he had tried to dance with her sometimes, so that Mr Garbutt had had to raise his eyebrows once or twice for the regulation one foot of space between them which he insisted on. But now there was not even one inch of space between them, and Barbara felt a little uncomfortable. Yet his conversation remained light-hearted and cheerful, although the heat from his body seemed to be mounting, and he was becoming a little breathless when he put his other arm round her, and his mouth was on her hair.

'You drive a man half crazy, Barbara,' he muttered thickly, and she looked up, startled, and saw that his skin was dotted brown like the underside of a fern, as if he had just brushed past one, and his smiling teeth, so strong and so white, were quite pointed. She stared at them, fascinated, as they descended dangerously close to her mouth, and his hands began to rove over her body, evoking thrilling feelings entirely new to her, feelings she did not know if she hated or really liked.

She could not swear how she might respond if their lips actually met. Before she could make up her mind, his slack mouth possessed hers with a suddenness and a ferocity which was quite shocking. Then, to her horror, his tongue forced her teeth apart and invaded the tender, private skin inside her lips. For a moment she was too shocked to move, and the minister's eyes, with that queer red flushed look in them, suddenly reminded her of Sandy's, that day in the hayloft at Starlochy when he had forced his attentions on poor little Jessie, and she knew in that moment why Mr Faulks was trying to bend her back into the bracken.

She tore herself from his grasp, forcing back the hysterical feeling that she had been violated in some way. She must be sensible. After all, what had it been? Only a kiss. In fact, she supposed she should be flattered, because the first real kiss of her life had been bestowed upon her by a minister.

'Perhaps we should go back now,' she managed to suggest quite calmly.

Mr Faulks seemed to have been holding his breath, for

now he expelled it in a long, shuddering sigh—almost of relief, she thought with surprise.

She did not relish the prospect of dancing with him again, and wondered how she could tell him so, in a way that would not offend him. 'It might be wiser if you danced with some other lady,' she said, as they were walking back over the lawns into the ballroom again. 'You have paid me so much attention already that perhaps people may remark upon it.'

'Indeed, that is very clever of you, Barbara. Besides, I should only want to kiss you again,' he said with a familiarity which made her shudder.

It was as though he were entering into a complicity with her, that he expected her now to be in some quite irreverent alliance with him. It was not at all what she had meant to convey.

All the rest of the afternoon, while the lessons went on, Barbara was very thoughtful. She had learned a great deal in the shrubbery, not least that she was now a thoroughly grown-up young lady and must expect that sort of thing from gentlemen. But not from Mr Faulks, for she could no longer trust what he might do, or lead her to do. No matter how sensible she was trying to be, she was sure that his behaviour towards her throughout these whole two weeks had been wrong somehow, although she had no yardstick of experience to match it against.

All she did know for certain was that it would never have happened at all if Jack had been there—never. She trembled at the very idea of his fury, if he knew; at the cold hard brilliance of his angry eyes, if he knew, and suddenly she began to miss him horribly. He looked after everyone so well. She missed him worst of all in the evenings, after they had all dined, and the golden lights of sunset had gone, and the sky became paler, mysterious and soft in that hour before it grew dark, when the lights glowed out of the doors and the windows of old Redayre on the guests wandering through the shadowy gardens in the still, scented air.

She had seen John Reid and Margaret once, standing

very close together with their arms round each other, and in a flash she understood now that this jolly couple shared a passion which was not comfortable at all, but burned like a fire. It was then that Barbara began to feel restless, and very often sad, filled with a longing she could not name.

Her feelings were by no means soothed when Sibylla told her, 'We have had word from Jack. His business detains him, but he hopes he may be back in time for the Ball.'

The Ball! But that was another two whole long days away, she fretted.

'What business is it that keeps him so long, Sibylla?'

'I do not know it all, my dear. But part of it is in connection with the linen trade, which is assuming so much importance in Scotland. He is having discussions with other landowners about the possibility of growing flax on the estate, with a view to starting up a mill, all of which would provide more work in the district.'

'Oh,' said Barbara. It sounded very dull.

'And, as far as I know, to make any profit from flax it must be dressed to prepare it for spinning—heckling, I believe it is called. It is a difficult craft, and if Jack proceeds with this idea, he will have to choose men to go as far away as Ayrshire to master it.'

'I can see that he has a lot to occupy him, Sibylla.'

'The roads are often so bad in the winter that when he is as far away as Dumfries at this time of year it is only sensible to attend to as much business as possible.'

'Yes,' Barbara sighed.

'Why, dear? Are you missing him?'

'Oh no,' she protested, half in a lie, and half because the little devil inside her was calling to her again, reminding her that there might not be many more days and nights of freedom from the watchful eyes of her guardian.

It kept reminding her of the closet, and the little hidden staircase she had never used. Barbara looked out upon the tall beech trees that stood gaunt and naked that summer night, their branches stirring softly like a whisper of things to come, and knew that she could stand it no longer. She must go and run in the moss, in the young green of the woods, and touch the ripples of the sea.

Lifting her gown above her ankles and tightening her sash at her waist to keep it in place, she tiptoed to the closet along the moonlit landing, and found her way down and out through the little door behind the ivy. Silent as a ghost, she ran down through the trees to the Solway shore. She danced along the shining sands and waded through the stream, climbed over the shingle banks until, breathless, with her heart beating fast, she scrambled up the rocks to Yawkins' Hole. A three-masted ship rode at anchor in the deep blackness of the creek.

Dumbfounded as she was, she had the presence of mind to flatten herself immediately upon the soft grass half-way up the slope, while her heart thumped and her spine crawled with fear. What was it doing here, this ominous black shape, so still, so eerily silent? She hardly dared to raise her head to look at it again, so great was some nameless dread upon her, and even as she did, her ears caught the creak of oars.

A little boat was making its way out to it. As she watched, it came alongside, and men were clambering up on the deck of the ship lying in the shadows. Perhaps they would go away, sail the ship away again, she thought hopefully. But no. They were returning to the rowing-boat, heavy laden with boxes and kegs which they passed carefully and silently from hand to hand, and then dropped down themselves to row for shore again.

A white-hot thrill of terror, and some primitive instinct, kept Barbara from moving. She hardly breathed. She was so near to them, as the boat glided past the rocks, that she could almost have put out her hand and touched the men in it. Of course they were smugglers, and there was something in their furtive yet powerful actions which told her that they would deal out short shrift to anyone spying on them.

In the moon's rays she saw that one of them had light curly hair, and he was broad and stocky. With a sickening shock, she recognised him. He was Alan Kerr, the Redayre groom, she was sure of that. It was as much as she could do to contain herself, to stop from racing back to the house then and there, to warn Sibylla and the others to send word at once to Jack.

And then one man stood up in the bows to guide them into the Hole. He was tall, and dressed all in black, looked slimmer than her lurching heart remembered. Her worst fears were realised when he turned his head to give an order to his men, and Barbara saw with a sick feeling that, in the moonlight, his eyes flashed and glittered like silver. It was Jack Jardine.

Jack Jardine, her brain repeated numbly, who was supposed to be away on business, who had sent word to Sibylla that very day.

She had no idea afterwards how long she lay there, not daring to move, while the rowing-boat plied back and fore, back and fore to the ship. It grew cold while she watched, sick and shivering, until it seemed the last trip had been made, for there was a long pause, and she heard the smugglers talking on the beach in low tones.

It dawned on her slowly that she must get away, and at once. They would all be returning to their homes, now that their secret work was done, and Jack Jardine would be going back to Redayre. Somehow she had to get there before him. Which way would he take? she asked herself wildly, and knew it would be the shortest way, over the rough tracks which radiated through the tussocks, and then over the fields. Silently she slid back down the grass on her stomach, small stones scratching and cutting her legs and her hands, until she reached the beach again where she had danced so happily only a few hours ago.

Then she ran—faster than she had ever run before in her life, so that her breath struggled in her lungs—through the shrubbery, and sobbing for breath, over the lawns until she found the little door under the ivy again. She was choking and gasping as she clawed her way up the staircase and arrived at last bleeding and dishevelled, in her room, to fling herself upon the bed.

It could not have been him! It could not! She would not believe it. She was mistaken. She was often mistaken, she told herself fiercely, like the time she thought she saw a long-haired woman in the minister's house. It had not been—it never was. It was all part of her imagination. Yes, she had imagined it all, and sobbing wildly she cried herself to sleep, for she knew in her heart that she had not been imagining the events of this night. They had really happened.

She got up next morning, listless and dull, and as the memory of last night flooded back, promised herself faithfully that she would never think of any of it again, never admit to it, not even to herself.

'Your hands, Miss Barbara!' Betsy exclaimed. 'What has happened to them? And your legs! They have been bleeding!'

'It is nothing. I fell outside, last night.'

'They must be soaked at once in hot water, and rubbed with salve. It should have been done at once. Why did you not call me?'

'It was very late, Betsy. I had been out for some air.'

'But I will attend to you at any time of the day or night, Miss Barbara. I live here now. I sleep in the attics with the other maids. Sit still while I run down to Miss Margaret for the ointment.'

'Make light of it, then, Betsy.'

'I can keep secrets! Do not worry, Miss Barbara.'

Afterwards, when she was dressed and composed, she went downstairs and arrived quietly in the dining-room. Half-way across the floor she became rooted to the spot when she met the icy grey eyes she had been forcing herself to forget.

'What on earth has she been up to, Sibylla?' Jack asked. 'She looks worn out to me,' as Sibylla rushed in consternation to her side.

'Have you been dancing too much?' he asked her coldly and accusingly. 'Go back to bed until you are rested.'

Her eyes hardened into blue daggers, and she gasped at the effrontery of the man sitting there, looking so tired and drawn himself, as any man would be who lived the two lives he was living.

'Thank you,' she said icily, and then, with a sudden surge of anger, 'it is lack of fresh air and Snowy's company which fatigues me. I find horses so much easier to understand than some men.'

The corners of his mouth twitched for an instant, and then he asked sternly, 'You have not been out alone on him, I trust, in my absence?'

'There was no chance,' she glared at him. 'I rode with the ladies once or twice, but that is no use to a horse of Snowy's spirit, just ambling along. He needs to be given his head.'

'There may be a good deal of truth in that,' he said. 'It would apply to a filly of uncertain temper, too, I dare say.'

'What was that I missed? Do tell!' Louise Favenel trailed in, yawning, and fastening her eyes on her host. Beautiful great blue eyes, too, Barbara saw with a savage pang.

'It was nothing. Merely a small discussion with my young ward,' Jack answered, while Barbara seethed, rebuked in grown-up company.

She observed how tenderly he passed Miss Favenel the toast. Very soon, she told herself acidly, he would be spreading the butter on it for her.

'Where do you and your players appear next?' he was asking her.

'At the Theatre Royal next month in Dumfries.' She glowed up at him. 'Of course you will come, Jack. Bring Sibylla and Margaret—oh, and the child as well, of course.'

Barbara got to her feet, her chair grating harshly over the floorboards, and flounced out.

Jack's head poked out into the hall from the dining-room door. 'Go and get ready,' he commanded. 'I shall take you riding myself this morning.'

She came out into the stable courtyard in a thoroughly

bad temper, fully expecting to find Miss Favenel there, mounted and in some magnificent riding-habit, with Jack. But he was alone, seated on the big brown chestnut who was tossing his head impatiently. Joe brought out Snowy and helped her up. Patting the horse's velvety nose, she asked innocently, 'Isn't Miss Favenel coming too?'

'I didn't invite her,' he said coldly. 'It is you I wish to speak to, alone and out of earshot.'

'What now?' Barbara wondered as they cantered off. Had he seen her last night as plainly as she had seen him? If he had, then she was riding straight into trouble.

'Right! Let them go!' Jack said, as his horse broke into a gallop along the flat hard sand.

With the sea wind in her face, the movement of her horse beneath her, the thunder of his hooves, the scent of the golden gorse, and the sound of the Solway coming in to them as the long surf rollers split themselves with a roar on the shore, Barbara forgot everything else. She felt free at last, and she lifted her head and laughed. They galloped across the open country until she heard a shout from Jack and drew in her reins. He jumped from the chestnut and held out his hands to her, and quite forgetting that she was placing herself and her trust into the clutches of the arch-criminal she had convinced herself he was, she allowed him to lift her down.

He tied the horses to a tree, where they frisked a little and then settled down to munch the grass.

'Sit here beside me,' he said, taking her elbow. 'The wind has whipped your hair into tangles.' The touch of his hand smoothing it back off her face was oddly tender for so strict a guardian. 'So, you went to see Mr Faulks?' he said at last.

She nodded, startled at this turn of conversation. 'Yes, with Sibylla.'

'Was he alone?' Jack asked, looking away from her over the sea.

'I think so,' Barbara replied. 'But he has a house-keeper, you know.'

'Hm. I do know,' he said in a strange voice. 'Did you see her?'

She hesitated. 'I thought I did.'

'What does that mean, Barbara?' he asked impatiently.

'I—I don't know,' she stumbled. 'I thought I saw her at a window, but she moved away.'

'Did you see anyone else?'

Determined not to repeat any more of the business of a man of God to a smuggler, no matter how much she liked the smuggler and disliked the minister, she shook her head. She would not mention the hoofprints, either, she decided, no matter how the smuggler's eyes could melt in that disturbing way to the softest grey, like the wings of a dove.

He laughed suddenly. 'I'm sorry, Barbie, if I have been abrupt. We had all better have an early night in our beds, before the Ball tomorrow.'

'Oh yes, the Ball,' she repeated vaguely, still remembering why he lacked his sleep. 'Did you not go to bed last night, then?' she ventured.

'Did you not notice,' he asked, his voice steely, 'that I am the one asking the questions, and you are the one who is answering? Why did you look so unhappy this morning, Barbara?'

She turned her face away, and felt the tears start at the back of her eyes. How could she answer that, when he was lying back there on the grass, so solid and—so safe? Nothing like a smuggler at all, and everything like her protector!

'Are you unhappy here?' he repeated, his voice gentler.

'No!' she burst out passionately, the tears sparkling on her lashes. 'But I do not like it when you are away,' she wailed truthfully. 'I do not understand what it is you do, or where you go.'

'No more questions, Barbie, and no more answers. I have found out more than I had hoped,' he said, brushing away her tears. But she had not, she thought rebelliously.

And then he was pulling her up, and for a breathless moment she hung in his arms and forgot that he had evaded her, before he lifted her back on to Snowy, and his eyes held hers in a look that had nothing to do with being her guardian.

'You ride well,' he said a minute later when he had mounted himself, in his usual cool tone. 'But we shall go back at a more sedate pace, I think.'

What had she told him, she wondered, and could not guess.

The evening of the Ball on the 25th of July coincided with Barbara's eighteenth birthday, a day she had dreaded not long ago. Now she put on the rose satin gown and stopped before the glass to see that it hung straight and smooth. She quite overlooked the beauty of her creamy skin, the pink flush on her cheeks, the brilliance of her eyes and her lips so full and red.

'Now, your hair, Miss Barbara,' Betsy said behind her.

'How are you going to do it? Not too tight, Betsy.'

'No, I have thought of a new way. I will brush it all up on the crown like this, and pin it with these little rosettes I made out of scraps of the rose satin. Then your hair can fall free behind.'

'What will you do, tonight, when we are at the Ball?'

'Oh, bless you, Miss Barbara, we are all dancing, too, out in the big barn. It is all cleaned and decorated for the occasion.'

'What will you wear? Have you a sweetheart? Tell me, Betsy, and don't brush so hard!'

'I'm nearly finished with the brushing. See, it is the polishing with this length of silk. No, I have no sweetheart, and yes, I made a dress. It is lilac.'

Betsy began to pin the pink rosettes in very firmly. 'Do you like them?'

'It was a brilliant idea. I knew you would have brilliant ideas. Why do you not have a sweetheart?—You are so pretty.'

'Oh, I don't want to marry,' Betsy laughed. 'I am happy as I am.'

'Watch out, Betsy Proudfoot,' Barbara said, and ran downstairs.

'Your gown is very pretty,' commented young William, goggling at its low neck and leading her with sticky hands to the dance floor.

Barbara forgot him almost immediately. She danced on wings of happiness, for out of the corner of her eye she saw that Jack was there, tall and handsome in the dark blue brocaded coat which sat so easily over his broad shoulders. Then she found herself dancing with Mr Faulks, his smile much too presumptuous.

'You are lovely, like a rose,' he said, and to Barbara the words in his velvet tones sounded almost indecent. Suddenly she felt overpowered and tried to edge herself away from him, and his masculine smell. An odd smell, even stronger than the scent he wore. It was strange how his thick brows met in the middle, like a bar of fur. She had noticed it before, but never so much as now, when his face was close to her own.

She looked around for some way to escape, some excuse, and found one almost at once, for the dance floor was clearing, the couples sitting down to make space for the belle of the Ball. It was Louise Favenel, in a dazzling gown of sapphire blue with silver trimmings, sparkling and shooting stars in the bright lights of a hundred candles. More sparkles were in her hair, and on her feet she wore concoctions which seemed to be made of sugar frosting. Worse, a thousand times worse than that, Barbara discovered, Louise was dancing with her guardian, every inch the Lord of Redayre, and they made a magnificent couple.

She had not known that she could hate anyone as much as she hated Louise Favenel at that moment, the way she pirouetted and turned to her audience, the way she swept her eyelashes up to Jack, who bowed and smiled and caught her to him over and over again so tenderly. But at last it was over, the clapping subsided, and with the striking up of the music again the minister had her in his grasp once more.

'We have a secret, you and I,' he whispered in her ear. Barbara smiled politely and looked away. 'Nobody shall know of it. You were so right, Barbara. We must keep it to ourselves for the time being.'

'Yes, indeed,' she agreed.

'But it may not be long now, before I can declare it to the world,' he murmured.

'What do you mean? I do not understand you.'

'Then shall we go outside again?' He strained her closer to him, and she saw that his eyes had taken on that hot red glow again. 'Before the music stops, so that we are not missed? Oh Barbara, you must come!'

His hand moved further up her back, over her hair, so that if he was not going to pull it and hurt her, she was forced to tilt her face up to his. For a hideous moment she thought that there, in front of all these people, he was going to kiss her again with his spongy lips. And then, mercifully, the music stopped.

'The next dance is mine, I think?' Jack said behind her, and she turned to him with relief.

'You are quite recovered, I see,' he observed, as the music started again.

Barbara glanced up at him, fighting against the wild racing of her heart, and struggling to conceal the nervousness which had nothing to do with his smuggling activities. 'Thank you, yes.'

'So formal?' His eyes glittered. 'You looked more kindly on your last partner, I think.'

She trembled as his encircling arm tightened a little. She had never danced with him before, and tried to appear calm and unconcerned. She found it unbearable, and the hand that held hers sent little shivers through her at every step. It was a new sensation, and she would not have released his hand for the world. She clung to it.

'You are angry, Barbara, aren't you? Angry and even rebellious, because of my efforts to curtail your liberty. Are you going to forgive me, just for the duration of this dance?'

She looked up, amazed at such an admission of weakness from Sir John Jardine, custodian of the coast with one hand, smuggler with the other, and met his eyes, amused and admiring. Even in her confusion she saw that it was the rings of jet black eyelashes fringing those unusually pale eyes which made the deadly contrast. They were piercing her heart so softly and so pitilessly. They were talking to her.

'I will forgive you,' she said with dignity. 'Just for tonight.'

Jack laughed, and his look intensified to a hard thrust. 'You do not know it,' he murmured close to her ear, so that her knees almost buckled, 'but I have sworn an oath to Robbie Burns. And I intend to carry it out.'

Barbara shivered. She had not forgotten the threat he had made that June night in Dumfries. 'Perhaps I over-heard it,' she answered, her eyes sparkling up into his with the boldness of the new-found liberation of her eighteen years. 'But will not the outcome rather depend on me?'

'I think not,' he said, tightening his hold on her. 'Before we are finished you will want it as much as I do.'

'Another threat?' Barbara flashed, her eyes darkly blue.

'No,' he laughed, and his lips brushed across her cheek, cool and firm. 'That is a promise—to my Lady Barbara.'

And then, good or bad, she was filled with a convic-tion and a confidence she had never felt before, and the rest of the evening was a nebulous dream she scarcely remembered when the Ball was ended.

The guests departed and Barbara went back to her room in the old house of Redayre, its boards creaking back to rest, and the noise of the music and the laughter fading into happy memory. note by note. She was happier than she had ever been before, standing at her window and looking out over the Solway sea, in the still darkness. She could not bear to take off her beautiful gown. She could not bear to think of Jack—not yet, so soon out of his arms.

She was too excited, her senses too aware, to sleep or

even to dream, and in that state of heightened perception the first tiny sound, a faint slithering sound, came to her ears. At once the hairs rose up on the back of her neck and she scented danger. The noise whispered nearer, ever nearer, and in the silent shadowed room blind panic seized her, and a desperate desire to escape. She flitted silently round the edge of her open door and into the closet, taking refuge behind the hanging cloaks and pressing herself close to the wall, then held her breath and tried to still her heart from beating.

The furtive shuffling grew louder, with now and then a pause as if to listen and to watch, and in Barbara's feverish imagination she saw Crafty, the old Starlochy dog again, stalking prey, saw his pads go down so carefully, heard the panting of his breath when now and then his tongue lolled out in his excitement, smelled the sharp odour of his fur.

Then she knew the door to her room was pushed ajar, knew it by the familiar little grating of its hinges, and then there was a padding and a silence, and the shuffling again, and to her horror, now only inches away, she heard a panting and a swallowing more terrifying than a howl of anger. Barbara froze into a column of fear, feeling her nose pinched with the effort of holding her breath, and then the sound moved and sighed, it retreated, dragging away, until her straining ears could catch it no more. She expelled her breath in a long quivering sigh, then gathered it again as she opened her mouth to scream. The scream rattled back in her throat, and suffocated as a hand reached out from nowhere beside her, and fastened like a clamp over her mouth.

She felt her face grow damp and cold, as waves of faintness broke over her. And then the hand was slackened, and in a shaft of moonlight through the little skylight up above them she recognised its owner, dressed all in black, with nothing to betray him but his cruel glittering eyes.

'Be quiet, Barbara,' Jack's grim voice muttered in her ear. 'For God's sake be quiet, or there will be murder done in Redayre tonight!'

# CHAPTER
# FIVE

IT SEEMED that the night grew darker, and colder, and
more mysterious in those long minutes while they stood
there together amid the creakings of the old timbers of
Redayre and the tiny scufflings of an adventurous
mouse.

'He is gone,' Jack sighed in her ear, 'our secret
visitor.'

'Who was it? What was it? Was it an animal?' she
moaned, trembling with fear.

'An animal in human shape, perhaps . . . A fox with
only two legs.'

What was he trying to tell her? The red-brown colour
of a fox, its pointed teeth . . . In her fevered imagination rose up the image of the minister. But, of course,
Jack could not possibly be hinting at him? Not Mr
Faulks?

'It is someone who is very much attracted to you,
Barbara, who is following you, stalking you as a fox
would stalk a frightened little rabbit. You must know
who that is?'

'No, I do not know him,' she said uneasily and un-
truthfully, for Jack's meaning was perfectly clear. He
must still be angry because she had been dancing so
much with the minister. She longed to tell him how much
she had disliked it. But, perversely, her mind concentrated on the last statement he had made. A frightened
little rabbit was she indeed? 'And I am not a frightened
little rabbit, Jack Jardine. I am more afraid of the
unknown than a mere fox, human or otherwise.'

'Then why are you trembling like that? And why are
you telling me one lie after the other? Is it because you

are as attracted to your pursuer as he is to you? Are you
perhaps trying to shield him, and his identity?'

'I am attracted to no one,' she whispered furiously.

'Another lie, Barbara?'

'Half a lie, perhaps,' she told herself, with a catch of
her breath. She could have been so attracted to her
tormentor, if only he had not been a smuggler. 'Anyway,' she said aloud, 'I would stop trembling if only you
would tell me who you think he was.'

'As to his identity, I know it, but I am going to keep it
the secret he believes it to be until I am ready to pounce.
But you are a woman, and that is a different matter. No
woman can keep a secret. You would betray the fact that
you knew him, if I told you his name outright, every time
you saw him. Come along, you are going to your bed.'

He dragged her, protesting, to the door of her room.

'I cannot sleep in there, Jack! Whoever it was, he has
been in there! How could I sleep? And you are wrong
not to tell me. To be forewarned is to be forearmed.'

But Jack had pushed her in and was tugging at the
curtains. In a flare and a sputter, he lit her candle and
went back to close the door.

'You are in your true guise, I see,' she said bitterly,
goaded beyond endurance, and eyeing his black trousers
and the tunic close up about his neck. This was the man
who was telling her she was not to be trusted! 'You have
been at it again, with your smuggling. The great Sir John
Jardine of Redayre—*smuggling!*'

Was it a cobra she had read in one of her books, she
wondered shrinking back, whose hoods came down like
that over its eyes before it struck? For Jack's eyes were
mere silver slits now, staring into hers, striking terror to
her very soul.

'What do you mean, Barbara Graham?'

'I mean, sir, that I have seen you. I went down to
Yawkins' Hole and saw you. You and Alan Kerr, for
only one of the men with you. I saw you quite plainly.
You cannot deny it!'

'No, I do not deny it,' he said scornfully. 'Why should
I deny or admit anything to you? What would be the use

of explaining anything to you?' His voice took a coldly savage note. 'I inherited you, Barbara Graham, whether I liked it or not, remember that, from my father, who wished to give you the protection and the care of a guardian. It was not my idea.'

Barbara regarded him incredulously, as his voice hissed on relentlessly. Then she was not wanted here in Redayre. She had never been wanted, in spite of all the Jardines' fair words, their welcome, their lavishing of attention, even down to providing her with Betsy Proudfoot.

'Then I can certainly relieve you of your responsibility, sir,' she blazed at him across the guttering of the candle, as they faced each other. 'I shall return to Starlochy in the morning.'

'You will do nothing of the sort,' his words lashed her. 'You know too much, for one thing. Or you think you do. You have never listened to one word I have tried to tell you, have you, Barbara?'

'I don't know what you mean,' she countered.

'How many times is it that I have told you, things may not be as they seem? Yet you will not take my word for it. You have never taken my word for anything, never obeyed the rules I laid down for your safety, never minded your own business.' He paused, and drew a hand tiredly over his eyes. 'I cannot trust you, you see, Barbara,' he said sadly, on a calmer note. 'And now I have found out, in this night's work, that you have made a dangerous situation a thousand times worse with your meddling.'

'I? Meddle? I have done no such thing, Jack Jardine. I saw you, and I told you, and I am glad to have it out in the open. I am glad I told you!'

He looked into her flushed face for a long moment, and then smiled enigmatically. 'I, too, am glad you told me, Barbara. But our discussion leads us nowhere, for I can explain none of it to you at present, and you are tired.'

It was true, she was tired to death, and cold, and so terribly disappointed.

'But I cannot lie down in that bed,' she said, cringing back in horror. 'He may have touched it. It will be dirty.'

'He did not have time to touch it,' Jack said, and his voice was gentle. 'Undress quickly, and I will come back and douse the candle when I have seen that you are all right.'

Barbara took off the rose satin gown, her fingers stiff and clumsy with cold and fear, and crept into bed. Her teeth were chattering, and she thought she would never feel warm again, as she lay shuddering under the bedclothes. It seemed a long time before Jack came back, and when he crossed the room towards her she saw in the flickering candlelight how tired and exhausted his face looked, as unhappy and as worried as she felt herself.

'Where are you going?' she asked, rigid with fright. 'Can't you leave the candle burning?'

'No,' he said. 'It would go out, anyway. But I will not leave you. I shall be close by, don't worry, in the closet for the night. And I sleep very light . . . the slightest noise, and I will hear it. Go to sleep, Barbara, and rest easy.'

She felt the warmth of his hand on her cheek, then the candle's light was gone and the room plunged into darkness. She heard his feet lightly over the floor, out into the passage, and the creak of the wicker hamper in the closet, and then a sigh. Closing her eyes, she fell unexpectedly into a deep and dreamless sleep.

Hours later she awoke, the light warm and bright in her curtained room.

'No, indeed, you cannot begin,' she heard Betsy's voice outside the door. 'Miss Barbara is still asleep, and I will not allow it.'

Barbara stretched out, tired and listless, and the memories of last night crowded in on her. She did not want to get up and face the day. Last and least of all, she did not want to face Jack Jardine. She lay still, listening to the wrangling in the passage outside.

'I have my orders, the same as you,' a man's voice said. 'Stand aside, or I shall have to tell Sir John.'

'What is it, Betsy?' Barbara called out. The door opened and the maid came in, then closed it again.

'It is one of the workmen, Miss Barbara. He has been ordered to fit locks on all the doors in this wing of the house. Sir John said so, before he left.'

'Left? Where has he gone?'

'I don't know, Miss Barbara. But it must have been very early, before I got up at seven o'clock, anyway.'

'What time is it now?'

'After ten.'

'Is everyone up, then?'

'Most of the guests have breakfasted and gone. Miss Sibylla would like to see you when you are ready. Shall I fetch a tray up here?'

'Oh Betsy, I wish you would. I don't feel like facing any of them just at present.'

But when the food arrived, Barbara could eat none of it, and drank only a few sips of tea, for by then her brooding had convinced her that her bed and board, food, water, even the air she breathed was doubtless grudged her at Redayre, and it was in a tearful mood that she knocked on Sibylla's door.

'Barbara! What is it, darling? What is wrong?' Sibylla fluttered with concern. 'Did you not sleep well? Your little face is so white and sad today.'

'Yes, thank you, Sibylla, I slept all night long. But . . .'

'But what, dear? Oh, and I had our day all planned out for us! It is so very pleasant to have you here with us at Redayre, Barbara, especially for me, for I have sorely missed companionship, with Margaret forever in her cooking-pots, now that Papa and Mama are both gone.'

Barbara's tears spilled over at these kindly words, so different from the harsh and bitter words Jack had flung at her last night.

'Perhaps the excitement of the Ball has been too much,' Sibylla said. 'Should we not go out today, as I had intended?'

'No, it isn't that, Sibylla,' Barbara sighed, and wiped

her eyes. 'Only tell me again that you truly want me here?'

'Goodness, child, whatever made you imagine that you are not as welcome in this house as the flowers in May?'

Barbara smiled, although it was a watery little smile, but there was no doubting her cousin's concern. 'I'm afraid I did something very wrong three nights ago, Sibylla. When everyone was asleep I could not resist going out in the moonlight, by myself, through the secret door down from the closet, and went to run along the beach.'

Sibylla frowned a little. 'But there was nothing so terrible about that, except of course that these sands can be so dangerous. But you did not go far, did you?'

'Too far, I'm afraid, Sibylla. To Yawkins' Hole, and there I saw some smugglers.' Barbara did not dare mention the fact that one of them was Jack.

'Oh dear, have they been back again? Well, Barbara, that was a very dangerous situation indeed,' Sibylla said gravely. 'But it has frightened you very much, I can see that. You will not be venturing out again, in the middle of the night, and all alone?'

Barbara shook her head, the tears flowing again at the graciousness of Sibylla's reproof.

'We will not mention any of this to Jack. It would alarm him near out of his wits if he knew. He is very fond of you, too, you know. We all are.'

'Oh, Sibylla,' thought Barbara sadly. 'If only you knew!' But all she said was, 'You are so kind to me, dearest Sibylla, and of course I will go out with you, if you want me to. I am perfectly well, and quite recovered now.'

'Well, then, this afternoon I shall be taking the carriage and going to some of the houses in the villages of Claremont and Port Elphin on the estate. Would you like to come?'

Barbara felt much better when they all sat down to lunch. Jack had returned from wherever he had been since early morning, and she stole little glances at him from under her lashes. He seemed just as usual, with no hint of their adventure of the night before. The table was set out with anchovy toasts, and rarebits, and a chicken in a devilled sauce, and in the centre was an appetising mound of pastry ramekins, their hot cheesy smell whetting all their appetites, very much to Margaret's delight.

'I have filled baskets with provisions, Sibylla,' she said, 'and there are some sacks of meal to take with you.'

'And Fanny has looked out blankets and clothing,' Sibylla said. 'What else shall we take with us, Jack?'

'Did you put in the medicines I spoke of, Margaret?' he asked.

'They are all packed, the medicines and the beef tea, and barley sugar too.'

'We shall leave as soon as we can,' said Sybilla. 'There is a lot to do.'

'Before you go, I must give you the keys to your rooms,' Jack said, taking them out of his pocket. 'These are yours, Sibylla'—handing her two—'and this is your one, Barbara.'

She saw that there was still one key left in his hand.

'I will hold on to this one,' he said, and she knew from the steely glint in his eyes when he directed these words at her, that he meant it was the key for the closet. Her nights of slipping out of the secret door were gone for ever, her voyages of discovery in the moonlight.

But as the carriage bowled down the drive of Redayre her spirits began to lift again, and the little devils of merriment came back to her eyes. There would be other ways, other times. Fortunately, Sibylla sat beside her, watched over by Fanny who sat opposite, so that it was only Betsy who saw her fleeting smile, and caught the sapphire flash of her eyes, and smiled back in return, as if in some conspiracy.

'How did Jack know where to send us, know where help was needed?' she asked Sibylla. 'Is there a grieve or a factor here, to supervise the estate, who tells him?'

'Jack is the only supervisor at Redayre. That is where he goes when he is away so much. He knows every man, woman and child in the district. And if any are in trouble or in need, he sees to it. He is determined that everyone on the estate should be provided with the work he needs to be independent, and he spares no effort to bring it in.'

Barbara digested this surprising information about the man she had thought to be an idle dandy. In fact, she had even told him so. Sibylla's idealistic view of Jack certainly did not match up with her own. But then, his sister was perhaps too close to him to see him with the fresh eye of an outsider like herself.

Barbara had worked all this out to her satisfaction, when a little hamlet came in view.

'This first one is just outside the village of Claremont,' said Sibylla, as Alan Kerr directed the carriage straight for a little cottage almost buried in the woods. A young woman appeared in the doorway.

'How is your mother, dear?' Sibylla asked, dismounting. 'Come with me, Barbara. And show Alan what to bring in, Fanny.'

They went into the little kitchen, and sat down by the low hearth, where an old woman huddled, wheezing and shuddering for breath.

'It is a bad attack this time, is it, Ann?' Sibylla asked her sympathetically. 'Miss Margaret has made up a syrup for you, and an inhalation. They always do you good.'

Old Ann gasped her thanks, croaking away to Sibylla, with her daughter repeating and interpreting every word, while Barbara looked around the room. The house seemed to be in good order, certainly. It was as clean as a new pin and there was a good fire in the hearth, and the smell of something delicious in the pot the girl was stirring as she spoke.

'Ann used to be a chambermaid up at Redayre,' Sibylla told Barbara when the old woman held out a thin brown-wrinkled hand to her as they were leaving, and the young girl bobbed respectfully. 'She is a widow with two daughters,' she continued in the carriage. 'One stays at home to look after her mother, as you saw, and we took the other into service when Jack pensioned off old Ann.'

And then on to two small houses joined together, which Sibylla approached and stood outside to speak to the women who came out upon the steps, for there was a fever and a rash on the children inside, and they could not allow her to enter. More baskets and bowls and bales of clothing were handed over.

'There is one last house we must visit today, at Port Elphin,' said Sibylla. 'The home of Tod Wilson, a fisherman.'

The coach had been travelling west all this time, along the highway, but now Alan Kerr was urging the horses down a narrower road, nearer to the sea, and they had turned round, heading back to Redayre again.

'We are making a circular tour today,' Sibylla raised her voice over the groanings and bumpings of the carriage on a road so poor it was scarcely more than two grey tracks made by carts, with humps of grass growing in the middle, and great potholes. 'Port Elphin is really only over the side of the Head of Redayre. Yawkins' Hole is on the other.'

The massive headland came nearer and nearer, sheltering a few fishermen's cottages, built in a semi-circle round a little natural harbour, and after more lurching and creaking, the carriage came to a halt outside one of them. Sibylla and Barbara climbed down thankfully, while the two maid-servants caught the rest of the boxes Alan Kerr was throwing down to them.

'Tod is a great friend of Jack's,' Sibylla remarked, as they walked up to the front door through an overgrown garden, and knocked.

A man opened the door, a thin, spare little man like a monkey, with a weather-beaten face pale beneath the tan, and his arm in a sling.

'Sir John said I should expect you, Miss Sibylla,' he said.

'What have you done to yourself, Tod? Take off that bandage, and let me have a look.'

She made him sit down on the stool beside the hearth, and asked Barbara to pour some of the water into a bowl from the kettle singing softly there. When the wound was uncovered, it looked purple and angry, and Sibylla asked again, 'How did you do it, Tod?'

'It was a fish-hook.' He smiled grimly, the beads of sweat standing on his brow at the touch of hot water with Margaret's herb infusion.

Barbara stared at his hand. It had been no fish-hook to gouge so deep into the flesh; more like a grappling-hook, she thought.

'When was this?' Sibylla asked.

'Three nights ago. It is beginning to ease.'

'You must bathe it with the hot water and herbs at every hour's end,' Sibylla said strictly. 'Will you do it yourself, or must I ask Mary Bryce next door to come in and do it for you?'

'Oh no, Miss Sibylla. Any sort of pain must be better than that,' the little man answered, and Barbara saw the ghost of the impudent merry fellow he must be to his ship-mates. Three nights ago, and he was a friend of Jack—yes, he must have been one of the smuggling party, and the grappling-iron must have caught his hand somehow between the rowing-boat and the ship in the Cove. He looked daring enough to be a smuggler any dark night.

'We have had enough of the coach, Alan,' Sibylla announced when they came out of the cottage. 'Miss Barbara and I will take the short cut over the Head back home, while you and the girls go back in the carriage.'

Alan waved his whip in salute, and the servants rumbled off. The sun was behind them, sinking westwards; the fierce heat of the day had gone, and the little breeze coming up off the Solway smelt of salt and seaweed.

Barbara took off her bonnet and threw back her ringlets, and made her cloak billow out behind her like a sail. 'I love the sea,' she said. 'I hope I may always live beside it.'

'It is beautiful, like a beautiful woman in a smiling mood, as it is today. But let her turn sullen or in a fury, and the sea can be as dangerous as it is beautiful. This whole coast, from east to west, as far as the eye can see, is Jack's responsibility now,' Sibylla told her, as they reached the top of the headland. 'When Papa died, he was sworn in by officials of the Crown to be Custodian here, and given the title "Admiral-Depute", responsible for supervising the disposal of wrecks. It is not an easy hat to wear,' she sighed, 'for there is a constant war between the beachcombers, always on the look-out for casks of brandy, even wood to build with, and ever in hope of treasure-trove—and the excisemen on the look-out for their taxes and duties.'

'Still, it is a very convenient hat for a smuggler to wear,' thought Barbara.

As if almost to read her thoughts, 'And, of course, the smuggling which is carried on all along the coast confuses the issue even further,' Sibylla continued. She pointed out the Crow's Nest, the topmost lookout point of the Head of Redayre, and the yawning cavern of Brandy Lake below. They climbed the Frenchman's Scar, walked round Barrel Bay and looked out at the Manxman's Holm, the green isle so conveniently situated just off it.

'The goods arrive from Europe and America to the Isle of Man, where they are exempted by a Royal Charter from all duties,' she explained. 'It is too great a temptation not to smuggle them over here to sell quickly at a high profit, when our own goods are so heavily taxed to pay for the war in America. The Solway shores are riddled with hiding-places. And so many people conspire with them to "jink the gaugers"—to dodge the custodians of the law such as Jack—and to ferry the goods away. Farmers, villagers, sometimes even unscrupulous ministers in their churches—ah, my dear Barbara, but you know all too well about the jinking and the Lingtowmen! I still shudder every time I think about that terrible night you told us about, when your Papa died.' And sighing Sibylla patted the small hand in the crook of her arm. They were climbing down now, round the cove.

'How did it get the name of Yawkins' Hole?' Barbara asked.

'After a certain Captain Yawkins, the most heathenish pirate ever to sail the Solway sea. Papa once saw his ship with his own eyes, trying to come ashore here. His vessel was named *The Black Prince*—supposedly after Satan, who gifted the ship to him to carry out blacker deeds of foulness and villainy than any mortal mind could ever conceive.'

'Tell me more,' Barbara begged, and was aghast at the terrible tales of Billy Marshall, tinker, gipsy chief, the Caird of Barullion, King of the Randies, and last of the Pictish kings.

'Surely that could not be the same Billy Marshall who arrived in the barns of Starlochy?' Barbara protested in horror.

'The same, or his son,' Sibylla assured her. 'Anyone else daring to use his name would not live long. They are close friends of Captain Yawkins, and other fiends of Hell from around here.'

Barbara was appalled to realise how near she and her Mother had been to rape and murder on that night of her Father's death.

'And there are the worst of all,' Sibylla was saying. 'The wreckers. The murderers who deliberately move the beacons and lure ships on to the rocks, and all the poor souls aboard. Jack is determined to find who the wreckers are here, and their ringleader. He has fixed his mind upon it, to the exclusion of everything else.'

'Could the wreckers and the smugglers be in collusion?' Barbara asked in fear and trembling.

'It is possible, although unlikely. Smugglers are not murderers, as a rule. Still, it would be a clever disguise.'

With a sinking heart, Barbara believed she had stumbled on the grim truth of Redayre Bay, and she walked across the lawns with Sibylla with her head cast down, bitterly disappointed and depressed. She could confide no more in her gentle cousin, and certainly never disillusion her about Jack, the brother she clearly loved and idolised.

But her dream that night became a nightmare, of footsteps crunching on the shingle, and whispered voices of men, and the screams she did not recognise for her own. For beneath the placid surface of the sea, on the sandy bottom, lay nameless skulls pressed down further by newer faces, white and bleached, with holes where eyes had been. And there were coins, too, once gold but now green, and the old bones of ships, and when she raised her head she saw the false lights flickering to seduce yet another shipload of men and women, with guineas in their pockets and rings on their fingers, ripe for plucking.

She woke up, trembling and weeping, and it was still dark, and all was quiet around the bay. It was then that Barbara knew she could not go on with such a burden as this, to bear alone. She must turn to someone, and if it could not be to anyone within the family, it must be to the nearest authority, the Church. She shrank from the very idea of having to confide in Mr Faulks. She *could* not. She could not be alone again with that man. Mama had brought her up to believe that the minister was the friend and the adviser of the family, the one with whom to entrust the most private innermost thoughts and secrets. But Barbara had had her doubts about the minister at home, with the smuggled brandy. She had her grave doubts about the minister at Redayre, too, for different reasons.

Then, as the sleepless night wore on, she remembered that Mr Faulks had not visited the house since the night of the Ball. Indeed, except for Sundays, she had not seen him at all. The hope stirred in her breast that he had forgotten about her. She became more and more confident that all that had passed between them had been a flash in the pan. Besides, there was no one else she could tell. Filled with this conviction, she lay back again and tried to sleep, but forgetfulness came no more that night to Barbara Graham. Her mind was filled with schemes and plans of how to see the minister, without anyone else to know.

Her chance came sooner than she had dared to hope. Sibylla was occupied that afternoon with visitors, and Margaret on one of her rare excursions into society, had gone in the carriage to visit the Reid family, and her beloved farmer John. Jack was nowhere to be seen.

'I am going out in the grounds with Snowy,' she told Betsy. 'I won't be long.' And not waiting for an answer, she put her horse at a gentle amble in the direction of the Willow Walk. She was nervous, and her hands holding the reins trembled almost uncontrollably, for this was a terrible mission for anyone to be on. But it had to be done.

The leaves sighed around her, green and cool, up the long vista to the summerhouse, and helped her to compose herself for the ordeal of the confession ahead. No Mr Faulks rose from his seat this time, and when she tied Snowy to a tree near the top of the incline, she saw that the summerhouse was deserted, and a little breeze blew softly, and lifted her damp ringlets off her neck. She found her hands were quite wet, too, but her mouth was dry with fear and dread.

She paused uncertainly for a moment, then plunged round to the front door with a grim determination and pulled at the bell. She could hear it pealing deep within the house, but minutes went by, and still no one answered. She pulled the bell again, and waited, quivering. This time, slow footsteps came towards the door, unwilling and somehow very disconcerting. Then there was the sound of bolts slamming back, slowly and grudgingly, and the door was opened. On the threshold stood Mistress Caldwell, with her greasy apron and her hair ragged about her face.

'Yes?' Her black eyes gleamed with hostility.

Barbara stood her ground, her chin up a little. 'I wish to speak to Mr Faulks.'

'He's not here,' the woman said flatly.

'Oh,' Barbara had not expected this, had never imagined it.

'Where is he?'

'That I could not say, I'm sure,' said Mistress Caldwell, folding her arms akimbo. 'He does not tell me all his comings and goings.'

'Will he be long, do you think?'

The woman shrugged indifferently.

'Well then, I shall come in and wait,' Barbara announced. 'I have something very important I must discuss with him.'

'He won't like it. He won't like you waiting here,' Mistress Caldwell said rudely and decisively. 'You'd best be off. The proper thing to do is to make an appointment to see the minister.'

'You had best stand aside,' Barbara said coldly, 'and let me in. He will not be pleased when I tell him of your insolence.' She marched past with her head in the air, and took her seat again in the front room which still slept for a hundred years. The atmosphere in it had not changed.

Mistress Caldwell's steps retreated down the passage, and Barbara sat still, waiting and looking about her. But there was nothing in the room to interest her, no paper with his writing on it, no book to read, no picture to dwell on, and after what seemed a very long time, she stood up and walked to the open door.

She was not mistaken. There were voices coming from the back of the house. Barbara tiptoed out into the passage, and they sounded a little louder. There were people in the kitchen, she was sure of it, and walking softly towards the sounds she strained her ears to hear the man's voice amongst them, for she was positive that it belonged to Mr Faulks.

When she got within earshot, she discovered there was no man's voice at all. They belonged to two women. One she recognised as Mistress Caldwell's, raised now and in a villainous temper.

'All I know is that she should not be here, poking her nose in where she's not wanted, Miss Barbara Graham of Redayre! I'm going to throw her out!'

'You fool! You'd better not, Sadie Caldwell. You know what he's like when he's riled.' This voice was deep, like a man's, guttural and so slovenly that Barbara could scarcely make out what she was saying.

'Oh, go to the devil, Kate Sharkey. You're soft-

headed about the minister. But you've never seen the
way he looks at her, as I have.'

'Looks at her? What do you mean? He's my man,
Sadie Caldwell!'

Mistress Caldwell's voice rose to a screech. 'Let go my
throat, you damned wild-cat! You're mad, that's what
you are—mad!'

There followed strings of oaths from both sides,
enough to blanch Barbara's cheeks. How could such a
person as Sadie Caldwell, with her dirty mouth and her
dirty ways be a servant to Mr Faulks? And who was that
other terrible woman she had called Kate Sharkey, there
in the kitchen with her? There were the sounds of
furniture scraping over a wooden floor, and crockery
rattling, and the crashes of a vicious struggle going on
between the two women.

There was no use waiting here, Barbara decided, and
walked back, as quietly as she had come, to the front
door. Just as she had her hand on it, the kitchen door
opened with a crash at the other end of the passage.

'Miss Barbara Graham of Redayre, is it? Let me get at
her! Where is she?' Kate Sharkey shouted.

Barbara caught one glimpse of a raddled face below a
mane of wild red hair before she slammed the front door
behind her and fled. There were no other horses here
that she could see as she looked round her on her way.
She had to get to Snowy before that dreadful woman
caught up with her. She heard the front door of the
North House opening again behind her, and heard Kate
Sharkey yelling.

'Browne is my man! Don't come back here after him!
He doesn't want you. He wants me!'

Casting a terrified glance over her shoulder, Barbara
saw that the woman was following her, and she could run
like a man. She reached the spot where she had tethered
Snowy, who was prancing nervously around the tree at
the commotion, and with shaking fingers, all turned to
thumbs, tried desperately to undo the knot. But it would
not come undone, and for a terrible moment Barbara
was sure that Kate would catch her, and then the reins

fell loose in her hands, she leapt on the horse's back, and kicking out at the woman's restraining hands, galloped back down the Willow Walk a great deal faster than she had climbed it.

Her mind was in a whirl all the way to Redayre. None of her impressions had been mistaken, after all. She had imagined nothing. Hard on the heels of a feeling of relief at this came the realisation that Kate Sharkey must have been living at the North House all this time, that she considered herself to belong to Mr Faulks, and he to her. It was too shocking to take in.

'Why, Miss Barbara, Snowy's all in a lather!' Alan Kerr protested when she arrived at the stables. 'What has happened? You look as though you had seen a ghost!'

'A noise frightened him, and he took off,' she answered with perfect truth. 'Oh dear, he *is* in a lather, Alan.'

'Well, don't you worry, Miss Barbara. I'll attend to him. But you had had best go and see Miss Margaret. She will make you a cup of tea.'

But she felt Alan Kerr's eyes following her curiously as she went.

In the days that followed this fiasco, she became very quiet, sometimes reading to Sibylla, sometimes writing down the stocks of linen and blankets, for it was time now to take stock against the winter.

'Is Betsy proving a good maid to you?' Margaret asked her one sunny afternoon when they were out in the lavender beds. 'Has Fanny had to teach her a lot?'

'She has had very little to learn,' Barbara assured her, burying her nose in the warm dry stalks and breathing in their clean scent.

'Well, we have gathered enough for the moment. We will take these armfuls into the scullery and tie them into bunches to be hung up to dry. Perhaps Betsy would have time to make the lavender-bags now, and replace the old lavender in the pillows, while this is so fresh?'

'I'll help her,' Barbara replied, and went slowly up-stairs in search of the maid.

But her heart was not in it, nor in any of the household affairs at Redayre, and she was glad when it was Sunday again and she could go to the church. Having success-fully kept quietly in the background and well away from Jack's scrutiny these last few days since she had blundered into the North House manse, she found herself seated again at his side in the Redayre pew, his face solemn and withdrawn.

Secretly she had been worrying in case Mistress Caldwell had told her master of her unhappy visit, and if Mr Faulks had ever come to find out about it without her knowledge. But nobody had said anything about it, and as for the minister himself, he was climbing into his pulpit without a glance in their direction. She breathed a long quivering sigh of relief, and Jack glanced down at her.

'You may well sigh,' he whispered, 'for the sake of these two poor unfortunates here today.'

It was only then that she saw the young couple being dragged in by the Elders, the girl sobbing, her face covered by her hands, as they were both thrown to their knees before the altar.

'What is wrong?' Barbara murmured to Jack. 'What is the matter with them?'

He bent his head down to her level. 'You shall soon see,' he said between his teeth.

Mr Faulks seemed possessed of a delight and an energy that morning, which she had not seen before. He radiated power, his voice soaring over every other in the singing of the opening psalm in all its verses. And when they bent their heads to pray, he launched straight into his favourite theme, which, without any doubt about it, was the wages of sin. From there it was only a natural progression to his real target, for he had only been warming up, Barbara then discovered, for the business of the day.

In the hush that followed, a pin could be heard to drop. Even the girl's tears had dried up in the quivering silence. And then the minister raised his right arm slowly, the sleeve of his black robe falling down to resemble the wing of some great crow above them, and before Barbara's hypnotised stare, the index finger of his hand stretched out and pointed at the hapless couple.

'Fornicators!' came the accusation from the pulpit in a bass whisper, far more effective than if it had been bellowed, and Barbara felt herself begin to quake, as though she had been the transgressor.

'May God help them!' she groaned inwardly, and felt Jack's warm hand steady upon her own. She clung to it throughout the terrible harangue, the spitting venom, and the scorn which rang and echoed from the rafters upon the heads of the young couple, their faces white now, and stained with tears.

Well pleased that he had torn them to shreds, the minister proceeded with his service. The two remained on their knees, their heads bent, while he thundered through his long sermon. Still clinging to his hand, Barbara glanced up once at Jack's face, but it was immobile, carved from stone.

Nobody was disposed to stand about the church door that Sunday morning in the sun to exchange pleasantries. With one accord the congregation departed silently, along their various ways. Jack tucked Barbara's hand firmly in the crook of his left arm and marched her off towards Redayre.

'That was dreadful, dreadful, dreadful,' she said despairingly. 'Those two are branded for life now, in this community.'

'Worse still, so is the child,' he said drily. 'And all because his parents were in love.'

'What will become of them?'

'In the old days he would have gone to sea and got himself drowned, or run off to leave her to drag herself and their child along somehow. Not many are strong-minded enough to remain together and face the world, not after that. I'm afraid Mr Faulks and his kind are enough to blight the tender feelings of any young couple in their predicament.'

'They will marry, of course.'

'Of course.'

'Will you look after them, Jack, in spite of this?'

He smiled down at her. 'What do you think, Barbara? In other times, in different circumstances, it might have been you and I on our knees before the altar today. Of course I shall look after them. And Mr Faulks as well,' he ended savagely.

She looked up with a little lurch in her heart, but not in any sympathy for the minister. '*It might have been you and I.*' It was a strange thing to say!

As they walked the rest of the way home, Barbara fell silent. She was thanking God that she had not betrayed this strong, kind man walking along beside her after all, whatever his own faults or crimes. She felt quite faint to think how close she had been to his possible undoing, to Heaven knows what castigation from the pulpit out of the mouth of the terrible minister, to whatever cruel punishment he would have seen fit for Jack with the authorities.

She clung to him more tightly. 'I will never leave you, Jack,' she said passionately. 'I will stay at Redayre, and help you all I can.'

'Even with my smuggling?' he laughed down at her. 'Oh, but you *will* leave me, Barbara. I have arranged it for next week.'

# CHAPTER
# SIX

'BUT I DON'T want to go away!' she protested, when she got her breath back.

'You will do exactly what I tell you to do, Barbara,' Jack said firmly, and he drew apart from her, hands on hips, and his face became stern. 'Sibylla is going to Dumfries at the end of the week, and you are to go with her. I have been having a discussion with her, and we are agreed that you have been too quiet lately.'

'Oh, but . . .'

'No buts. I have decided it, so you will not argue with me, miss. Sibylla is in some silly lather about sheets and tablecloths, and she assures me that you are in need of new dresses. You have bloomed, it seems, since you came to Redayre.'

Jack's eyes travelled from her face down to her toes, and then back again, a strange little smile playing about his mouth. 'And I agree with her. That gown you are wearing has become positively indecent.'

Barbara pulled her cloak together hastily, and blushed. It was true, she had noticed it herself, how her figure had blossomed out, so that the summer dress Mama had made for her six months ago now revealed far more of her bosom than it should. Jack laughed wickedly.

'Oh, it is very pretty, Barbara! But hardly ladylike, and I am determined to make a lady of you yet. So you will go to Dumfries. Sibylla has been invited to stay with her friends, the Favenels, the next time she is in Dumfries.'

'Oh, no!' she exclaimed. 'Not the Favenels!' She regretted the words almost before they were out of her

mouth, but how could she endure it, to stay with that
awful Louise, powdered and painted, and ogling at Jack
from morning to night?

Jack glared at her. 'They are very nice people. Louise
Favenel, in particular, is one of the most fascinating
ladies of my acquaintance. You would do well, Barbara,
to spend some time observing her.' His eyes looked past
her disdainfully, no doubt conjuring up this wonderful
creature. Barbara scowled.

'When?' she asked, resignedly. 'And for how long?'

'This is the beginning of August, and from this month
onwards we can no longer trust the weather or the state
of the roads. Sibylla will be ready by Saturday next, and
is sending word ahead to the Favenels that you will
accompany her, with Fanny and Betsy in attendance, of
course.'

'Why?' she said. 'Are you not coming too?'

'Not on Saturday. I cannot stay away from here so
long,' Jack answered, with a bleak look on his face. 'I
shall try to find the time to come perhaps on the Thursday after.'

Barbara considered this in silence. Stay with the
Favenels she would not. Somehow she must think up a
plan to get out of it.

'And, by the way,' Jack added, 'I want it clearly
understood that, in Dumfries, you will never set foot
outside the door without Betsy. Young ladies do not go
abroad alone.'

They went to remove their outdoor clothes, and then
directly into the dining-room. Before she had left for the
church service, Margaret had prepared a trout, and set it
to cool. It waited in its pale amber jelly on the sideboard,
while they took their seats, and Nessie and Jean came in
with the small new potatoes, cooked in their skins, and a
fresh salad sprinkled with mint and thin green beans.
The conversation was all of the forthcoming visit to
Dumfries.

'Why do you not come, Margaret?' Barbara asked.

'Someone has to stay at home and look after Jack!'

'What nonsense! She means she cannot bear to go too

far away from John Reid,' Jack teased.

'I will go some other time,' Margaret answered, more interested to see how her pastry had turned out, a butterscotch tart under a crisp and lightly browned meringue of egg-whites and sugar, and served with little bowls of cream.

Barbara went to sit with Sibylla in the afternoon, to read to her out of the bible, long passages they both knew by heart already.

'I know we should not be looking at any other book on the Lord's Day,' said Sibylla, 'but I have one I have been meaning to give you ever since you came.'

Barbara took it, intrigued to see that it was written by Robert Burns. On the flyleaf was printed 'His Poems, The Edinburgh Edition', and was signed by the author himself.

'It is his latest publication,' Sibylla said, 'most of them made into songs, like "Auld Lang Syne". And I see he refers so often to his Clarinda, a lady in Edinburgh. He gave the book to Jack, really.'

'I cannot take it, Sibylla, since it was a gift.'

'Why not? It will not be going out of the family.'

Barbara read a few stanzas aloud, then her voice faltered and stopped. 'Sibylla,' she asked after a little pause, 'have you written to Miss Favenel yet?'

'Not yet, dear. I shall do so this evening.'

'Would it be very wrong and impolite of me to ask to stay with Mistress Flora Cowan instead, in the High Street? I stayed there before, on my way here. She is the sister of Mr James Aitken, our grieve at Starlochy. Perhaps she may have news of Mama to tell me.'

Sibylla's eyes softened. 'I cannot see anything wrong in that at all. You would be well chaperoned, between Mistress Cowan and Betsy. I shall ask Jack tonight.'

'Thank you,' Barbara said gravely, and went out into the garden smiling to herself, to cut flowers, although those in her room were not yet faded. The cutting of the flowers was a peaceful thing, soothing to her unquiet mind, and the very touch of the petals, the long green stalks, and laying them in the basket banished some

of her restlessness, while she contemplated the forthcoming holiday.

It would be a relief to get away from some aspects of
Redayre. In particular, she did not know if she could
face going to the church again, which the family must do,
at least once every Sunday. For she had made up her
mind now. She did *not* like Mr Faulks. He was cruel, not
at all the man she had thought him to be at first, with his
smooth voice which could edge to a honed blade, to flay
people apart. She did not like his ruddy colouring, his sly
innuendoes—nor his smell, come to that. She did not
trust him and would be glad to get away from him, even
if it would be for only one or two Sundays.

Leaving Jack Jardine behind was quite another matter, and the hand cupping the dark red petals of a rose
trembled a little at the prospect. How she had changed,
she thought, in the space of five short weeks! For now
she could not imagine herself feeling secure, or safe, too
far from his silver gaze, those eyes which could melt to
the softest grey when he looked at her, or pierce her with
just one steely glance when she had not conformed. The
fact of the matter was that now she *did* trust him, respect
him, and honour him. He had succeeded in extracting
the second promise from her, whether he knew it or not.

Barbara stopped cutting the flowers, and stood lost in
thought while she saw in her mind's eye his now familiar
profile, the straight nose, those firm lips, and the hard jut
of his jaw—and quite forgot he was a smuggler.

Yet, on Saturday morning, when she leant from her
bedroom and felt the sun on her face, and saw the clear
bright sky with a sharp gloss about it because the wind
was in the east, she began to smile and laugh with Betsy,
with all the guilty excitement of two conspirators. The
excitement was infectious, and when she and Sibylla
climbed into the carriage and sat down side by side, with
the two maids opposite, prim in their black bonnets, the
whole household was out upon the steps to wave them
goodbye.

'You know where to stable the horses, Alan?' Jack

asked. And with his head in the window of the coach, and his eyes on Barbara, 'I will see you on Thursday. Take care.'

They had scarcely reached the end of the drive when she began to miss him, and turned her face to the side and gazed forlornly out of the window, slowly but surely coming to the realisation that, smuggler or no smuggler, she would rather be with him than without him. Half-way to Dumfries she still mused and dreamed. He had not spoken again about the Favenels, and somehow it was just taken for granted that she and Betsy would be staying with Mistress Flora in the High Street. Perhaps Sibylla had used her considerable diplomacy on her behalf with Jack. Barbara didn't know, didn't ask. She only knew it would be a very long time till Thursday.

And then the coach lurched violently in a deep rut and threw them all of a heap together, before it righted itself and at the same time shook her addled brains free. *Why had he got rid of her?* It was a revelation and a disenchantment which took her all of five minutes to assimilate, before her cheeks took on a distinct flush and her eyes a dangerous flash of blue fire.

She was too quiet, indeed! In need of a holiday, a whole week at least! And then packed off in the charge of no less than three females, like a little donkey with a carrot dangling before her nose, by the lure of new dresses! She fretted and fumed the rest of the way into Dumfries, along the High Street, past Greyfriars Church and a little way north along the Edinburgh road, where the coach came to a halt.

It did her temper no good to see Louise Favenel coming to greet them at the door of her large red sandstone house, her hair crimped into a thousand tiny curls, and her gown apparently composed of a dozen filmy shawls. Barbara looked on sourly while Sibylla kissed her friend, and Fanny alighted in a fuss to count the boxes and to see that none was left behind.

'We need not come in,' Barbara said, when Sibylla turned to fetch her out of the coach. 'We may as well go back to the High Street to our destination.'

'What nonsense, darling child!' Louise Favenel's
voice had all the velvet tones of an old violin, rounded
and mellow. In fact, Barbara thought, Louise had everything. Beauty, maturity and, far more than that, a
personality which simply did not allow the slightest
hostility against her to matter at all. 'Of course you must
come in! I have been waiting for you so long!' She smiled
up at Barbara through the open door of the coach.
'Besides, you must give me your opinion of this glorious
man in my drawing-room—my new leading man. His
name is Courteney Carrington, and I believe I am in love
at last!'

Entirely disarmed by this last statement, Barbara
condescended to alight from the coach, and followed
Sibylla into Miss Favenel's house. Mr Courteney
Carrington was everything Louise had pronounced him
to be, large in stature, lavish with his gestures, with a
long mane of light orange hair which reminded Barbara
of a lion. She wondered if it had been coloured, and
decided it was. Both he and Louise wore rouge on their
cheeks and their lips, and little black patches on their
cheeks. They were larger than life; they were actors.

Nevertheless, over tea served in thin little cups, along
with wafer biscuits, she began, grudgingly, to like them.
They laughed a good deal, and were so entertaining, and
there was no doubt they fitted together like a hand in a
glove.

Louise Favenel's scent wafted around Barbara when
she bent to whisper in her ear, at the front door as she
was taking her leave.

'You see, you had nothing to fear after all. Come and
see me again, won't you?'

Thoroughly abashed and remorseful, Barbara
climbed back in the coach and sat down beside Betsy.

'We shall meet outside Greyfriars at eleven o'clock
tomorrow morning,' Sibylla reminded her, and Alan
Kerr walked the horses smartly up the High Street, and
deposited Barbara, Betsy and their boxes at the house of
Mistress Cowan.

Next morning they took their places high up in the

visitors' gallery in Greyfriars Church, where the light streamed in gold and red and blue through the stained glass of the windows, and the minister spoke gently and hopefully to his congregation about the kingdom of God where one day man would live at peace with man. It was all quite different from the services at the Kirk of Redayre.

On Monday and Tuesday they consulted Sibylla's lists and exhausted themselves completely in the choosing and the buying of the new linen.

'We are to spend tomorrow afternoon with Louise,' Sibylla said. 'She is having a little garden-party. It will be restful, after this.'

With Betsy at her side, Barbara set off on Wednesday afternoon to walk to the Favenels' house on the Edinburgh Road, glad that she had chosen to wear the pale lavender gown made down for her from the hamper in the closet. It was cool, and floated in the warm breeze, for the day had turned out hot again. She trod daintily along the High Street, lifting her skirts over the little heaps of rubbish where the hens picked, careful of her pretty lavender slippers, while Betsy steered a way through the crowds of townspeople, for the town was busy.

They passed the 'Dumfries Fly', the Edinburgh coach, as it emptied out its passengers on to the Plainstones, and were in the thick of the crowd milling and thronging around the Midsteeple, when Barbara thought she recognised a woman passing. Who was she, with her friendly, smiling face? Realisation dawned on them both at the same time.

Barbara hesitated a moment to speak to her, and Betsy came back to stand at her side, a respectful pace behind. 'It is Miss Park, is it not? How are you?'

'It is the young lady who looked out of her window over at the Globe! I remember Robbie was so taken with you! But I do not know your name.'

'My name is Barbara Graham, and this is my maid Betsy. We are staying at the same house again for a few days.'

The girl who had been swollen with child in June was slim now, and somehow older, and a hurt look came into her eyes. 'I had my bairn, Miss Graham. Robbie's bairn,' Anna Park told her. 'I named her Elizabeth.'

'She is well, I hope?'

'She has gone to live with Robbie's wife, Jean Armour, and to be brought up by her. I could not bring her up myself, you see. I am only a barmaid in my uncle's inn, the Globe.'

'Oh,' said Barbara. 'And Mr Burns, is he still in Dumfries?'

'Yes. He's not been well, this while back, and he is drinking with a lot of hot-heads. They all come in to the Globe to drink. And that Kate Sharkey—Kate o' the Vennel, we call her—she's back. She was there that night as well. But I don't suppose you saw her? She is notorious around here.'

'No,' Barbara said slowly, 'I would not know her. And Kate is so common a name.'

'Perhaps you may see her from a distance, with her terrible face and her long wild hair. It's red—or it would be, if it was clean. Keep well clear of her, Miss Graham, if you do.'

Barbara was thoughtful as she and Betsy continued on their way to the red sandstone house, and round to the large walled garden where there were voices and laughter, and little tables and chairs set out in a large ring beneath the chestnut trees, and fashionable ladies stood under their parasols with gentlemen in little groups.

'Thank you, Betsy. You may leave me now, for here is Miss Sibylla.'

'Oh, here you are, dear,' said Sibylla. 'I suppose you are surprised to see that Mr Favenel is still here?' She smiled from Barbara to Philip Favenel.

'Yes,' he said. 'I have decided not to go back again to London, but to live here now. The London air does not suit me as well as the air here. Nor the company,' and he smiled broadly at Sibylla as he said it. His eyes were for no one but her.

How well they are matched, Barbara thought a little

dispiritedly, and made her excuses to wander off over the smooth lawns to the rough grass beyond, which sloped down to the River Nith. A luxuriance of tall grasses bowed gracefully in the balmy breeze, and here was a little wilderness of wild flowers, where the river meandered, its waters fast and dark, deep and secret. She sat down to listen to the water splashing and tinkling through the reeds, and the drone of the bees.

If it was the same Kate as at the North House manse, how had she got to Dumfries? It would not be too far on horseback for anyone used to riding, Barbara mused. And the raddled red-haired Kate of the North House had been the one with the Lingtowmen, well used to horses, and hard living and hard drinking. That Kate would certainly be the kind of loose woman to go into a hostelry alone to drink.

But then, she thought, as she lay down on her back with a blade of grass between her teeth and contemplated the sky, it did not have to be the same Kate. Yet she had a sneaking suspicion that she was, which grew rapidly into conviction. From what she had overheard between Kate and Mistress Sadie Caldwell, it was quite possible that Mr Faulks had got rid of her, whatever the truth of their relationship—in much the same way as Jack had manoeuvred this trip to Dumfries for Sibylla and her, come to that. Her eyes narrowed as she thought for some reason for it. It *had* to be the smuggling.

When she got up and brushed down her skirt with her hand, she knew she had found part of the answer at least, and in her imagination the three-masted ship was even now lying in at Yawkins' Hole, and Jack Jardine was in his black disguise again.

And so it was even more surprising when his voice spoke in her ear. 'So here you are, Barbara! I have been looking all over for you, high and low. What are you doing down here, hidden away?'

His face looked fresh and composed, and his clothes were immaculate, pale fawn buckskin breeches, short cream waistcoat and ruffled white stock under the darker jacket, and they gave him an air of severity.

She shivered and dragged her eyes away. He looked more handsome than ever.

'I thought you were not coming until tomorrow,' she murmured in confusion.

'And there were no other gentlemen that you could speak to?' His hand gestured towards the assembly on the lawn. 'You were waiting for me, me alone to talk to, is that it?'

'Of course not!' Barbara said indignantly. 'I was thinking about something quite different.'

'I do not believe you, Barbara.' He looked down at her, amused and tender, and laughed as though she were a silly girl. She hated him for it, and with a sudden intuition she knew the question that was coming next, and her hands grew hot. 'If you were not waiting for me, and dreaming about me, why did you look at me just now as though you wanted me to kiss you?'

She took a deep breath and steeled herself to gaiety. 'Oh, for the sake of your bright eyes, Jack Jardine! Do you not know I cannot resist them?' And she met his glance without a tremor.

He laughed at that, and caught her hand, and crumpled her fingers. 'Grown up, in the space of so short a time? You're glad I came a day too soon, aren't you?'

'Yes,' she said recklessly, not minding, and they stood there laughing at each other until Jack put his arm round her shoulders and led her further away from the garden-party, along a little path beside the river.

As she walked along beside him in the sultry heat, Barbara's mind and senses were in a turmoil. His arm round her pulled her so tight to his side that she became more and more aware of the movement of his hip as he walked. It seemed to press into her body, and she felt herself grow weak, her flesh grow soft, to accommodate him. She did not dare to look up. It was as if she watched herself at a magic lantern show, for she knew what was bound to happen if she did look up; it was inevitable, for it was as if she were on fire, burning, melting.

'Barbie,' he said softly, and then his face came down, and his eyes looked first into hers, then moved down to her mouth, before he kissed her for the first time, a soft gentle little kiss, and he drew back to look at her again, and then his mouth was not so gentle next time. She felt the tips of his fingers on her neck, travelling to her shoulders in tiny burning trails, and suddenly she had the strangest sensation that her legs would no longer support her, and her whole body was weakening. It was the most natural thing in the world to reach her hands up to his shoulders and cling to him even closer.

'Then you did miss me, Barbara? As much as I missed you? Why do you think I could not wait until tomorrow?'

Whatever answer she might have made was captured and then forgotten for several moments while she thought she would swoon, and when he raised his head again it was to run his lips across the hollow at the base of her throat. Barbara realised that the lethargy threatening to overpower her now was becoming very dangerous.

Why indeed had he come a day too soon? She turned her face into the warm hollow of his shoulder, and pushed lightly against his broad chest. Jack's hands slipped reluctantly from her waist to release her, and now there was a smile of faint indulgence to make his hard mouth very gentle.

'Beware the dark smuggler, is that it, Barbara?' he laughed, and kissed her lightly again, and she laughed with him, wondering at herself. Was it only half an hour ago that she would never have believed she could possibly feel so light-hearted, and certainly not about him? But here she was, with the laughter bubbling up inside her, and Jack was dragging her back to mingle with the guests at Louise Favenel's garden-party.

'Your little ward looks different today,' their hostess greeted them half-way across the lawn. She looked at Barbara with narrowed eyes, and in that minute the girl knew that she had guessed what had happened. 'She does look very pretty, does she not, Jack? Perhaps it is that dress.'

'I see an improvement every day,' he replied gravely, but there was a laugh behind his voice.

Barbara treated Louise to a brilliant smile, and her eyes were sparkling like blue stars. This afternoon she did not give a fig for Louise Favenel or anyone else on earth. Jack had kissed her, which was far more important. Nothing could be more important, more dazzling, than that. Her entire world was upside down.

'Then it was a good party, Miss Barbara?' Betsy asked her, as she brushed out the long black ringlets that night.

'Can you tell?'

'Yes!' Betsy smiled at her in the mirror. 'It is something about the eyes. A softening, a change.'

'Did I tell you Sir John was there? He arrived a day early.'

'You did not need to tell me, Miss Barbara. I can see it for myself.'

'We walked by the river, where it is quiet and cool. Alone.'

'Yes, Miss Barbara?'

'But you need not mention that to Fanny, or the others.'

'No, Miss Barbara.' Betsy's voice was grave, even shocked, but there was a ghost of a smile on her face.

'Are you dreadfully shocked, Betsy?'

'No, Miss Barbara. I have been waiting for something like this,' Betsy laughed.

'Then you guessed all the time! How did you know? How could you tell?'

'Oh, something about the way you walked home, nearly danced, when I saw you from the window. And your eyes, even bluer than they were before.'

'And what have you guessed, Betsy?'

'That it has happened at last, and that you and the master have fallen in love. I have been hoping for it.'

This time Betsy tried to hide her smile no longer, she relaxed for the first time with her mistress, and Barbara knew she need not be always on her guard before her maid any more. She was her friend, her ally, and she could trust her to the last.

'It is our secret, Betsy.'

'Safe with me, Miss Barbara, as I do not need to tell you.'

At two o'clock next afternoon, they all met at the Burnett Halls, and proceeded inside where many ladies and gentlemen had foregathered under the splendid glass cupola which extended far over the roof to let in the light and the sun. Between the marble columns all around the hall, rows of chairs had been placed, and in the middle was a long raised platform, running almost to the door.

'The Dress Collection is brought here every year,' Sibylla told her. 'The young ladies walk up and down the platform to show off the gowns.'

They sat down and waited in a buzz of conversation. Then slowly it died down, and a splendid gentleman attired in a long wine-coloured coat, with a sash around his waist in a deeper tone and a white curled wig, made the opening announcement, and the Show had begun.

Of all the gowns they saw paraded before their eyes, only the sapphire blue satin took Barbara's eye. Already she and Sibylla had chosen three day gowns each, but this was a gown for the evening, and Sibylla had said she must choose one.

'It is far too old for her,' Jack said decidedly. 'Magnificent, I agree, and one at last with some colour, but much too old for my ward. It is for a matron. Show us something else, my good fellow.'

The splendid gentleman clapped his hands, and gowns and more gowns made their appearance until they were all giddy, and Jack put a stop to it.

'No, no!' he said. 'I do not care for any of them. They are all much of a muchness, too insipid, and not at all what I had in mind for Miss Graham. Can you not see how vivid she is? Is there not a gown that is different?'

Vivid, indeed, thought Barbara a little rebelliously, as the man hesitated. However, she conceded, Jack's own clothes reflected his impeccable taste. Perhaps, now, she had better trust him in the choice of hers. And it was true that the gowns they had been shown were all rather dull, mostly pastel coloured, with hardly a spark among them—except for the sapphire blue satin, of course.

'I have one last one, Sir John, that is certainly different, which is why I hesitate to show it to you.'

'Let us see it, for God's sake, man,' Jack said impatiently. 'We cannot sit here all day!'

After five minutes or so, and a lot of agitation behind the velvet curtains, a young lady walked out, attired in a dress which took Barbara's breath away. It was made of silk, the skirt and the sleeves brilliantly green, with the low-cut bodice and the deep frill around the hem dark blue and lilac and green checked. All the ribbons were of the same checked silk, like a tartan.

'Ah, yes,' said Jack. 'The very thing. "Green Sleeves and Tartan Ties". Yes, we'll take it.'

'There is also a little stole to go with it,' the man said, and produced a wide green scarf trimmed with the same tartan.

'Wrap it up, along with all the other gowns the ladies have chosen, sir. I will come with you to pay for them.'

'What did you mean?' Barbara asked him when they were back out on the street again and walking up to Mistress Flora's house. '"Green Sleeves and Tartan Ties"? Just right?'

'Perhaps you do not know that song written by Robbie Burns?

> "Green sleeves and tartan ties
> Mark my truelove where she lies;
> I'll be at her or she rise,
> My fiddle and I thegither.
>
> Be it by the chrystal burn,
> Be it by the milk-white thorn,
> I shall rouse her in the morn,
> My fiddle and I thegither."'

His eyes pierced into her, and his mouth was tender and smiling. 'I will call for you at seven o'clock this evening, Barbara.'

'He means you to wear it this evening, dear, when we go to see the play in the Theatre Royal,' said Sibylla, at Jack's other side. 'It is the Gala Performance of *As You Like It*, with Louise Favenel and Courtenay Carrington in the leading parts.'

So that was why Jack had come to Dumfries on Wednesday. It was to see Louise Favenel acting on the stage.

'Oh, how beautiful, Miss Barbara!' Betsy exclaimed, when they took the dress out of its box and hung it up so that there would be no creases.

'Ay, it's bonny, right enough,' said Mistress Flora, who had come up to the bedchamber to see. 'It's cost a pretty penny, I'll warrant. But come away now, and we'll have a bite to eat before you go.'

Downstairs neither Barbara nor her maidservant did justice to Mistress Flora's little light cheese pastries, which she served with a flummery of apples, but they drank a refreshing cup of tea before they ran excitedly back up again, to get ready. Barbara felt that everything was suddenly running away from her. It was all going too fast, while Betsy dressed her in the new gown with great care, combed her ringlets around her fingers, and set them behind her ears. Then they heard a knock upon the front door, and were thrown into a panic at the sound of Jack's voice below.

'Miss Barbara,' Flora said, coming half-way up the stairs. 'There is a gentleman to see you. He's in the parlour, dearie.' Barbara ran down, lifting her delicate skirt.

'There's no hurry,' Jack said, his eyes admiring her. 'But I see that I was right. I came early to give you these. Your dress demands them.' He handed her a small long box.

'What is it?' Barbara said, opening it, and gasped. Inside sparkled a pendant of sapphires and diamonds, and along with it the ear-rings of the same set. She stood speechless with the box in her hand, while in her imagination she saw iron-hooped chests hauled out of a broken vessel, and pouches of sovereigns snatched from lifeless forms. 'I cannot take them,' she cried, imploring him with her eyes. 'What was their origin?'

'They belonged to my mother,' Jack smiled calmly, 'and I brought them from Redayre for just such an occasion as this. I always meant that you should have them, from the first moment I saw you, Barbie. They are exactly the same colour as your eyes!'

Her mother had once said those words to her. Hearing them again from Jack's lips reassured her oddly, and she allowed him to fasten the pendant around her neck, and place the blue stones in her ears with his firm, sure fingers.

'Yes, that completes the picture,' he said, brushing her forehead with his cool lips, and went to open the parlour door. 'Betsy,' he shouted. 'Come here with Miss Barbara's stole!'

Betsy and Mistress Flora both came running, and Barbara felt the drift of soft silk about her shoulders, and then they were out upon the High Street, she and Jack, plunging into the laughing, jostling crowds, all heading towards the East Barnraws and the Theatre Royal. But it was a slow, shuffling business to get inside, with no order about it, with everyone pushing. Jack put his arm round her, to protect her while they waited, moving forward to the entrance, step by step.

At last they reached the alley at the corner of the theatre, and looking up the narrow close Barbara saw two figures. Even in that dim light she recognised them, could not mistake them, as the strange couple she had seen that night in June passing by in the lights of the Globe Inn, when she saw on her way to Redayre.

The woman was the red-haired woman, Kate Sharkey, who had been at the North House. 'Kate o' the Vennel', Anna Park had called her, and her companion was dressed once more in the long dark cape, his queer flat hat pulled well down to screen his face. It was only a glimpse, as they pressed forward, and at last inside and into one of the only two boxes the theatre afforded.

'We can thank Louise for this,' Jack said, shutting

the little door and settling Barbara beside him in her seat.

'Oh, it is wonderful,' she said, awhirl with excitement. 'I have never been in a theatre before.'

'There are a lot of things you will see and do, with me, for the first time, Barbara,' he said softly, and together they looked across at the gallery and down into the pit, and it seemed right and proper to her that he should hold her hand, and that the whole world should see her at his side, Sir John Jardine of Redayre.

'Oh,' Jack said, with a wave of his hand, 'Robbie Burns is down there in the pit. Do you see him?'

'Yes,' she said, blushing when Burns waved back, and pointed delightedly to her new gown. 'You like him, do you not?'

'He is a great friend of mine, and I admire him and his works very much, although I cannot agree with all his ideas.'

'Why? What are they?'

'Revolutionary, I fear, and against the Government. He even supports the Revolution in France, although so far not openly, thank God. Perhaps it all stems from his grandfather, who was a Jacobite and certainly opposed to the King. He believes in freedom for all, and, above that, that every man is born equal.'

'But I believe in freedom, too, Jack.'

'We all do, in this country. But there is the paradox, that we may live freely only so long as there are the constraints of the law. Otherwise crime would rule, and there would be freedom no longer, certainly not from violence and fear. Why do you think, in a small way, that I lay down the law to you, Barbara?'

'It is for my own protection, I understand that.'

'And, sad to say, we are not all born with equal chances into this world, although Burns cannot see it.'

'What do you mean?'

'Some are doomed to the gutter before they see the light of day, others to gilded palaces. And even Burns himself was born with a gift greater than gold, a gift none of the rest of us possesses, was he not? The gift of words,

to live for ever? Words of passion, whether in love, or in
his beliefs.

> "For a' that, and a' that,
> The man's the gowd, for a' that."'

'And yet Mama told me that he cannot live by writing
his poetry alone.'

'It is how he should live, and like a king, if he were
paid accordingly, which he is not.'

'And you have given him money, have you not?'

'I have offered him money, but he is too proud to take
it. He has currently applied for a position as an excise-
man.'

'And will he get it?'

'If he watches his step. It is Government business,
after all. We are all behind him, never fear, but he is so
hot-headed. I know the feeling,' Jack went on, with a
change in his tone. 'You make me feel hot-headed,
Barbara. You are the most outstanding lady here
tonight,' he murmured in her ear, and he loosened his
tight clasp upon her hand to put his arm round her
shoulders and draw her close to him. 'The best dressed,
and the most beautiful.'

'Then it is only right and fitting that I should be here
with the most handsome man,' she said, and felt his
cheek burning against her own and the soft slide of his
lips across it until he found her mouth, as the lights
dimmed.

Then the curtain went up and the play unfolded, and
they became engrossed in the story, and the colour, and
the superb acting of their friends, Louise and
Courteney. Scene followed scene, all the acts, and all the
intervals—all over far too soon.

'Oh, she was glorious, Jack!' Barbara cried, and
clapped her hands until they were sore. 'Did you not
think Louise was wonderful?'

'Of course. I always told you she was. She is a born
actress, on or off the stage.'

'So alive! She brought her part to life!'

'And yet she is on the wrong side of thirty.'

'She cannot be!'

'But she is, and quite desperate for a husband. But perhaps she has found one now,' and he pulled her to her feet to sing 'God Save The King'.

It had been a wonderful performance, the theatre still ringing with applause, the curtain calls, the heat and the cheering, and now in the solemn anti-climax the singing of the National Anthem. But it was distorted, in an interruption of shouting and the drumming of heels from the pit, and the music stopped and the audience stopped singing, shocked into silence.

'What is it?' Barbara asked Jack.

'*Ah, ça ira, ça ira, ça ira,*' came the chant.

'Oh, no,' Jack groaned. 'They are calling for the song of the French Revolutionaries, Robert Burns and his cronies! How could they be so foolish? There will be trouble now. Come, Barbara, you have looked so happy all evening, and I will not allow that to be spoiled.' He grasped her arm and they left the box quickly.

They pushed their way through the uproar already in the streets, a noise in the High Street which lasted far into the night, long after he had escorted her back to Mistress Flora's, and Betsy had taken off the sapphires and her new gown and left her ready for bed. But the whole town was seething, restless, and Barbara could not sleep.

She sat in the window, and once again watched the comings and goings at the Globe Inn, wondering if she would see the strange couple who had never been away from the back of her mind all through the Shakespeare play, until weariness and the excitement of the wonderful evening overtook her.

But sleep did not come easy to her, even when all the noise had died away. She tossed and turned long after the town of Dumfries lay dreaming under the stars. The little scraps of the picture in her mind did not fit together; there were large pieces missing, so that it did not make a whole that she could understand.

Why, if he was Custodian of Wrecks, was Jack not

doing something to put an end to them? She sat up in bed, wide awake now, for she felt sure she was at the crux of the matter. If she could only answer that, she would understand it all.

Why was he a smuggler, then, wasting his time? It could not be for the money—he was immensely rich already. Yet she must believe the evidence of her own eyes, and she had actually seen him, unloading the boxes and kegs into Yawkins' Hole, dressed for the part!

*Dressed for the part!* If she had never been to the theatre, she would never have thought of it. That was it. He was only pretending! But why? What good did it do, when whole shiploads of people were still being lured to their death on the jagged rocks round Redayre Bay?

She still could not understand it, there was yet one huge piece missing when, thoroughly exhausted, she fell asleep at last.

Sibylla called in the morning, not long after Barbara was dressed. 'Jack is taking us all to Mrs Mackie's Coffee House,' she said. 'He says you cannot be in Dumfries for a whole week and not visit Mrs Mackie's Coffee House. It is the thing to do.'

'Will this dress be all right?' Barbara asked.

'No, dear. Go and put on one of the new day-gowns. This is Friday morning, market day, and all the town will be abroad.'

By ten o'clock they were making their way down the Friars' Vennel to Mrs Mackie's establishment, and found Jack waiting at a table reserved. 'You are not wearing a new bonnet!' he accused her, after inspecting her with an eagle eye.

The formation of a little plan was conceived in Barbara's brain at that moment in a flash of inspiration. She achieved a look of patience and long-suffering, and a tear sprang in her eye. 'I have not any money,' she said sadly.

'Deuce take it! Confound it, Barbara! Do you have to be so damned tricky? Why did you not ask me?'

She gazed at him reproachfully. 'I am not so frivolous

as you would make me out,' she said, managing a tiny quiver in her lip.

'Here, will this be enough?' Jack passed her two guineas.

Barbara sighed. 'Bonnets are very expensive.'

'Five, then! Will that do?'

Her eyes smiled at him like two patches of blue sky appearing from behind the clouds.

'They had better be the most superlatively foolish concoctions in all the Stewartry of Dumfries and Galloway, at that price,' he said, and they turned to join the others drinking coffee, black, and in the gentlemen's case laced with whisky, with the cream on top in swirls.

'The town was very noisy and restless last night,' Sibylla observed. 'It went on for hours. We could hardly get to sleep.'

'It was the commotion at the theatre which started it,' Jack said. 'They have arrested Robbie Burns and his friends.'

'Oh, no!' Barbara cried.

'It was a foregone conclusion after their little exhibition. I am going shortly to meet with some other men, better friends of his, to see what can be done to get him out of this latest pickle he has landed in.'

'We had planned to visit all the abbeys round here this afternoon,' Sibylla said. 'It is Philip's idea. He is very interested.'

She smiled up at her companion, and Barbara saw that the look on his face was tender and very loving. 'They are so happy together, so much in love,' she thought, and suddenly felt the atmosphere in the Coffee House too close, and when Jack left, a little depressing.

'Jack has had to go back to Redayre in a tearing hurry,' Sibylla said, when she and Mr Favenel called for her in their coach in the warm and humid afternoon, thunder hanging low over Criffel's dark blue peak. 'It seems there is some trouble at home.'

Barbara's head reeled. 'Not more trouble?'

'He did not say. But he has gone, and left word that we

are not to alter our plans for staying here. He has ordered Alan Kerr not to drive us back until Sunday, after church, and he will try to come back himself if he can.'

'Two days,' Barbara thought, her mind racing. 'Between the two I must put my plan into action.'

'Are you ready to come with us?' Sibylla asked. 'Louise is not coming. She is resting for a few hours.'

'I am a little tired myself,' Barbara said. 'It is the thunder. No, Sibylla, I had better stay here and lie down, I think, to see if it will clear my head. Anyway,' she smiled, 'it will leave you and Mr Favenel alone for once. I think he will be pleased.'

'He is in no hurry for that, Barbara. And you had better get used to calling him Philip. We will have the rest of our lives together, to be alone.'

'You mean . . . ?'

'Yes, dear,' Sibylla smiled. 'He has already asked me to marry him.'

'Dearest Sibylla, I feel so happy for you!' Barbara hugged her cousin. 'Does Jack now?'

'Oh, yes. Philip has asked him for his consent, as head of the family. As you may imagine, last night when it all came out, he laughed and teased us a good deal.' She sighed. 'But now, today, we are furthest from his thoughts, I am afraid.'

An hour later, Barbara got up from her bed and called for Betsy. 'You and I are going for a walk,' she told her maid.

'Yes, Miss Barbara?' Betsy's calm eyes regarded her a little doubtfully. 'Do you feel better, then?'

'I did not feel ill. I lay down to think. And no, I will not feel better until I have told you what I thought about. But there is no time to lose, so I will explain it to you on the way to see Miss Louise Favenel.'

'Miss Louise Favenel?'

'Miss Louise Favenel, I am sorry to say. I have thought about it, and thought about it until I have nearly stunned myself with thinking. But now I have made up my mind. I have worked out a plan. And, like it or not, I must speak with Miss Favenel, Betsy, for she is the only one I can think of who can help me now.'

# CHAPTER
# SEVEN

THEY SAT in Louise Favenel's drawing-room, and
Barbara came to the end of her story.

'And so, you see, it is this Kate Sharkey who holds the
key to the mystery. I do not know how I know it, but I
do. I must speak to her, to find out, and it must be
tonight, as long as there is the opportunity.'

'Yes,' said Louise. 'And you would do anything,
wouldn't you, to help Jack? You are in love with him. I
saw it from the beginning.'

Barbara looked into Louise's large blue eyes, narrowed now, and wondered—was there bitterness there,
and jealousy? Had she made a terrible mistake, a complete error of judgment, to come here and throw herself
on the mercy of this woman?

'Yes,' she said quietly, raising her chin proudly. 'I love
him, and I would do anything to help him.'

Louise threw back her head and laughed, and admiring the long long line of her graceful throat, Barbara
thought, 'Why, everything she does is practised—she
does that on the stage,' and waited, despairing, while
Louise got up from her seat and paced about theatri-
cally. And then she stopped and grasped Barbara's
hands.

'Well, it is a bold scheme, to be sure! And quite
audacious enough to succeed. Of course I will help you,
Barbara Graham. I like you. You see, it is as I told you,
you never had anything to fear from me. For one thing, I
could never bury myself in the country. The bright lights
of the towns and cities are where I should be. And for
another, you are a girl after my own heart, one with
some spirit.'

Barbara leaned back in the chair, sighing in relief, and laughing. 'You have given me plenty of frights, Louise.'

'That is a great compliment, I am sure. I have so few women friends. Somehow they do not take to me.'

Louise looked away when she said this, and there was a pathetic little droop to her shoulders. Barbara studied her profile closely. It was true what Jack had said. Louise Favenel was much older than she had at first appeared. There were little lines radiating out from the corners of her eyes which no amount of powder and paint could hide.

Of course, she might only be putting on an act again. But even as this suspicion passed through Barbara's mind, Louise turned her face back to her and the tears in her eyes were genuine. They struck a chord in Barbara's sympathetic heart; the actress was a very lonely woman. All the same, came a little warning voice, Jack had said only last night that Louise might have found a husband at last. What had he meant by that?

As if in reply to Barbara's question, Louise added, 'Mr Carrington agrees that women would not like me.'

Barbara laughed again. 'Of course they do not. You are so beautiful, and they fear for their men.'

'You are very honest, my dear, and very young, and we are wasting time. Some other time we will talk, and become the greatest of friends. But in that meantime, we have this business to attend. I take it you do not care to have Sibylla know about it?'

'Oh no! Nor your brother either. I do not think they could keep a secret from each other.'

'Well, then, I will attend to the make-up. But you must allow me to enlist Mr Carrington, he is the expert on the costumes. The best plan would be for us to say we are leaving for the theatre early this evening. And so we shall, to get the things we require and bring them to you. Shall we say about six o'clock?'

'If all goes well, I can never repay you for this, Louise.'

'Ah, but you shall, little Barbara Graham, if you will be my friend.'

As they walked back to Mistress Flora's house, Barbara asked Betsy, 'Well, what did you make of Miss Favenel, when you were sitting behind me, so quietly?'

'She is a very lonely woman, Miss Barbara. And a very beautiful one.'

'You are right, Betsy,' Barbara sighed. 'And, as Sir John said, she is indeed fascinating. She has the ability to put the people she likes quite under her spell.'

'We will have to warn Mistress Flora,' Betsy reminded her.

'More than that, we must take her into our confidence, I'm afraid, and I am not sure how she will respond to it.'

But, to their surprise, Flora entered into the spirit of it all, even to preparing the evening meal an hour earlier than usual. 'If you are going over there into that heathen den, nae doot to drink a pint of ale, you will be in need of something in your stomach first,' she said, 'or else it will go straight to your head and ruin everything.'

They sat down at half past five to a plain omelette, and Barbara drank a little milk.

'That will put a lining on your stomach,' Mistress Flora said with satisfaction, and then a knock came to the door and two message-boys stood on the threshold holding a large cane basket by its handles. 'Bring it in here,' she commanded, and ushered them into the parlour, and while the front door was still open, Louise accompanied by Mr Courteney Carrington arrived, radiating energy and confidence, so sure were they of their stagecraft.

Mr Carrington pulled out a pair of breeches from the basket, and ran a practised eye over Barbara's slim figure. 'They are too wide, of course,' he said. 'But we will use padding round your waist. And they are two inches too long,' tossing them over to Betsy to alter.

And then there was the fitting of the shirt, and the dark blue coat, until finally the dressing was accomplished, except for the hat. 'I will deal with the hair and the hat,' said Louise, and within minutes Barbara's hair was screwed into a plait, and doubled up, and a three-cornered hat sat upon her head.

'We took some old grease-paints, nearly done,' she went on, 'so it does not matter if we do not get them back,' while with a few strokes she widened Barbara's jaw, hardened her eyes and darkened her eyebrows. 'But you must walk like this,' she said, stamping around the parlour, 'with longer strides, and your back very straight, and remember to scowl and look very fierce and proud, like all men do.'

'Now, on your way over the road, practise it,' said Mr Carrington, 'so that you enter the Globe with a flourish. We will watch you from here.'

'Good luck,' said Louise, and pushed her out of the door.

The only things Barbara was not sure of were the silver-buckled shoes, ill-fitting and hurting her most abominably. But she marched resolutely across the street, remembering all she had been told, and after a little hesitation, pushed open the door of the tavern, and found herself immediately inside the tap-room.

The air was thick with smoke, so that it stung her eyes and she had difficulty in seeing across the little room. It was filled with men, some sitting, some standing or leaning across a wide wooden counter, and each one seemed to be smoking a pipe, a little white pipe with a long stem. On every peg around the walls, and from the back of every chair, hung three-cornered hats like the one she kept firmly on her head, while she looked to left and right in a haughty manner, remembering to pull back her shoulders as she strode up to the bar, for she knew that to appear irresolute would be to betray the weak, silly attitude of a woman.

She cleared her throat, preparing to drop her voice down to its gruffest note, and sat down on a high wooden stool.

'It's a fine night, sir, very fine,' remarked the landlord, polishing a mug with seemingly rapt attention. 'And how may I serve you?'

'A pint of your ale, Landlord,' answered Barbara.

'Yes, it is very fine. Another good season, then, for the farmers round about?'

'Ah, now, I just knew you to be of farming stock, sir, as soon as you came round that door,' the landlord said triumphantly, 'and I'm never far wrong. Which part of the country would you be from?'

'From east, along the Solway, but here to look around,' Barbara answered, sticking to the truth as far as possible. 'There is good land here, I can see that.'

The landlord waxed eloquent, and Barbara had only to listen with an interested expression, while her eyes raked the taproom. There was a fair sprinkling of farming folk among the townspeople in the crowded, noisy room, she saw uneasily, fearful in case the landlord drew any of them into the conversation, for then she would soon be found out for a fake.

There were also a few women, but none of them ladies, and Anna was busy, rushed off her feet serving the customers round the small tables. It was not difficult to manage to spill some of the ale over her knees, for the pint-pot was too heavy for her to lift with any ease.

'Sit still, sir!' the landlord commanded, for by this time Barbara's willing ear had made her a firm favourite. 'Sit still, and I will bring my niece with wet cloths to mop that up. Anna!' he shouted.

'Don't look up, and please don't look surprised,' Barbara breathed in her ear as the girl bent to wipe up the ale. 'It's me, Barbara Graham. I must speak to Kate o' the Vennel. Is she here?'

'In the other room,' Anna whispered.

'Move me out of this corner then.'

'We'll have to move him out of this corner, Uncle,' Anna said, with no change of expression in her voice or in her face. 'He is sitting in a puddle. Is there not a free table through the house?' she asked, and the landlord went to look, flapping his cloth as he disappeared. 'What is this?' She turned back to Barbara. 'What a fright you gave me!'

'Thank God, you did not show it,' Barbara said.

'Ay,' the landlord said, arriving back a moment later.

'It's thinning out a bit now. Go with him, Anna, and see that he is made comfortable, and well away from you know who. Oh, your name, sir? I neglected to ask.'

'Smith,' replied Barbara.

'Ay, a good name, that, hereabouts as well. Smith, now let me see. You wouldn't be connected with Sir Matthew Smith, would you, sir?'

'No, no. Just plain Smith,' Barbara replied, hastily following Anna.

'But all the same, that's no chiel among us, that one, mark my words,' she heard the landlord remarking to his cronies. 'Gentry, to be sure. Did you not see his hands?'

The table which Anna led her to suited Barbara's purpose better than she could have hoped, and she sat down with her back to the wall in the dim corner of the snug.

'I canna be long,' Anna said, perched for a moment on the opposite chair. 'What is it you could want with Kate o' the Vennel?'

'That's her, isn't it?' Barbara whispered. 'That's Kate Sharkey, over there?'

'Oh, that's her, all right. Kate o' the Vennel. Just look at her!'

Barbara cast a sidelong glance at Kate's face, coarsened with drink, dirty and sourly spiteful. 'She knows me,' she said, averting her face again. 'She knows Barbara Graham. She has seen me at Redayre, and she did not like me. That is why I came here in the guise of a man. She seems to be very drunk.'

'Ay, she's well on tonight,' said Anna. 'She's boiling up for something, got it in for someone, God help them. She's as mad as the Devil.'

Kate was muttering and cursing into her drink.

'I've got to speak to her, Anna,' Barbara said.

'Na, na, lassie. Ye canna do that!'

'How can I arrange it?'

Anna stared at her, and saw that Barbara was in deadly earnest. 'Not just now, not in her state! She can turn violent.'

'I *must* speak to her,' Barbara repeated. 'Will you help me, somehow?'

'Well, before long, she will be under that table, fast asleep,' Anna whispered grimly after an anxious pause. 'As a rule, we throw her out. Tonight I'll keep her, if you like. When she sobers up, she'll be quiet. That's when she'd do anything for a few coppers, for another drink.' Barbara groped in the pocket of her trousers, and fished out one of the guineas Jack had given her for the bonnets.

Anna looked scandalised. 'Not all that!' she said. 'I will change it, and bribe her little by little to follow me, more like. Where to?'

'To Mistress Cowan's opposite.'

'It'll be late, mind, after closing-time.'

'I'll wait, Anna,' Barbara said, got up casually, and swaggered out, for she felt she had succeeded.

But as the evening wore on into the night, still and very dark, she grew anxious, and the ticking of the longcase clock in the hall of Mistress Flora's house seemed to grow louder every minute.

'Calm yourself, dearie,' she advised Barbara, 'and I'll away and make a drink of warm milk before we go to bed.'

'Oh, Betsy,' she said, when they were left alone. 'What can have happened?'

'It will be a miracle if Anna Park ever gets her sobered up, and pointed in this direction, if it is as you described it to us, Miss Barbara.'

But the words had scarcely left her lips when there was a small knock upon the front door, and with her heart in her mouth, Barbara, still dressed up as a young gentleman, moved back instinctively into the furthest shadows of the parlour. Betsy rose calmly and unhurriedly, and took the chair between her and the door, and Flora ushered in two figures clad from head to toe in long black hooded cloaks.

'I thought it best to let no one see us coming here,' said Anna, throwing back her hood. 'I have brought someone to see you. It is Mistress Kate Sharkey, who has been telling me some bonny stories. You want to tell this gentleman, too, don't you, Kate?'

Kate did not offer up her cloak, for which Barbara was thankful, as she had noticed the filthy state of the hands which clutched it close, and her feet below. When the woman jerked her head, for one agonising moment they all thought she was going to spit on Mistress Flora's best rug. But after a rumble from Kate's throat, they made out the word, 'gold'.

Barbara dug into her pocket again, and threw a coin to Betsy in a contemptuous manner, to place upon the table, and Kate clutched it with dirty claws and sat staring up at them from pulled-down brows, wary, and waiting for someone to speak.

'Who is the fine gentleman, the one who is your friend, with his long cloak and his flat hat?' Barbara asked.

At that, Kate o' the Vennel burst into a guttural torrent of speech in a dialect far removed from the soft Lallans of Dumfries. Barbara could scarcely decipher one word of it, and gazed imploringly at Anna.

'She says it is her lover. He lives somewhere further west. He is going to inherit a big house, and marry her, and make her a fine lady.'

Barbara nodded. 'What else?'

'He has killed two people already for it,' Anna interpreted, and they watched in horror the expressive twists of grimy hands, and the fierce, laughing face opposite.

'Which tribe are you from?' Barbara asked next, at which Kate emitted a rattle of oaths and mutters, clearly furiously angry, and bit by bit Barbara began to understand the woman's speech, heard it again, as if she were back in the hay in the barns of Starlochy.

'Billy Marshall,' came out loud and clear, and 'Left him, left him. Sandy Powe's the big man now. The fox is running with Sandy Powe.'

So there had been a quarrel among them all, in the tribes of the Lingtowmen, Barbara surmised, while Kate fell silent, muttering bitterly to herself. Flora leapt up, grasping the opportunity to hand round the hot milk she had brought in earlier, leaving one mug on the sideboard, and reaching in for the brandy bottle. The very sight of it was having a wonderful effect on Kate Sharkey.

Flora poured a liberal amount into the last mug, and Kate sat up straighter, the glazed look beginning to leave her eyes, and with every gulp her tongue became looser.

'Gold for the hire of a horse,' she said.

'Where to?' asked Barbara.

'To the man,' Kate grinned evilly.

'But where? Where is the man?'

'Watch her!' Anna whispered. 'Don't press her too hard.'

'Tell me where, Mistress Sharkey?' Barbara asked for the third time, and she jingled two golden guineas in her hand.

'Redayre,' shouted Kate.

'Get her out of here,' Barbara whispered to Anna, who had risen to her feet.

'Well then, Kate,' Anna addressed the gipsy. 'I told you you would not regret this night's work. One more drink at the back door of the Globe, and you can go and find a horse.'

Kate rose with alacrity, and in a moment all that was left of their visitor was a strong, strange odour.

'I must open the window for a while, and fetch something to get rid of the smell,' said Flora, disappearing.

'What have you found out, Miss Barbara?' Betsy said, her face anxious and tired.

'It is worse even than I feared, for she is indeed the red-haired woman I saw in the North House manse, and there must be a man she associates with, in the district of Redayre. A murderer, as you heard.'

'How did she ever come to be in the North House, at all?'

'If you had ever seen Mistress Sadie Caldwell, the minister's housekeeper, you would not be surprised at the sort of maidservant she would have about her, Betsy.'

'I did not understand what she meant when she spoke about a fox, Miss Barbara.'

'No,' she answered thoughtfully, 'but perhaps that is not important. What is important, although I shall not relish it, is that Mr Faulks should be warned about her when we go back to Redayre.' And she thankfully breathed in the clean scent of the smouldering lavender Mistress Flora waved about on a shovel.

On Sunday morning they were astir early in Mistress Flora's house in the High Street, for in the afternoon Alan Kerr would bring round the coach, and there were still last-minute preparations to make for leaving. They were at breakfast when they heard the sounds of a horse clattering upon the street outside, and stopping outside the door.

'Mercy me, who can this be at this hour of a Sunday morning?' Mistress Flora cried, rushing out and drawing back the bolts. 'Oh, James!' they heard, 'James, dear brother, what brings you here?'

'Now, now, Flora,' James Aitken laughed. 'I hope you are well, and there is some breakfast for me?'

'Come awa' in,' said Mistress Flora. 'Come in, James, and tell us the news. We needna' be standing here speaking on the doorstep.' The Starlochy grieve came into the dining-room, younger, brighter and happier than Barbara had remembered him.

'It is you I have come so far, so early, to see,' he told her. 'Sir John sent word to Starlochy that you were to be here in Dumfries this week, but we have had every man, woman and child out at the harvest, and I could not stop, except for the Sabbath Day.'

'Tell me about Mama, and the boys, first,' she begged him.

'All well, and so is Starlochy. Times have changed.'

'For the better, I can see that.'

'Your Mama wanted it to be a surprise. She gave me very strict instructions before I left.'

'What surprise?' Barbara asked, with a dawning suspicion.

'She hopes you will be as happy as we are, my dear, to know that she has done me the honour of accepting my proposal of marriage.'

'That's twice, the news of a wedding, in as many days,' Barbara thought, shaking his hand warmly, and laughing and crying. 'There is bound to be a third.'

'Oh my, oh my!' cried Mistress Flora, thrown into a tizzy of excitement. 'When?'

'As soon as it can be arranged.'

The clock in the hall struck the half-hour, and Betsy said gently, 'It is time, Miss Barbara, to get ready for the Kirk,' and in her best new gown, and one of the little lacy bonnets Betsy had hurriedly made up for her when she had seen the fate of Sir John's guineas, they stepped out upon the High Street and went to Greyfriars Church.

It was hard to keep her mind upon the minister's sermon that Sunday morning. There was so much to think about. Mama, to be married to James Aitken! She could not think of any happier news, for all their sakes: for his, for Mistress Grace's, and certainly for her two little brothers who had never known a proper father in their lives. He had said as soon as possible, and of course it would take place at Starlochy, and without doubt that meant that she would have to return to her old home, for she could not bear that she should not see dear Mama on the happiest of her days for many years. Perhaps Jack would arrange it.

But first, this afternoon, to ride in the coach back to Redayre. Barbara discovered she was filled with apprehension, and all the pleasure of her previous thoughts evaporated. She wished, suddenly, that she was going back home on Snowy, to Starlochy, into her own room again, and Jamie and Robbie would come rushing to her, and she would hold them tight, and forget all about the dangers of Redayre, the wreckers and the smugglers, and Kate o' the Vennel in particular, who would be there already.

She sat quietly beside Sibylla, watching the tiny motes of dust hang quivering in the long slanted shaft of light from the coloured window of the church. The red-stained picture of a saint turned the wood of the pew to rusty brown, glowing and alive, and idly she began to wonder again why Jack had made her stand before him in his library while he drew the fur, every particular hair, of a fox. Why had it been a fox, and not a rabbit, or a squirrel, or any other creature who lived among the trees? Kate, too, had said something about a fox. What had she said? For the remainder of the service Barbara racked her brains, until she recalled the gipsy's words, 'The fox is running with Sandy Powe', and bitterly chastised herself for not pursuing what that meant.

They came out of the church to stand upon the steps in the bright sun, and Jack Jardine was there to meet them. He pulled her hand into the crook of his arm. 'Is it wise of you, do you think,' he asked softly, 'to put all this temptation before a smuggler? Who can tell how a bonnet like that might excite a man of violence?'

'You are laughing at me, as usual,' she said. 'Besides, you are not really a smuggler at all.'

'Ah, and what theory have you worked out now, Barbara? Who have you been talking to, to come to that conclusion?'

'Nobody,' she said, in an agony because Sibylla was still talking with the Favenels. If only she would let them go, before there could be any little slip of the tongue in front of Jack about her performance last night. 'Well, yes,' she added quickly, to divert his attention. 'Mr James Aitken is at Mistress Flora's house. He arrived this morning, with news that he and Mama are to be married.'

'And that is good news, is it not, Jack?' said Sibylla, hurrying up to them.

He laughed. 'There will be a third, mark my words. Everything goes in threes, does it not, Barbara?' He looked at her an instant, and then away again, and she knew at that moment that he understood her, because he felt as she did, the same flame, the same longing. 'And when is it to be, this wedding of your Mama's?'

'Mr Aitken says as soon as possible.'

'Then so be it. And I shall invite them to have the

ceremony at Redayre. In fact, I must insist upon it—for Margaret's sake, if for no other reason. We must make her dreams come true, at last!'

She knew what he was thinking. How Grace Jardine, twenty years ago, had run away, not waiting to leave her home a bride. There had been no splendid feast for her, none of the happy excitement of a young girl preparing for her wedding. He meant that she should have it this time, and he would foot the bill.

'What is the matter?' he said quietly, breaking in upon her thoughts. 'Do you not like the idea?'

'I was thinking how pleased Mama will be,' she said, 'to go back to Redayre.'

'And you—Will you be pleased to go back there this afternoon?'

'Of course, if that were all.'

'Yes, I know, I could see that by your face.'

They walked back along the High Street from Greyfriars, Sibylla tranquil as ever, and smiling to herself, on Jack's right side. Barbara became aware how close he was to her, upon his left, their shoulders touching, their hands tight clasped, and that he was smiling again in his secret way at her. She was filled suddenly, there in the street, with a brazen, shameless longing to be closer still, with his lips on hers and his hands behind her back, as it had been beside the river one afternoon. She looked away from him, up towards the Midsteeple, struck dumb with the flame that had arisen in her, and began to pat her ringlets and her bonnet, silly little gestures she knew would not deceive him for a moment, but gave her a little feeling of disguising her naked self, on a Sunday morning in the middle of Dumfries.

They sat down to cold meat at one o'clock, Betsy eating with them, and looking shy at such a turn of events.

'I must ride back directly,' said James Aitken. 'For the minister is reading the banns for the first time at the evening service at the Powfoot Kirk, and I must be there to sit beside my future wife.'

'We must have them read in both counties, in our Kirk

as well, then,' Jack said. 'I will arrange it, so that they are also read this evening at Redayre. I will see to it directly we go back. Then, the wedding will be in three weeks' time? And you, Mistress Flora, what of you?' he added, turning to his hostess.

'Oh, I could not travel alone, sir,' she said, sadly.

'Would you do something to please me, Mistress Flora?' he asked.

'Anything, sir, that I could,' she said, a little tearfully.

'I want you to leave this house today, and come with us—now, this afternoon.'

Flora stared at him. 'But I cannot! I have made no preparations. I would have to pack up my things, my boxes!'

'We will allow you one hour,' he conceded, and at once all was bustle and confusion—Betsy running with heaps of clothing, the strapping up of boxes, while James ran to neighbouring houses with food left over in case of attracting mice. Then he mounted Negro and rode off laughing, and Jack doused all the fires and locked up all the windows.

Alan Kerr arrived, rumbling over from the Plainstones with the coach. It came to the door, and they bundled inside with packages, rugs, pillows, and the luggage on the roof.

'I will go on ahead,' Jack shouted, and mounted up on the chestnut. 'Take your time, Alan. There is no more hurry now.'

Then they would miss the evening service at Redayre, Barbara thought thankfully, leaning back beside Flora while they swayed along. She would have liked to hear the reading of Mama's banns, but there would be two more Sundays yet to attend in Redayre Kirk, while Mr Faulks proclaimed them.

For the next two days, Jack went about shaking his head and laughing, while they unpacked the boxes, and re-arranged themselves, and acquainted Margaret of every detail of the holiday.

'Women!' he said. 'How you love to dramatise everything, tear it all into fine shreds, and add it up again, two and two making five. Is it not enough, that a man and a woman love each other and want to marry?'

'How can it be as simple as that, Jack?' Margaret asked, her merry face all beaming. 'There is so much to consider. What shall we wear? What shall we eat?'

'And whom shall we invite, and whom leave out?' Sibylla put in, with a note of anxiety. 'We cannot accommodate more than twenty in this house, you know. You will have to advise me, Jack.'

'Oh, no!' he said, 'I leave it all to you. There are more mundane matters I must attend to.' He went away.

It was on Wednesday, after dinner, when Sibylla had gone into her sitting-room, and Mistress Flora had followed Margaret into the kitchen for yet another discussion of the forthcoming wedding feast, that Jack held out his hand to Barbara, and in it was a key.

'We may not have much more time,' he said. 'There may not be another chance, when the moon rides high over the Solway, and the night is balmy, as it is tonight. Here is the key.'

She hardly had to ask. 'It is for the closet?'

'By eleven o'clock they should be all abed. I shall wait for you, behind the ivy.'

'Why? Where are we going?'

'To have an adventure, to have a picnic, in the middle of the night, just you and I. You will like that, won't you, Barbie?'

Why must he always treat her like a child? She stood before her wardrobe, pondering which gown to wear, and dressed in this one, and then that, until finally it was all to her satisfaction, and she took out the grease-paints left behind by Louise Favenel that she had brought with her, and carefully painted her face. And then, in the end, in a panic when the stable clock struck half-past ten, and the harvest moon hung low and red outside her window, she caught a glimpse of herself in her mirror, like a painted whore, raddled and cheap, reminding her of Kate Sharkey. She wiped away all the paint and stripped off her finery, and put on instead her old white muslin gown, and over that her long dark cloak, and with her elaborate hair-style all brushed out she let herself down out of the closet.

Outside, the ivy was mysterious, rustling, and in the shadows inky-black. Then one of the shadows moved, and she saw it was Jack, dressed in his black clothes, with his finger to his lips, and even in the darkness she felt the colour flare into her cheeks with a quick thud of her heart at the sight of him, before it drained away.

He grasped her hand, and they tip-toed softly over the gravel. Then out upon the lawns he dragged her faster, and they broke into a run, and laughter bubbled up inside her and she hid her face in her cloak until they arrived breathless in the shade of the trees.

'You did not keep me waiting long,' he said.

'I did not think I should dress up,' she lied.

'You understand now, Barbie, how simple life becomes when gowns and bonnets and mirrors are forgotten,' he said, and she laughed secretly inside herself, remembering the gowns tossed aside on her bed, and the grease-paints scattered and left in an untidy heap.

'Yes,' she said. 'It becomes quite simple.'

They came out through the trees and walked over to where the stream flowed out between the high shingle banks, and the boat that was waiting. They stepped in, and he took the oars and pushed downstream, watching her as she sat in the bows.

'There are the lines,' he nodded with his head, 'and the bucket of worms. Fix some on the hooks.'

She picked up a wriggling worm, frowning as she concentrated on her task, and jabbing her finger on the hook, swore beneath her breath.

When she glanced up, she saw that Jack was laughing at her.

'I used to be able to do it,' she said angrily. 'Why must women be so useless?'

'I will do it, when we get out into the open sea,' he said.

'I want to do it for myself,' she answered furiously. 'I will not give in. I never give in.'

'Never?' he said, laughing, and then began to whistle, and when he turned his head to look for his direction, she seized the worm again and fixed it on the hook, while his eyes were off her.

'There it is,' she cried triumphantly. 'I have it. Look, I have it!'

'So you are making progress. I will make a fisherman of you yet, along with everything else.' He rested his oars, took a large stone fastened to a long rope, and heaved it overboard.

There was a faint ripple on the glassy sea, and the boat moved gently on it, up and down, while they sat, one at either end, and threw out their lines. He did not speak, and she sat there with him in the companionable silence, in their little world of water, while the moon glowed and the sea reflected a blood red path below it.

Was it on a night like this that Mama had run away? Still and warm and filled with excitement? Mama had never told her about those events, had always kept the knowledge of things that were best forgotten or frightening away from her. But she had not been able to hide the smuggling at Powfoot, or the bands of Lingtowmen, or any of the terrible events that followed.

The one thing Mistress Grace had made her children very aware of was the danger of the sands, quivering, shifting all the time beneath the sea, Barbara shivered when she imagined again what their quivering might uncover, dead men's bones and skulls, along the changing bottom. And here was Jack, peacefully sitting there beside her, intent only upon this business of fishing, while perhaps around the next rock men might be scrambling to hide a beacon, and a large ship might be deceived into sailing too close to the shore.

'What is the matter?' he said quietly, breaking in upon her thoughts. 'Do you not want to fish any more?'

'I was thinking of the wreckers.'

'Wreckers? What do you know of the wreckers, Barbara?'

'Nothing,' she admitted, 'until I came to Redayre.'

'There will be no wrecking tonight, for the moon is too bright. Otherwise I would not be out with you now, upon a different adventure.'

'Why? What have you to do with wrecking? Why must you be mixed up with it?'

'I believe you have a fish on your line,' he replied, and she felt a pull, a tug upon the hook. 'If you cannot bring it in, hand over your line to me.'

'I do want to bring it in,' she said.

'Very well, then. Haul in your line, gently to begin with. Don't let him slip off the hook.'

She began to pull, slowly at first, and then faster as she felt the weight of the fish upon the end of the line, thinking as she hauled how conveniently it had come to bite the worm, and allowed Jack to slip off another hook instead.

And still the moon sailed high above, while her fish flapped and squirmed, and with a little twitch lay still upon the bottom of the boat, and they threw out their lines again. There was not a sound, not even a sea-bird or a curlew, except the little slaps of water against the side of the boat. Barbara wondered where all her little devils had gone; there were none left now as she sat in perfect peace beside Jack. It was because of his presence, she knew.

'That's plenty,' he said, as the fourth fish landed in the boat. 'We will go back to the shore, and find a place to build our fire.' He steered them back to the high shingle banks, and over to a little clearing at the edge of the wood.

'Will this do, Barbie?' he said, and she caught the gleam of his pale eyes in the moonlight. 'It is a favourite spot of yours, is it not? This is where the fox stood, and watched you out there splashing naked in the sea.'

'Yes.' She bent her head to hide the quivering shyness which was threatening to engulf her, and took a steadying breath. 'But I am not afraid of foxes.'

'No?' The dreaded hardness was back about his

mouth. 'But they are sly and vicious creatures, are they not?'

'Foxes!' she said, taking the sticks from him, and building them one against the other. 'I have heard of nothing but foxes, from here to Dumfries.'

'Oh?' he asked her softly. 'And what did you hear about foxes in Dumfries?'

'That they will run first in one direction, and then another, so that it is very difficult to catch them.'

Jack went off to the water's edge to clean the fish, and she felt alone and frightened, and glanced over her shoulder into the wood. But there was no sound, only the leaves whispering behind her, and he came back and knelt down with his flint and tinder and lit the fire.

'Still,' he said, continuing the conversation, 'I am going to catch that one, the one who lives about here. Have you ever before cooked a fish outside?'

'No.' She was smiling at him over the flames, all feelings of nervousness gone now that he was back beside her. 'We always carried them home.'

He took the flat stone he had brought up from the water with the fish and placed it at the edge of the fire, and two fish upon that, with his knife at the ready, and soon he was able to turn them with it, their skins turned brown, and their smell delicious.

'I have not forgotten something to drink on our picnic.' He went down to the boat, and came back with a bottle in his hand. 'But I had no glasses, only these two mugs.'

'They will do,' said Barbara, and got a large leaf ready to catch the baked fish, while he poured out some wine, and put the next two fish to cook.

'Oh, it is a wonderful picnic,' she laughed, 'the best I ever had.'

'It is the best one for me, too, Barbie,' he said, and came to sit beside her, with his shoulder touching hers, as they ate and drank. Soon the fish on the fire were done, too, and they burned their fingers on them, and laughed into each other's eyes.

Barbara knew she had never felt happy before, never

until this moment, when he put his arm round her, and kissed her slowly, lingeringly, and she turned to fling her arms around his neck.

'Are you happy, too?' she asked him. 'It is like a dream, out here, with you.'

He looked down into her shining eyes, the ghost of a smile on his lips.

'Yes,' he said, 'I am happy. And you, Barbie, you must stay as long as you can in your dream world. That is for women. But men cannot afford to dream. They must stay alert, and fight, and have sons, to carry on where they left off.'

'Sons?'

'Oh yes,' he said. 'I shall have a son before twelve more months have gone.'

There was a silence between them, and now as the fire died down the night grew chilly, and the orange-coloured moon sank to the rim of the sky and slowly disappeared.

'Why is it that everything that is beautiful lasts so short a time?' she flung at him bitterly.

'There will other times for you, Barbara,' he said quietly, stamping out the ashes of the fire. 'And you will think that they are beautiful, and exciting too. Did you enjoy our picnic?'

'Oh yes,' she said, suddenly cold and very tired.

They did not speak again until on the way back they were almost out of the woods, and the lawns spread out before them, around the dreaming house.

'It is too quiet,' said Jack. 'There should be the crying of an infant for its mother in the night. And by day the noise of children rushing here and there, as it was in the old days, as it always was at Redayre.'

'And who is she, this mother of your sons?' she sighed in a whisper, as they crossed the lawns.

'I am not ready to tell you about her, not yet,' he said coolly, and held open the little door in the ivy for her to pass through.

She stole into her bedchamber and lit the candle on the table beside her bed, staring at the mess she had left behind two hours ago, a life-time ago, when she had been so joyful and tremulous, with her fingers all thumbs because she was going out with Jack.

Now she swept aside the grease-paints with a gesture of contempt for her own stupidity, so that they all scattered and rolled across the floor, and after the grease-paints she flung down the tangled heap of gowns. Why should she care, now? She had always vowed that she would never marry, anyway. She had always wanted to be free, not burdened down with babies.

And then, unbidden, the question came into her mind—What would any son of Jack's look like? What colour his eyes? Silver, like the cruel, hard steel of his father's eyes, to pierce a woman's heart, and wound her as deep as this, or would he take after his mother, whoever she was?

The tears spilled down her face, and turning her face into her pillow, Barbara sobbed the same anguished sobs she had heard from her mother's bedchamber when she had lost her lover.

# CHAPTER
# EIGHT

'WHAT HAS HAPPENED?' Betsy asked, eyeing her pink and swollen eyelids in the morning.

'I did not sleep,' Barbara said listlessly, and watched as the maid started to unravel the untidy heap of gowns and hang them up, and gather all the grease-paints from the floor, and afterwards fling back the curtains to open the window a little way.

'The weather is changing, Miss Barbara. The sky is overcast, and there is a great smell of the sea everywhere.'

'Sooner or later we shall have a storm, and it will be a bad one,' Barbara said as soon as she saw the mood of the Solway. 'And that reminds me, before it comes and when we get the chance, we must go to the North House to speak to the minister. But not today—I could not face it today.'

She was greatly relieved that Jack did not seem to be about when she arrived downstairs in the dining-room, to pick at some bread and drink some tea. In the next few days she became adept at avoiding everyone, keeping to herself as much as she dared. From her bedchamber she watched the weather hovering over the sea, then lifting, then lowering again, to fill her with a great unease and a depression of the spirits.

'I'm afraid our lovely summer is coming to an end,' Sibylla said. 'Let us hope this storm will break soon, if it is going to break at all, and be over before your Mama and the others arrive from Starlochy.' She peered into Barbara's face. 'You are looking quite pale, my dear. Is it the weather?'

'It is nothing, Sibylla, that some fresh air would not cure.'

'Put on your cloak, then, and I will send Fanny for mine, and we will go down to the sea. There will be plenty of fresh air there.'

Down on the shore Barbara breathed in deeply. Betsy had been right, the smell was strong, a smell of seaweed and brine.

'The swell is deep below the waters,' she said, 'and it is moving the seaweed. It is always a sign of danger when you can smell it so far inland, so the fishermen say at home.'

They approached a slimy, quivering patch of sand, and she grasped Sibylla's arm, every nerve aware, and dragged her over to the dunes. As far as her eye could see over the long flat stretch of the bay, the sands were quivering and blistering, and down below them, almost where they had trod, tiny bubbles ballooned up out of the sand, and popped, to show where they were boiling underneath. They were building up until soon they would be shifting, moving, sucking downwards, their inexorable jaws wide open for the unwary, in their grotesque dance of death.

'Along by Powfoot, it can simmer just like this for days, or explode within hours.' Barbara shivered, and under the lowering skies they watched the sullen sea creeping in ever further with the flowing tide, conspiring with the sands to conceal their deadly secret.

'We should have gone the other way,' Sibylla said, with a shudder. 'I do not really like the sea, as I have told you. It is too cruel and too fierce.'

They turned back, and Barbara began to speak of the thing she had brooded on ever since the midnight picnic. 'Who is she, the lady Jack will marry soon?' she asked, and waited with a sick feeling to hear the answer.

'There is no lady, as far as I am aware. Why, Barbara?' Sibylla said in surprise.

'Oh!' she expelled a long breath. 'I thought he meant he had it all arranged.

'Why, what has he been saying to you now?'

'He said Redayre needed children, and he would have a son soon.'

'Well, I hope that may be true, Barbara. Redayre certainly should have an heir, and Heaven knows what Jack has been thinking about, near thirty and not married yet, nor even the prospect of it. But there is no use marrying only for the sake of marrying, and I suppose he has not met anyone so far he loves.'

'But it is very refreshing to walk along the shore, is it not, dearest Sibylla?' Barbara said, her feet suddenly light, as if she could dance.

'Well,' she answered, laughing, 'it has certainly brought the roses back in your cheeks, my dear. But perhaps Jack has been giving it all some serious thought, since the death of our parents and the business of Redayre was thrust upon him so suddenly. They were in perfectly good health, you see.'

'Yes,' said Barbara, not wishing that Sibylla should be upset, and steering the conversation firmly back to Jack. 'And if Jack were to have no sons when he married, but only daughters, would the oldest one inherit Redayre?'

'Oh no, Barbara, certainly not. The whole estate is entailed in such a way that only the male next of kin can inherit, and the title too, I think, although I am not sure of that. Papa saw to it.'

'Why?'

'He had it written down in his Will, and our Agent in Dumfries, Mr David Simpson, came here and read it out to us. I can remember his words by heart, I believe.'

'What were they?'

'He wrote: "It has pleased the Lord to bestow on me the land estate of Redayre—the greater part thereof the ancient property of my progenitors—and some lands I have purchased of others, so that while kept together it happens to be somewhat greater than any in the South of Scotland, or ever was, which makes me unwilling to divide it among my daughters, in the event of the death of my son, John Jardine, or his son, and so on through the line. These daughters may have the best natural right, but thereby my name and my family becomes extinct, and whoever the next nearest male kin should inherit, he must do so in the name of Jardine.''' '

'It sounds as though he had some premonition,' Barbara said. 'But now I understand Jack much better.'

They walked along in silence, while Barbara kept her head bent, deep in thought, until she said, 'Who would be the nearest kinsman, Sibylla?'

Sibylla sighed, and said, 'The Reverend Browne Gilmour Faulks, dear. Not a direct heir, certainly, since the relationship was through Mama. He is her sister's son. But that is who would be the next master here, if anything happened to Jack.'

Barbara might have been struck dead, frozen in her tracks. She was too dumbfounded to speak, and a thousand things flashed through her head, a few words here, a fleeting glimpse of something there, before she found her voice again.

'Mr Faulks?' she cried. 'Oh no, not him! I do not like him. I do not like him at all!'

'I'm afraid none of us does,' Sibylla answered sadly. 'But he is still our cousin, you know, whether we like it or not.'

'Yes. I beg your pardon, Sibylla. I should not have said that, especially of a reverend gentleman.'

'I doubt very much if he is a reverend gentleman, Barbara, and so does Jack, although he is so learned and so clever, and was the tutor on and off for years. Then, when our dear old minister died last year, our cousin Browne persuaded poor Mama that he was a minister of the Church and that he had studied for his degree in Edinburgh, so Papa allowed him to fill the vacancy.'

'Most assiduously, I would say,' Barbara remarked.

'Nevertheless, dear, he is the minister here, and as such we must treat him with the great respect of that calling,' Sibylla said unhappily. 'Forget everything else, Jack says, unless it can be proved otherwise.'

'Of course,' Barbara agreed, and went up thoughtfully to her room, to put off her cloak and join the others for a cup of tea. A small chill wind was blowing in through her window, and she went across to close it, noticing how the trees were bending, for the wind had shifted to the south-west. 'Now it will blow up,' she thought, staring at the sea, heaving leaden-grey and mutinous.

Downstairs, the servants had already lit the fire in the sitting-room.

'I shall not be in for dinner this evening, Margaret,' Jack said, striding into the room.

'No,' said Margaret, with a sudden, anxious look.

Sibylla got up and looked out of the window, shuddering. 'It is coming, then, the storm?'

'The wind is rising from the south-west, and you know what that means.'

'Yes, that is what I feared,' said Sibylla, and Jack went out. They heard him in the hall, shouting for Alan Kerr. He had not spoken one word to Barbara, only glanced at her with the cold implacable hoods down over his eyes.

Then it was five o'clock ringing, and a whole hour still before dinner, and the household was quiet, Mistress Flora busy and happy in the kitchens with Margaret, and Sibylla up in her own sitting-room. Every minute of that day had seemed an hour to Barbara.

'I cannot bear it,' she said to Betsy, when she called her. 'There is the terrible feeling of something hanging over us. I suppose it may be the storm, but I fear it is also my conscience. We have not yet been to see the minister.'

'No,' said Betsy.

'I do not really want to go.'

'I know you do not, Miss Barbara.'

'But perhaps it would be better done, and off my mind.'

'I shall come with you, Miss Barbara. You cannot go alone.'

'Then fetch our cloaks, while all is quiet here.'

They crept out of Redayre through the front door, because of Margaret and Mistress Flora in the kitchens so near the back, and skirted the house on the grass, until they came out of the shrubbery and on to the little path which led to the church. The wind was in their faces, making little snatches at their hoods, so that soon they were forced to hold them on their heads with one hand, and the skirts of their cloaks together with the other.

It was dark, even although it was still quite early in the evening, with the clouds hanging low, and they reached the shelter of the Willow Walk thankfully, quite out of breath, and started to walk up its dim path. But as they neared the top, and made out the outlines of the summerhouse, their footsteps dragged.

'You will stay here, Betsy, in the shelter of the summerhouse. Round here,' Barbara said, leading the way to the side nearest the North House, the east side, away from the wind. 'I shall not be long. Ten minutes at the most. Wait for me.'

Then, once again, she stood upon the doorstep of the manse and pulled the bell, shivering and expecting to have to wait and wait, as before, and then to ring again. But instead, the door opened almost immediately, and Mr Faulks himself stood there, the light behind him shining into her face.

'Barbara! You have come! You have come, at last!' he said, and there was a strange exultant laugh in his voice.

'May I come in, sir, for I have something I must tell you?'

'Did you think I would let you go—*now?*' he asked, and closed the door behind her. It seemed to her that it clanged, like the door of a cage. She saw his teeth flash in his smile, those pointed white teeth, and his eyes glowed with such fervour they seemed like coals. 'But not into my front parlour this time, I think. It will be cold in there, and cheerless without a fire. I have been sitting in the kitchen. Come and see where I really live. I call it my den.'

But even as she followed the minister down to his 'den', Barbara became more and more dubious, and fear followed her every footstep.

Fleetingly she wondered why Mistress Caldwell had not lit the fire in the minister's front room, when at any

moment some parishioner might call to consult him for
guidance from on high. But nevertheless she followed
him down the dingy passages, past closed doors which
perhaps were never opened, until he reached the one at
the far end and, throwing it open, stood back for her to
enter.

She stood in the middle of the floor, aghast at the
squalor and the dirt which met her gaze. The flagged
floor was littered with rubbish, the room lit by three
candles, while a low turf fire smouldered on the hearth,
and a loaf of bread beside a bowl of dripping was all that
was on the table.

The kitchen was blue with peat-smoke, and it hurt
her eyes and made them smart. Peering around, she
saw no sign of Mistress Caldwell. She was alone with
Mr Faulks.

'Can I offer you something to eat?' he asked. 'No?
Then I shall fetch us something to drink, for an occasion
such as this is worth celebrating, is it not, when Miss
Barbara comes to call!'

He went across the flags to a big cupboard behind the
panelling, and took out a bottle and two glasses. 'The
very best brandy, no less, for Miss Barbara,' and poured
some out for each of them.

'I do not drink brandy, sir,' she said, alarmed at
something sinister in his tone and facing him across the
table, from the chair he had pulled out for her. She held
her hands in her lap so that he should not see them
tremble. 'I have come here to warn you about your
maidservant, Kate Sharkey.'

'I have no servant here, except for Mistress Caldwell,
and even she is not here this evening,' he answered
softly.

'But I saw her! I saw Kate Sharkey, the last time I was
here, at the window. And I have come to tell you to
beware of her, for when I was in Dumfries I found out
how wicked she is, and goes with some man in this
district, a murderer. She confessed it. You could be in
such grave danger!'

He poured himself out another glass of brandy, and

she saw with terror that he was angry, the veins standing out upon his forehead.

'Kate Sharkey? Kate o' the Vennel?' he laughed contemptuously. 'Oh yes, she came here, but I sent her away. What would I do with a woman like that? No, Barbara,' and he leaned towards her, 'I have had my eye on you, since ever you arrived in Redayre, how you would look with silks and satins on your back, and jewels at your throat, and in your hair, the grandest lady in all the Stewartry. And, tonight, it will all be within our grasp.'

For an eternity it seemed she stared at him, as he leered at her from across the table. She got to her feet, and backed away from him as he came towards her, never taking his eyes from her face, taking papers out of his pockets and opening them out,

'Look,' he said. 'Look at these! They are maps, and notes of all the expeditions I have managed, all along the coast, in this last year.'

'Expeditions?'

'Yes,' he said. 'They bring the news to me about the sailings of the ships, so that I know exactly what course they are on, and how to divert them, for the gold. I am a rich man already, Barbara, but this prize tonight will be the most lucrative of all. And I have promised the Lord that, having delivered it into my hands, it will also be the last!'

He fell silent for a moment, gazing at his empty glass. He picked it up, and put it down again. 'No,' he said, 'I'll have no more at present, I must keep a clear head until later, when I come back. Then you shall join me, Barbara, I insist.'

He placed one of the candlesticks upon the table, spread out the papers, and fell to studying them, muttering all the while. Barbara edged towards the door, got her hand upon the handle, but he was too fast for her.

'Where do you think you are going, Barbara? Here you have come, and here you shall stay, for it is what you have always wanted. You knew it, and I knew it, from the first. You and I are partners now at last!'

He held her arms pinioned to her sides, and laughed into her face, and she smelled the unpleasant odour of his breath with revulsion, saw how the beads of sweat stood moistly on the freckles of his skin and turned them to dark-brown pin-points, and reared back her head as his short sharp teeth came nearer, threateningly. But instead he kissed her savagely and cruelly, with his hot damp face pressed upon her, and she was filled with horror. She tore her mouth away, feeling sick, unable to breathe.

'But I have not the time at present,' he said, and the words uttered in his silkiest tones were infinitely revolting and degrading to Barbara, with their lustful implication. He dragged her back over to her chair, and pulled her hands behind her back. She felt a rope around them, digging into her skin, and kicked with her feet before he grabbed them too, and tied them to the legs of the chair.

'Wait there, my little bride,' he shouted exultantly in his voice he used for preaching, and then he stuffed a rag cruelly across her mouth and tied the ends behind her head.

'The Fox is going hunting,' he laughed evilly, and her eyes watched him as he donned a long dark cloak which fell right down to the floor, and a queer flat hat with a very wide brim.

He went out and slammed the kitchen door behind him. It made the candles gutter and they almost went out, but after a second they burned up again so that she could see. How filthy, how disgusting, this madman and the house he lived in! For now she realised that the Reverend Mr Faulks was mad, he was demented—but worse even than that was her own stupidity.

Why had she not seen it long ago? Almost from the very first day she had come to Redayre, when Jack had even drawn it in a picture for her, the drawing of a fox, a Faulks, the Reverend Mr Faulks. Then Jack, at least, had known it all along. Even Kate Sharkey had spoken of the Fox. And now he had gone out upon the prowl, and there would be another wrecking under cover of this storm, and Jack's life was in mortal danger.

But the harder she pulled at her cords, and the deeper they dug into the flesh of her wrists and ankles. She could not shout or scream. She sat there helpless, and thought of Betsy. How long would she wait? But even if she came and rang the door bell, there would be no one to answer her and she would go away, not understanding her mistress any more and blaming her for a long cold wait in a deserted summerhouse.

And then she heard a creaking floorboard, and a tiny rustle, and the hairs stood up on the back of her neck as she watched the handle of the kitchen door turning very slowly, and the door opened. The last person she had expected in the world stood there looking at her, had been listening all the time, and her face was livid with rage and hatred. Kate Sharkey had a knife in her hand.

In those next few moments, which Barbara believed would be her last, she could think of nothing and no-body, nobody except Jack, the man she loved and had tried so hard to help. Where was he now? Out there, somewhere in this storm, up in the cliffs, perhaps, not knowing that a murderer was behind him. And dimly, as Kate advanced towards her, something whispered in the back of her mind. 'He will be killed, and I am sitting here as helpless as a trussed chicken, and I can do no more.' Once again she struggled feverishly to loosen her bonds.

But Kate, it seemed, was in no hurry to see the end of her, and besides, her eyes had gone past her and fastened on the brandy bottle, and the full glass beside it that Barbara had not touched. She drank it at a gulp, and, as before, it had the same effect, and she began to talk.

'Brown Fox, he does not want you!' She spat furiously in Barbara's terrified face. 'He wants Kate Sharkey. Kate Sharkey will be a fine lady, in silks and satins and rings, plenty of rings, and a fine house—the Big House, Redayre—and plenty of servants!' and she laughed and lurched about on the flagged floor in a ghastly charade of a lady's walk.

She bent down and peered into Barbara's face again. 'Brown Fox is a clever man. He is a minister. He is my man,' she shouted. 'I will kill anyone who tries to take him from me!'

Then the Fox and the minister were one and the same, and it was as though she had known it all along. But she could not think about it, not then, while Kate fell to drinking, and kicking the leg of the table fiercely from time to time, and then to muttering. 'Gold! Gold!' Barbara made out, and then with a sudden leap Kate threw herself at the cupboard behind the panelling where the brandy had been kept, and began to grope inside it. She became more agitated still, and dragged across a stool, and stood upon it to search the shelf above, and with a terrible scream stood back in front of Barbara, the knife raised in her hand.

'Gone! Gone! The gold is gone!' she shouted. 'Where is it?'

Barbara shook her head violently from side to side and tried to speak against her gag, but nothing came out except her muffled moans. Kate raised the knife and slashed behind Barbara's head, and the rag fell to the floor. She found that she could not speak anyway, for her lips were too numb with fear and her throat too parched to utter even a word.

Why had Kate not killed her, there and then? Of course, it was because she thought Barbara knew where the gold was. The gold was even more important than the Fox, after all.

'Here,' said Kate, and put the glass of brandy up to her lips. Barbara drank a sip, and then another, and felt it glowing down through her body, hot and reviving.

'He has betrayed you, Mistress Sharkey,' she said calmly, 'and gone with all the gold. But if you got it back again, you could still be a fine lady and marry any man. It need not be the Fox. There are other men, better than he.'

There was a pause, while Barbara prayed, and another glass of brandy was gulped, as Kate considered this. Then, 'No!' she cried, dashing down the glass on the table and smashing it to pieces. 'It need not be the Fox. The gold!'

'Where has he gone?' Barbara asked, knowing that she had the better of Kate now.

'To strip the ship, the wreck.'

'And then?'

'Back here, for you,' Kate glowered.

'But if I am not here?'

'To lie low, with Sandy Powe, north by Dumfries,' she said with an evil look of cunning, before she bent her head of long, matted red hair and fell to muttering to herself again.

Barbara's heart was beginning to fail her. She had come this far, found out this much, but of what use could it ever be now? Her eye fell on the maps and papers still left lying on the table.

'Get a horse, steal a horse,' Kate was mumbling, and then Barbara saw her chance.

'Untie me,' she said, with a note of authority. 'If you untie me, I will give you my horse from the stables of Redayre.'

Grumbling and doubtful, Kate Sharkey slashed the ropes round Barbara's wrists and ankles, and the pain was terrible as the blood returned. Kate smiled cruelly when Barbara rubbed them, her face twisted with the pain, before she got to her feet.

'Come, Mistress Sharkey,' she said coldly. 'Put that knife away, and remember, if you are seen around Redayre you will be hanged, as like as not. You will have to keep beside me, for I am the only one for whom they will open up the stables.'

They left the North House by the back door, leaving it ajar, and plunged into the night, round the side of the house until they reached the summerhouse. Where had the knife gone to? She had seen Kate hide it somewhere in her skirts, Barbara thought uneasily.

'Betsy,' she called softly. 'Are you there?'

'Here, Miss Barbara.' A figure materialised out of the shadows, and even in the darkness, Barbara could see the look of horror on her maid's face at the sight of Kate Sharkey.

'Run on ahead with these,' she said, thrusting the

maps and papers into Betsy's hands, 'and put them in a safe place—in Sir John's hands, if he is there. Warn Alan Kerr I shall require Snowy at once, saddled and ready to go.'

Then Barbara took the long, terrifying journey down the Willow Walk alone with the gipsy woman, the shock of the cold air making Kate reel drunkenly, so that with a shudder of distaste Barbara took her arm and dragged her along. The full force of the gale whipped savagely round their backs as they emerged on to the little path to Redayre.

Somehow they arrived beneath the stable clock, and Snowy was out upon the cobbles, with Betsy at his head, holding his bridle firmly.

'Here you are, then, Kate Sharkey,' Barbara said. 'Look after my horse, do you hear? If any harm befalls Snowy, I will see to it that you get it back a hundredfold.'

Kate leapt on the horse's back, and grasped the reins expertly. A quick dig from her heels in his flanks, and they were off, galloping away into the night.

'What excuse did you give Alan Kerr, Betsy?'

'None. He is not here, nor Joe. Neither is Sir John, Miss Barbara.'

'Why, where have they all gone?' Then, when Betsy shook her head, 'What time is it?' They stared up at the clock in the courtyard. 'It has stopped, Betsy, it must have. It does not even point to six yet.'

'It has not stopped,' Betsy replied. 'It is ringing the hour now, and you will have to go into dinner.'

It seemed to Barbara that it could have been a week instead of the short hour they had been gone. 'Take my cloak,' she said, and smoothed her hair, and went into the dining-room.

'There are only us, this evening,' Margaret said. 'No gentlemen, only four ladies, so Mistress Flora and I made the meal quite light. Are you hungry, Barbara?'

'I don't think any of us are, are we?' she said, looking at the three anxious faces of Sibylla, Margaret and Mistress Flora.

A constraint fell upon them, and it was a quick,

uneasy little meal, the food turning to dust in Barbara's mouth.

'If you will excuse me,' she said, 'I believe I shall go up early. I am very tired.'

She lit the candle beside her bed, and noticed that the little drawer of the cabinet was askew, as though it had been opened and closed carelessly, or in a great hurry. When she pulled it open, she found the maps and papers from the North House lying there inside, where Betsy must have thrown them before she had run back to saddle Snowy. Barbara closed the drawer thoughtfully, and after a long look at the boiling seas in Redayre Bay, sat down beside the other window, the one which faced out to the west, the only one in Redayre House to face west, where the weather was coming from.

She was the first to hear a soft moaning in the wind, and then a sudden unholy shriek as it gusted, and her blood froze in her veins. She had only ever seen this once before in all her life, when the sea rushed in like a wall, faster than wild horses could gallop, and once, long ago, a whole village was engulfed in its fury and disappeared. Houses and families and animals had been sucked out on its backward draw, lost for ever in the ravening quick-sands of the Solway Firth.

But now it was boiling and raging like a devil un-leashed, its fury lashed by the tearing wind, its howls the howls of the hounds of Hell. And high up on the cliffs of the Head were sparks of light, tiny will-o'-the-wisps, all moving and dancing. Those were men with torches, she realised. But of the large yellow light of the Redayre beacon there was no sign.

Barbara surveyed the vicious cauldron of Redayre Bay with a strange calmness, cold and calculating. Betsy could not be involved again, not tonight. This was something she must do alone, and with her face set grim and pale, she put on her cloak again, and slipped out of the house by the little secret door of the closet, for Jack had never asked for the key back again.

It was blowing hard, and now the storm-clouds had opened to release their driving rain, and soon her hair hung in wet strings for she could no longer hold her hood on, and even her bodice was soaked through in minutes. She came to the gully in the shelter of the trees, where she had walked with Sibylla, and tried to find the path, putting out her hand to touch the bank, for she could not see more than a few yards in front of her. Her fingers came at last upon stems of sodden grass and the grit of sand in front of her, and she climbed up, stumbling over stones and scraping her legs with hot searing pain.

Once upon the high bank, the roaring of the surf became thunder, as it crashed down upon the shingle, and the stones screamed as they scattered and dragged back with the sea. In the darkness the white froth of the spume rearing up and back marked out for her where the cove of Yawkins' Hole was. Somehow she must climb up around it and onto Redayre Head, where the beacon was—where Jack was, too.

She began to creep forward uncertainly, foot by foot, climbing up all the time, grasping tufts of grass and pulling up her body over the slithery slopes. She must keep the edge at least three feet away on her left hand, for if she slipped she would fall on the rocks in the raging seas below. Yet she could no longer see the curve of the Cove, if she kept further away from the edge.

Up here the rain was pitiless. Once, she thought she saw a light up ahead and put up her hands to push her hair back, and because of this did not see the dark figure crouched half in a ditch in front of her until she crashed into him, and the breath was knocked from her body.

She stared up into the face of Alan Kerr, his fair hair now black strings dripping down his forehead.

'Oh, thank God,' she said. 'Thank God it is you!'

'Miss Barbara,' he said, staring at her out there in the screeching storm. 'What in God's name are you doing here? Does Sir John know about this?'

'He soon will,' Barbara said. 'Take me to him directly!' And when he hesitated, 'Don't be a fool, Alan. I know he is out here somewhere, and I shall look for him myself if you don't show me.'

'Then I hope it is something of importance, Miss Barbara, at a time like this.'

'It is important. And it is because of a time like this that I am here. Would a lady do any such thing in the usual way?'

He laughed, 'Come on, then, it is this way,' and dragged her on, and round, to the other side of the Cove where there was a dip in the land, and they had to climb down almost to the level of the sea. After a while her eyes became accustomed to the gloom, now that the rain had eased to a miserable drizzle. She could make out the rocks almost at the water's edge, and the shadowy figures round them.

Alan Kerr dragged her down, and muttered, 'Oh Lord, get your head down, Miss Barbara. There they are—the wreckers! Now the time is coming!'

'What do you mean?'

'We can go no further at present, to spoil Sir John's plan. Our men are dotted all around. He is here somewhere himself. Keep your head down, and be quiet.'

Then she saw that the shadowy figures around the rocks had faces, pale faces, every one turned out towards the foaming sea, silently peering and waiting. Something in their crouched stillness was infinitely sinister to Barbara, so few yards away.

From out of the blackness all round there was a faint slithering noise, and then Jack was there in the hollow with them, his face hard and set.

'What the devil is she doing here, Alan?'

'She appeared out of nowhere. She said she had a message she must give you.' When she looked up again, Alan Kerr had melted into the dark.

'God save you, Barbara, I could not believe my own eyes when I saw you! Do you not know the danger here, on this hellish night?'

'It is worse than you know,' she answered in a whisper. 'I have found out the wreckers' master, the one who plots it all, the ringleader.'

'It is one thing to know, and another to prove. Oh,

thank God,' he said, lifting his head. 'They have repaired the beacon, and set on the light again.'

'I have the proof, Jack, in my bedchamber.'

'What proof, hang it, Barbara?'

'Maps and plans I took from the North House! Pray do not argue about it now—I am too miserable, and too wet.'

He clapped his hand over her mouth. 'Lie still for God's sake, Barbie. It is all beginning now,' and they heard the fast hoof-beats of a horse coming up behind them, and then going past, scattering the loose stones on the path down to the sand and over to the little knot of men. At once it seemed to Barbara that a hundred torches flared into light, in a ring round Yawkins' Hole, and then they were descending, drawing closer and closer together, as they converged upon the little beach beyond the cave where the waves boomed and surged deep inside.

The torches lit up the faces of the men, and the long flapping cape of the horseman and his reddish hair. 'He must have lost his flat hat somewhere. Perhaps the wind blew it off,' Barbara found herself thinking foolishly and inconsequentially.

'Come! We have him, and all the rest, at last,' Jack said, dragging her up to her feet, and scrambling over the rocks.

But with a shout of fury the little group of men, five of them, leapt into a boat bobbing round from behind the rock, and in a scramble for oars began to row desperately out to sea. At the same time, Browne Faulks turned his horse into the breakers alongside them, got beyond the ring of light, and disappeared into the foam.

'They are lost and drowned, for certain,' Jack said. 'And now the Fox will never be brought to justice. I shall never have his brush.'

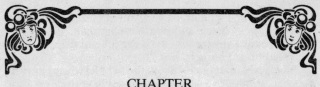

## CHAPTER
## NINE

'THE FIRST thing to be done is to get you out of those wet clothes,' Jack said, and carried her in his arms up the little staircase and through the closet into her room.

Barbara stood shuddering and dripping on the mat where he had set her down in front of the fire, while he lit her candle and threw another log on the ashes in the grate. Her hands were too stiff with cold even to unclasp her sodden cloak, and he moved over to the washstand and whipped off every sheet hanging from its rails, and set them on the hearth.

'What are you going to do?' she asked through chattering teeth.

'Undress you, of course.'

Nothing could have been guaranteed to set the blood coursing through her veins faster than those words, and her cheeks burned with flaming colour under his gaze. Furthermore, she found suddenly that she had got back the power of speech, for it was easier to speak than remain silent before those strange crystal eyes looking at her in that disturbing way.

'I am not a child any more,' she said.

'Indeed, I am very well aware of it. You have demonstrated that to me on more than one occasion, as I recall.'

'And I believe I can manage to remove my own clothes,' she added, trying to ignore his meaning and undo the clasp at the neck of her cloak with fumbling fingers, and failing dismally.

'It has always been a mystery to me, that as they grow older, women become more helpless,' Jack observed, snapping open the clasp and peeling off the cloak.

'Besides,' she said, 'as a gentleman you should know better than to enter a lady's bedchamber, far less to attempt to disrobe her—even if she is your ward.'

'You know that you are talking nonsense, hang it, Barbie! What would you have me do? Leave you here to die of a chill in the middle of the night? Or shall I go and rouse Betsy, and thereby all the other servants, and so all the house?'

'No,' she said, and placed her hand on his shoulder to keep her balance while he pulled off her shoes and stockings.

'Hold up your arms, then,' he commanded, and unceremoniously hoisted her gown over her head. Before she caught her breath his lips had pressed a teasing kiss upon her cheek, and then moved with a sudden thrust to cover her mouth. Flooded with emotion, and the passionate desire to return his kiss, she felt his hands untying the ribbons of her petticoats.

'But you can't!' She pulled her mouth away. 'What are you going to do next?' Her voice trailed away uncertainly under the silver daggers of his eyes.

He laughed softly, and picked up a sheet, warmed now by the fire, wrapping it round her. 'No, not yet, Barbie, perhaps. But the time is coming, and soon, I swear it. Take off the rest of your things and rub your skin hard with the sheet.'

Barbara stripped to the skin under the protection of the sheet, and turned her back to him. The water dripped down over her arms and between her breasts, and she began to rub herself dry. She heard his sharp intake of breath behind her, and then she felt the glow from the firm friction on her back as he helped her.

'You have a beautiful body, Barbie,' he murmured. 'But I had not forgotten it, from the first time I saw you naked on the sands.'

She felt herself go bright pink all over. So he had seen her, after all. She snatched up her nightgown and flung it over her head. 'Thank you,' she said. 'Now I am warm and dry again, and perhaps it is better that you go and dry yourself off, too.'

'I intend to,' he said coolly, as he pulled off his clothes except for his tight black breeches, and began to rub down his chest. 'Although nothing would give me greater pleasure than to crawl now into that bed beside you for what remains of the night, I am afraid I can stay with you only a short time, Barbara, while we talk.'

He whipped a blanket off the bed, and pulled her down on to the cushions before the fire which had blazed up in a little shower of blue sparks, and spread the blanket round both their shoulders, so that they sat huddled together in a little tent, and she felt the same peace and contentment as on their midnight picnic.

'It will be dawn in a few hours.' He threw the words like a stone into a calm pond. She felt ripples of uneasiness breaking over her, and a presentiment of more to come.

'And then?' she asked.

'And then I must send for the dredgers.'

She received this news with a sickening lurch of her stomach. The dredgers! That meant exploring the terrible sands at the bottom of the bay. 'Then you believe that they all perished? That they are all lying there, drowned in the bay?'

'It is in case they are *not* all drowned. Five men escaped on that boat, and one other on his horse. I cannot rest easy until we have laid six bodies on that beach out there.' She shuddered at the gruesome picture in her mind, and he went on, 'If we find six of them, the wreckings and all our troubles are at an end, and I can begin to live a life of my own, even, at last, to asking that lady I told you about to marry me.'

'Oh,' Barbara said, her voice flat with despair, and thought how lucky the lady would be to live with him for ever. 'And if you do not? If you find only five?'

'That is what I fear, that we will find only five. But the sooner the search is made the better, now that the wind had eased. By dawn the sea will be running off, and the sands settling; because undoubtedly they will have shifted, we must work fast before they bed down hard in their new position.'

'Then you believe Browne Faulks escaped?'

'Like any other fox, he is too cunning to be caught easily. And now, Barbara,' he said, a note of sternness creeping into his voice. 'I want you to tell me of all your adventures at the North House. It is a question I should have asked you long ago.'

'But they were still continuing, until six o'clock tonight,' she said.

'Last night,' he corrected her, as the hour struck one on a thin high note, and she began to relate the events which led up to her confrontation with Kate Sharkey at the manse.

There was a silence when she faltered to an end. His hand, which had been resting round her shoulders, came down to cup her breast. 'You should have been born a boy, Barbie, as your Mama said. But I am so very glad you were not.' And beneath his fingers her heart raced at frightening speed. 'You have been exposed to so many dangers, my darling. None of it would have been allowed to happen, with my knowledge.'

A little pang of guilt darted through her. He did not know the half of it. With God's help he would never need to know. Jack bent down and kissed her very gently, and then with a determined effort, he rose and pulled her to her feet.

'Will you be all right now?'

'Yes, I shall be all right.'

'You are trembling, and near to tears.'

'It is just because I am cold and tired,' she said, with a little gasp of her breath, wishing fervently that he would hasten and go, so that she could give vent to her feelings, and sob out the tears behind her eyes. Why had he not waited for her? Why did he have to meet that other lady first?

'Get into bed,' he said, and when he had spread the blankets back over her, he bent down to look at her searchingly. 'It is not just just because you are cold and tired, Barbie. It is worse than that. I can see it in your eyes.'

'It is to be a weak, silly woman,' she burst out at him,

not caring any more, because the tears were spilling down now over her face, 'half-child, half-woman in your eyes, no matter what I do. And, worse still, to be your ward, for I cannot stop you doing what you will with me, as you constantly threaten. I do not even want to stop you, God help me. But this lady of yours, the one you will marry, you do not treat her in such a way, of course. But then, I forgot—*she* is a lady, and very beautiful, no doubt.'

She stared up bitterly at his broad shoulders, at his black hair, and his pale eyes which held such a strange expression now after her outburst, and felt completely desolate, as though her heart would break. Jack smiled and stroked her hair back off her brow.

'Yes, very beautiful,' he said, 'and never more so than when she is so angry that she must cry.'

And then he snuffed out the candle and left her alone. She heard the door close, the key turn in the lock, and knew no more until the morning, when she heard the key turning again from the outside and Betsy came in, her arms full of clean sheets.

'Good morning, Miss Barbara. Sir John left me your key, and said you would be requiring fresh linen.' Her calm blue eyes surveyed the sheets of last night, dirty and still damp on the floor.

'What time is it?' Barbara asked.

'Nine o'clock. I did not let you sleep too long. There is a lot of traffic in the bay today.'

Barbara rose and leaned out of her casement. 'So they are here, the dredgers.' She watched as the long flat boats plied busily back and fore, back and fore, with their dredges down, criss-crossing as they swept the sandy bottom of the bay.

'What are they looking for, Miss Barbara?' Betsy asked as she helped her to wash and dress, and Barbara told her the events of last night, because she owed Betsy that much at least, she thought, up to the point when she had entered her room in the company of Sir John. All the rest of the morning she watched, as the monotonous work went on. And then there was a signal, far out

beyond the rocks of Yawkins' Hole, and down below
Redayre Head. One of the boats stopped there, and
stayed for a long time before it raced for the shore. Two
men staggered from it, splashing through the shallow
ebb-tide, and she saw that they carried a heavy burden
between them. Then they laid out a body on the beach,
and returned for another, and another. 'Three out of
six,' she thought, and turned from the window with a
sigh. The dredging went on as before, a grim and grisly
business now that the summer gale that had whipped the
sea for twelve hours without ceasing had blown itself
out, and the sky was cloudless, hard and blue again, and
the sea was left quiet and strangely still.

For the rest of that day everything that was said to her
lacked reality, and after breakfast Margaret and
Mistress Flora looked after her, puzzled, when she went
out, for she seemed almost like a sleep-walker who did
not fully understand what was said to her. She met
Sibylla, cutting roses in the garden, with Fanny close
behind.

'It is dreadful, how it all hangs over us,' Sibylla said.
'Nothing will feel right again until the dredgers have
done their job and gone away.'

'Where is Jack?' Barbara asked.

'He is down there, dear. He will not be back until
darkness falls.'

But Jack did come back, just as the setting sun
dappled the water with orange and crimson, and
Margaret and Mistress Flora were in the thick of preparing their evening meal. Barbara saw him from her
window, and as he left the shore, the dredgers came
about and left Redayre Bay, for they had done all that
they could do that day.

She ran out to meet him as he crossed the lawn. 'What
has happened?' she asked.

'It is as I feared,' he said, and the signs of strain lined
his face. 'We are not finished with it yet. They found the
five wreckers, but of Browne Faulks there is not a sign.'

'He was not drowned. He did not go any further out
into the sea,' she said with sudden conviction.

'I never thought he did.'

'Ah!' She gave a long sigh. 'Then you will need the papers and the maps from the North House.'

'Bring them to me, Barbara,' he said tiredly, 'in the library after dinner.'

The sky darkened, and the moon rose, and a small chill night wind whispered in the trees. It whirled away the smoke from the tall chimneys of Redayre House, and one by one the lights appeared in all the windows, as the candles were lit inside by the servants with their long tapers, held in cupped hands.

Betsy had piled the logs upon her fire when Barbara reached her room, and fetched hot water in the tall jug on the wash-stand.

'What gown shall I lay out, Miss Barbara?'

'I shall wear the blue wool dress,' she said, and then because a feeling of things still to come, but yet a separation, stole around her heart, 'and the sapphire pendant Sir John gave me in Dumfries.'

There was no more said, as the washing and the dressing, and the brushing of her hair was accomplished, until Barbara stood before the mirror, ready to go downstairs, touching the dark sparkle of the sapphires in her ears.

'You have changed,' Betsy told her. 'You are older.'

'I can see that for myself,' Barbara said as she took the papers from the drawer.

He was waiting in the library when she brought them to him, and sat down beside the fire. 'I watched you all through dinner,' he said, 'with that sad, thoughtful look upon your face.' He spread the papers out on his desk.

She smiled back at him, but did not answer, and leaned back upon the couch, watching how his lean, strong fingers smoothed out the creases in the maps, and the way a little line of concentration gathered between his dark brows as he studied them intently, and a silence fell, broken only by the occasional hiss of a log as it slipped down into the embers and flared up for its brief spell.

Her Mama had lived here, she reminded herself. Walked into this very room, and sat perhaps on this very chair. But the man she had loved had not sat behind the desk like that, his elegantly dressed figure so imposing, but had belonged outside beyond those windows, about the farms and stables of Redayre, his arms strong enough to crush a slip of a black-haired girl, and his eyes as blue as the summer sky. Mama should not have married him, Barbara realised suddenly. It was not true that there was only one man in the world for one woman. Especially if all the love was on the woman's side, as Grace's had been, and as now her own was for Jack Jardine. She sat up, straight and cold, her head clear when at last he spoke. She felt emotionless.

'It is of no importance,' he said, 'whether you understand any of it or not, for it need not concern a woman. And yet, I do not even believe that, myself, because you have a mind of your own, and a quite considerable brain.'

'Oh yes,' she said, and sat with her hands folded upon her lap.

'You did not believe for long that I was really a smuggler.'

'No.'

'But by engaging a ship from the Isle of Man, and hiring men to sail her, I brought some goods in, and I did indeed smuggle them into Yawkins' Hole. And all the Redayre men were with me.'

'Yes, so I saw.'

'And, bit by bit, we came upon the runners and the informers who formed the wrecking bands. We could have taken them months ago. But we did not, and all the time more ships were being lost, cast upon the rocks and more dead men going to the bottom.'

'Then why, Jack? Why did you allow it to continue?'

'To find the ringleader, the brain behind it all, who planned every wrecking, not only here at Redayre, but all up and down the Solway Firth.'

'And you have found him?'

'Oh, we knew it, long ago. But we could never prove

it. Not until now, and by his own hand, with these papers. And that was thanks to you, Barbara.'

'But still you are not satisfied, even yet,' she sighed.

'I had hoped to see him hanged for something else as well.'

'I know. The murders of your mother and father.'

'How did you know that?'

'It was from Kate Sharkey, that as well. She knew about it. And she hates Browne Faulks enough now to testify that he killed two people. I just didn't realise at the time who they were.'

'You have had your share of Kate o' the Vennel, Barbara. Now it is my turn.'

'Why? What are you going to do now? Where are you going?' she cried, as he gathered together the papers.

'The Fox has prowled these shores quite long enough. Now it is the hound's time to hunt, for him and for his vixen, too.'

'Can you not just let justice take its course, Jack?'

'That is exactly what I intend to see,' he said savagely. 'He will pay, at last.'

'How was it that he killed Sir Robert and the Lady Elizabeth?' she asked. 'Why was he not brought to justice then, at that time?'

'When we came upon the coach the shafts which hold the wheels had been half sawn through. From the time it left Redayre it was only a question of time before it came to grief, and they were both crushed. Alan Kerr, being on the outside, could jump clear. And the Fox was always hanging about the stables. He had been there for a long time that morning. But we did not see him, and we could prove nothing. No, I will see to it that he will pay, if it is the last thing I do.'

'The last thing I do', rang in her heart like the clang of doom. If Browne Faulks got to him first . . . She could not bear to think about it. She saw that in the end she would lose Jack anyway—if not to the other lady, then to murderers who would stop at nothing, and she was filled with utter despair.

'How long will it take?' she asked.

'For ever, if need be. But, if the gods are kind, perhaps only a few days, once I get the news I am waiting for now.'

'What news is that?'

'Which bolt-hole the Brown Fox has run into now; which den of vice.'

'It will be the same one that Kate Sharkey was heading for when she left here on my Snowy,' Barbara said, tearful as she thought of her horse. 'Poor Snowy, I miss him so much.'

'And where was that, Barbara?'

'She said it was to the camp of Sandy Powe.' Her mind was far away, still occupied with memories of her white horse, how he had obeyed instantly her slightest touch upon the rein, and galloped with her like the wind when she slackened it. She sighed, and shook her head sadly. 'I do not know who Sandy Powe is,' she said, 'except that he must be some new leader of one of the packs of Lingtowmen, and I think she said he lived somewhere north of Dumfries, up in the hills.'

Jack stared at her with an expression she found impossible to fathom. It contained shock, and disbelief at something she had said, and above everything else, a bitter pity. She found herself becoming nervous, even a little frightened, under his gaze, and crept back into the couch when he rose from behind his desk and came over to sit beside her.

'Oh, Barbie,' he said, taking her hands in his, and holding them so tightly that she understood in a flash, before he spoke again, that he was trying to protect her from his words, 'then now it must come out, for Sandy Powe will be caught with all the others. He will be hanged. It is only a question of time.'

'Why?' she cried. 'Why are you looking at me like that? Why are you telling me—warning me—about Sandy Powe?' She became filled with a dawning horror, a terrible suspicion. 'What has Sandy Powe to do with me?'

'Sandy Powe, Barbie. Powe. Powfoot. Sandy of Powfoot,' he said gently.

'Oh no,' she breathed, shrinking away. 'No, not Sandy. Not my brother.'

She felt a heat break over her, then drain away to leave her icy cold, and then Jack's face became a blur, and there was a singing in her ears, and for the first time in her life she fainted clean away.

She was lying flat on the couch when she came to, with Margaret waving something under her nose. It had a sharp and shocking odour, and she shook her head to escape it.

'There now, lassie,' said Mistress Flora, rubbing her wrists, 'you'll be all right. Just lie still for a wee while.'

Barbara found that she was unable to do anything else. Every time she tried to lift her head waves of sickness threatened to engulf her. Why were Margaret and Mistress Flora here, anyway? They had not been here before when Jack told her . . . when Jack told her . . . What had he told her? It was something dreadful, she thought dazedly, and struggled to remember.

The shocking truth came back to hit her twice as hard this time, and she looked round wildly for Jack through tears pouring down her cheeks.

'Why did this have to happen *now*?' she implored him. 'Now, when Mama could be happy again, at last! She must not be told.'

He came back, and took her hand again. 'It was your Mama who let me know,' he said. 'She sent word with James Aitken, when we saw him in Dumfries last Sunday. She hoped, and I hoped, that you would never need to know.'

'It is better that I should know,' she said, sitting up shakily.

'You are going to your bed now in any event. You have had too many shocks and you have been doing a great deal too much lately. You are in sore need of some rest.' Jack swept her up in his arms, and Margaret raced to open the door. 'Get Betsy,' he said over his shoulder as he marched towards the staircase.

She did feel tired, deadly tired, and as she caught a glimpse of herself in her mirror, she saw the great dark smudges underneath her eyes, and how pale her face was.

Jack laid her down gently on the bed, and kissed her, a soft brush of his lips upon her forehead. 'Here is Betsy,' he said. 'Just lie still, and she will undress you. Tomorrow you will not get up at all.'

Unutterably weary, she did as he said, and straightaway began to doze. She felt gentle hands move over her, was aware that she was tucked up under the covers, before she gave way finally to a healing blackness and blessed relief.


'Can you sit up now, Miss Barbara?' She heard the words dragging her back again into the world. 'You have slept peacefully for a long, long time. And now it is the middle of the day, and time to eat. See, Miss Margaret has prepared a tray for you.' Betsy plumped up the pillows behind her.

Barbara sat bolt upright as events swam back into focus. 'But it is Sunday, and we have not been to church.'

'There is no minister to preach in it,' Betsy reminded her.

Left alone, Barbara surveyed the tray. Little forcemeat balls with thinly carved lamb, and a dish of fluffy apples. It was one of her favourite meals. She set the tray down carefully at the foot of her bed, and swung one leg out.

'Na, na, lassie! Back in you go.' Flora's voice was behind her. 'You're not to get up before the evening meal, if then, and I am here to see to it that you eat this one.' She replaced the tray firmly under Barbara's nose. 'Come on, now! Eat up, for today there is good news to tell you. James and your Mama and the twins will arrive next Sunday, to stay for a week before their wedding.'

'Next Sunday! Oh, Mistress Flora!' Barbara cried happily.

'And in two or three days a new minister is coming, to see if he will like it here at Redayre, and if the people like him.'

'Who is he, do you know?'

'It's Mr Favenel. Sir John is laughing a good deal, and Sibylla is quite excited.'

Barbara considered the dizzying speed of this event. 'They will be married, and live happily ever after,' she said with a sigh.

'You seem to be doing quite well in that direction yourself,' said Mistress Flora, and threw back her head and laughed. Barbara could not resist her. Their laughter echoed in the room, peal after peal of merriment, until their eyes ran with tears.

'Wh-what are we laughing at?' Barbara gasped.

'Your night-shirt,' Mistress Flora said, wiping her eyes.

'What night-shirt?' Barbara asked, glancing down at her nightgown, to find it was not a gown she wore, but one of Jack's shirts, the white one with the wide balloon sleeves, and it was open near to her waist.

'Oh!' she said, her face scarlet. 'He did that for devilment. But Betsy was here all the time,' she assured Mistress Flora, who smiled again, then broke into laughter, and once again they were submerged in gaiety and giggling, and Barbara held her aching sides.

'I feel much better now,' she announced.

'Then eat up,' said Mistress Flora, 'and towards evening you can rise. But tak' your time and dress bonny, for that same fine gentleman is pacing the floor downstairs, waiting for you to get better.'

Afterwards, Barbara leaned back in her bed and made up her mind not to think of unpleasant things any more. Browne Faulks had gone, and for that she could only feel thankful, whatever became of him. Kate o' the Vennel had gone too, and would never be seen again, she hoped. And as for Sandy, he would come to a bad end, she thought with a shiver, but he had brought it all upon himself. If he had turned out good instead of bad he would have been in Starlochy now, the master there.

Starlochy! In one week's time she would see her family again. In two, she would see her Mother wed. And then perhaps Margaret, having cooked her celebration meal, would consent to marry John Reid at last. Margaret would leave Redayre, she realised. And if Sibylla and Philip Favenel married next, there would be only one Jardine left in the great House, Jack himself. She lay and watched as the dying sun slipped further and further down outside her west window, until it vanished out of sight and left the sky a hazy orange-red, and the evening star began to flicker.

'Who undressed me last night, Betsy?' she demanded, when her maid entered to get her ready to go downstairs.

'I did, of course, Miss Barbara,' Betsy said primly.

'Was this Sir John's idea?' she asked, pointing to the shirt.

'He said you needed something to cheer you up, Miss Barbara. And it would serve to remind you of your future.'

'Oh, he did, did he?' she said, flinging back the bedclothes. 'We shall see about that.'

She sensed the atmosphere of subdued excitement as soon as she entered the dining-room. To Barbara it had never looked so elegant before. Fresh candles had been placed in all the sconces round the walls and glowed long and tall in the candlesticks up and down the table, and around them Sibylla had massed the late roses in huge bowls. She felt a fierce pride for the old house of Redayre, for the kindness and the grace of all who lived there. For the first time in her life, she felt completely at home.

'How beautiful it is,' she said, as she went towards the little group of Jardines grouped round the fire.

'I do not know how we are to deal with it, Barbara,' Jack said, rising to his feet at the sight of her, his eyes possessing her so that her heart thudded, as it always did at the very sight of him. 'For it seems there is nothing but romance in the air. Now it is Sibylla's turn. She is fairly swooning with delight at the mere mention of the next incumbent at our Kirk. Mr Favenel has been called, it seems.'

'Pay him no attention, Barbara,' Sibylla said. 'He has been teasing me unmercifully all day, and it was he himself who called him to the charge in the first place.'

'But where will he stay?' she asked, as they took their seats, and the picture of the dirty smoke-filled kitchen of the North House flitted before her eyes.

'He will stay here,' Sibylla said, 'perhaps on Wednesday, until we see.'

The bantering continued, and once a little draught blew all the flames of the candles sideways, with tiny plumes of smoke, before they righted themselves again to burn up brighter than before, 'They are like the Jardines themselves,' she thought. 'They will always survive, however tenuous their hold seems, here at Redayre,' and she looked at their faces, Margaret's so plain and rosy, and so happy, Sibylla's so gentle and serene, and Jack's so commanding at the head of the table. No, he would never give in, never give up Redayre and their way of life, he prized it above all else, she saw, as his teeth gleamed in a laughing retort to Sibylla, and Barbara leaned back in her chair and admired the Master, the Lord of Redayre.

And then his eyes found hers, down the length of the table, and dazzled her, pierced her through and through.

'We will go riding tomorrow, you and I, Barbara,' he said casually. 'He is not so fine as your beloved Snowy, and nothing like him, but he is a loveable and good-natured creature, our old Dapple.'

There had been a tiny speckle of frost, a sparkling trifle through the night, enough to make her stir and hug the blankets round her in her dreams. But the morning was magnificent, fresh and alive, and everyone in Redayre was up and about early, the dogs barking with some excitement in the courtyard, and a quiver of bright cool air through all the house.

'We shall turn our faces to the east,' Jack said, 'and go to visit Squire Marchbanks and his lady. It is sadly overdue.'

They walked the horses at a gentle pace, and the air blew in their faces, bright from the east.

'We have not got over it,' Mistress Marchbanks assured them in the morning-room over coffee. 'We had set our minds on asking you, at the Kirk yesterday, to come to our little party next Saturday night. What a disgrace to have no minister!'

'We shall have one next Sunday,' Jack said. 'And we will come to your party. We are in sore need of one. Tell us about it, pray do.'

'You picked the right one there, I always said it,' Squire Marchbanks said to Jack, when he came in, and eased himself into the spindly chair next to his wife. 'Damme, she is more beautiful than ever! Her lines are beginning to show! Can't beat breeding, eh?'

'Really, George! You must forgive him,' said his scandalised wife. 'He grows worse with age, Barbara.'

'She has the makings of a Jardine, certainly,' Jack said, and as Mistress Marchbanks poured out the coffee into tiny fluted cups, Barbara could not decide if he spoke with derision, or pride, when he said it.

And then, on Wednesday, Mr Favenel arrived, tall and slender and bespectacled, and was deposited upon the steps of Redayre House. Sibylla took charge of him immediately.

'Take his bags,' she directed Nessie and Jean. 'Come, Philip, and I will show you to your room.'

Nevertheless at dinner that evening, listening to his conversation at the table, for such a gentle gentleman Barbara decided his looks belied him. If Philip Favenel accepted the charge at Redayre, it would all be very different from the days of the Reverend Mr Faulks.

'But first, tomorrow, you must see the Kirk,' Jack said, 'and, sad to say, the manse of the North House. It was a fine house once. But go with Sibylla, and then you must tell us what you think.'

Breakfast at Redayre was always a solid occasion. Barbara lifted the silver lids of the ashets uninterestedly, as Jack lounged at the fireside, to discover ham under one, and pork chops under another, and there were cold meats, and fish and a ring of boiled eggs. She chose an egg, poured out a cup of tea, and took them to the table.

'Philip and Sibylla have gone to see the North House already,' he told her, 'and there is no other news. And I see you do not eat much; I have observed that already.'

'It is every woman's fate to marry,' Barbara answered crushingly, 'sooner or later. Few gentlemen would choose a bride who is too fat. Besides, this is all I care to eat.'

'Your shape, I assure you, is delightful. So you do intend to marry, do you, Barbie?'

'Not in the foreseeable future. Perhaps when I am old, nineteen or twenty.'

'As old as that?' Jack's lips twitched. 'But that's a very long time away. Too long, would you not agree? We must postpone this interesting discussion, however, for I see they have come back.'

'The North House is in a shocking condition, Jack,' Sibylla cried, removing her bonnet on the way in, and fanning herself with it in an agitated manner. 'Have you seen it recently? Mama would be so shocked if she saw it!'

'And yet it is so fine a building,' Philip said. 'It could be restored quite easily.'

'Do you think you will accept the calling, then?' Jack asked.

'I believe I shall, providing the congregation accepts me.'

'Then let us all go back there now, and see what can be done, and how you would have it arranged, Sibylla. I take it that you intend to make the North House your home?'

'Oh, Jack,' she said, and flung her arms about her brother's neck. 'I have always loved the Willow Walk, and the house in the trees!'

'Well, then, let us go and open it up. It will be in need of some fresh air, I do not doubt.'

The back door still hung open when they arrived— Barbara wondered if it had been open ever since she and Kate Sharkey had run out of it. They walked in through the dimly lit passage, cheerless with its cold stone flags and narrow rickety staircase, leading up perhaps to the servants' rooms, and entered the squalid kitchen.

'Faugh! The room smells like a pig-sty,' Jack said,

fumbling with the catch. It was jammed, of course, with lack of use, and probably had not been touched for months, and then he flung open the window to let in the sun and the fresh air.

'It would be better knocked down,' he said, looking around the shambles with distaste.

'Sibylla will have a new kitchen,' Philip Favenel said decisively. 'This one has the smell of evil about it, over and above the stench.'

They went about the house, opening up doors to rooms which seemed to blink their eyes, and come awake in surprise, for no foot had crossed their thresholds for so long. The stuff upon the chairs was faded, the curtains hung full of dust at the windows, and there was a smell of decay about the place, and soot, where it had tumbled down the chimneys and spread out across the floors.

But the long front rooms were graceful in their proportions, and from the upstairs windows the sea was a shining ribbon far below.

'Our carpenters can start tomorrow,' Jack said.

'After Sunday,' Philip smiled quietly. 'After that we can make a start, perhaps, if I am accepted here. And I am not a poor man, Jack. The workmen will be paid, and Sibylla can buy whatever furniture she chooses.'

He would be accepted, Barbara thought, for here was a man who commanded both trust and respect. How could she once have attributed them to Browne Faulks? She watched Sibylla and Philip wandering off hand in hand into the garden. Yes, they would be happy here at the North House, she thought, sighing.

'So sad, Barbara?' Jack's hand was on her shoulder, his voice in her ear, 'Or do you see ghosts?'

'Together, Philip and Sibylla will exorcise them,' she said.

'Yes, together. But then, that is what marriage is about, is it not?'

## CHAPTER
## TEN

Two days came and went, days without hours or minutes, and during them she must have dressed and undressed, gone outdoors and eaten at the table, and all the while it was as though she were in a dream, a world of unreality, as though she stood outside and saw herself, some other woman they called Barbara. She had watched her in the mirror, this Barbara, in an emerald silk dress, with its plain green sleeves and its tartan ties, someone who looked like her Mama, saw her leave the house and sit in the coach with Jack, and Sibylla and Philip, and Margaret and John Reid, heard her speak to them, laugh with them, and go to the party at Squire Marchbanks's house.

But she did not think of it, there were no thoughts in her head. At one time she looked down from the little gallery which ran right round the Squire's hall, and she admired it, as she would a painting or a beautiful scene, but she felt no part of it. The floorboards gleamed pale honey in the soft candle-glow, and the ladies seemed to her like flowers, crimson and pink, carnations perhaps, when they sank down in their curtsies, their skirts billowing, before the gentlemen.

And then there was another time, as she danced with Jack, that she knew she spoke and smiled, for he was smiling down at her, and his grey eyes were laughing and tender, and she felt as insubstantial as a feather, floating, floating, as all the other ladies watched, and spoke behind their fans.

She recalled she went to Redayre Kirk with them all, next morning, but if it was warm she did not know it, or if it was cold she did not feel it. She listened to the voice of

Mr Favenel as he preached from the pulpit, and she did not hear a word. Up there he was no longer Philip, who would marry Sibylla soon. He was part of the unreality, calm where there had been so much rage before, gentle where there had been so much cruelty, and when his eyes shone down on them, they shone with God's love, they did not glow and burn.

But she did not listen to his sermon. She could not, for the thing that was preoccupying her mind came out in that serenity, and stared her in the face. Only a few hours now, and Mama would be here. Only one little week more, and Mama would be married. And what then? Would Mr and Mistress James Aitken take her back with them to Starlochy? Were these to be her last few days and nights in the house she now thought of as her home, in Redayre where she wanted to live for ever, with Jack, for the rest of her days? But no understanding came to her that morning, and when she left the Kirk there were still no answers to her tortured questions, and at three o'clock she found herself upon the steps outside the front door of Redayre still in a dream, when a coach drove up and stopped, the horses steaming in the still air, and she heard Jack say, 'The Starlochy coach, Barbara. Your Mama is here.'

The Starlochy coach! But there had been no coach at Starlochy for many years—there had been no money for that—and this one was bright and shiny, and brand new.

Her twin brothers broke in upon her long reverie. They bounded out, so big now! Barbara could not believe how they had grown in so short a time. They halted, suddenly shy, Robbie standing in his accustomed place, one pace behind his brother, and searched the faces before them for one they knew.

She ran to them, and hugged them, and James Aitken was out upon the drive, laughing and letting down the little step for Mistress Grace to put her foot on as she alighted.

'Oh, Mama,' Barbara cried, and put her arms around her. 'What changes!'

'There is a change in you, too,' Mistress Grace said. 'A big change!' She turned to greet the others, but her swift, close scrutiny did not deceive her daughter. Mama had much more to say, and she would say it in her own time.

It came later, when they had put the boys to bed, and in that hour before it was time to dress for dinner.

'Come to my room with me, Barbie,' her mother said, and they went to Mistress Grace's old room in the middle of the house, almost above the front door of Redayre, where all her boxes had been unpacked for her and her gowns hung up.

'It is just the same, the same as the day I left it,' she said, and they stood together at the casement, and Barbara wondered what was in her mother's mind. Was it the ivy she had climbed down that she was staring at, or the ghost of the young man waiting below, on a night when the moon was out? Mistress Grace was swift to disillusion her.

'It was always the same, with you, my dear. You were born with an imagination far too vivid. You are too clever,' she said sadly. 'Sit here beside me, and tell me what you have been up to this time?'

Barbara received these words like a douche of cold water over her, bringing her smartly back to life and to reality. Her mother had never failed to have a perfect genius for it! She sat down with a sigh, and began to relate her story since she had left Starlochy, knowing full well it would not do to try to leave out any part of it, no matter how scandalous, not when Mama's grey eyes could see right through her, as they always had. Nevertheless there was one part of it, the most important part, she kept to herself.

There was a silence when she came to the end of it, while she awaited her mother's sorrowful remarks, but, to her surprise, none was forthcoming.

'All of that I could have expected, Barbie,' said Mistress Grace. 'That all took place a few weeks ago, when you were still a child. It is not important. But now you have grown up, you are a woman, and you cannot deceive your mother. There is something else you have not told me.'

No, she could not deceive her mother, Barbara thought, for she was the one who was clever, and could read her like a book.

'It is nothing,' she said, 'and now it is late, nearly time to go down and join the others,' and left to go across to her own room, to begin to dress.

On Monday morning Redayre House sat up, alerted out of its accustomed leisurely pace. It took on a sprightly air, as the people in it became so brisk, running here, running there about their business. Robbie and Jamie provided the background noises to all the stir, as they explored its corners and played out their fantasies together in the little world which belongs only to those who are born together, each sufficient unto the other, with no need of anyone else.

The workmen had made a start to the North House, and Sibylla and Philip were always there, constantly supervising, and, according to Jack, driving the men quite mad, while they debated between them the proportions of a window here, or the width of a passage there, and where they would position the furniture when it arrived.

'I do not believe it will ever arrive,' Jack said, 'because they spend so much time in wondering, and if it ever does, it will be sent back, because they will have changed their minds a hundred times since it was ordered.'

But it was in the kitchens of Redayre that the hub of activity was taking place, with two of the pantries cleared out and set aside, and there was the hard swish of the scrubbing-brushes as the little kitchen-maids scoured all the shelves to be in readiness to receive the food for the wedding feast, as it was prepared. Margaret's face took on a sterner expression, Mistress Flora looked a little anxious, and Mama and James kept out of their way. They went to visit the Squire in the coach, and old friends Mistress Grace had not seen for twenty years. Barbara went with the chambermaids. to open up the east wing and prepare it for the guests.

The day before the wedding the house was in a turmoil, with as much coming and going as if there were to be five hundred guests instead of the fifty they expected. Tradesmen and errand-boys called continuously at the back door, and Mistress Flora was at her wits' end and Margaret almost in tears over the straw and manure that were being tracked into the kitchen, in spite of the sheeted floor.

By mid-day a good deal of intemperate language was drifting in from the stable yard, where Jack and Alan Kerr and Joe were backing the horses out and into different stalls or over to the barns, to make way for the visitors' beasts, and indoors the staff were here, there and everywhere, laden down with great boxes of candles for all the rooms, or tottering piles of linen, or trays of wine-glasses with the inevitable nightmare crash as some of them met their doom.

It was while Barbara was with Sibylla, filling the great urns with flowers to place upon the pedestals between the long windows, that Jack came in and found her.

'It has come,' he said, 'the news I have been waiting for, and, as we might have expected, just at this most inconvenient hour.'

'When must you go, then?' Barbara asked, her heart sinking, and fear in her eyes. 'I have been dreading it.'

'Why?' he asked. 'Because of the wedding?'

'There is that, of course. But I was more concerned about your safety, where you are going.'

'And you care, do you, Barbara?'

'I care very much,' she said, turning away to hide her trembling lips. 'Of course I care. What would become of me without you? If I were to lose my guardian, I should have to return to Starlochy next week.'

'Ah,' he laughed. 'So that's it. Well, you will not lose me, never fear. And I will guarantee it, that you will not go back to Starlochy next week. Not unless that is your wish, of course?'

'I want to stay here with you, Jack, as long as it may be convenient, until the lady arrives to be your wife, that is.

I do not think she would care to have me living here as well.'

'No,' he said, laughing again. 'I don't think she would. We will talk about that when I return, however, for the longer I delay here, the later I shall get back.'

'When will you come back?'

'In time for some part of the wedding tomorrow, I hope.'

She wandered disconsolately down into the kitchens, and through to the pantries to admire the pots of marbled ham and potted pigeon, the bowls of brawn and shrimps, great dishes of trout in jelly and beef in cider, and a huge cured ham baked in a pastry crust. The bowls for the junkets and the strawberry fools still lay empty under their muslin covers, waiting until the morning, but Flora had excelled herself with her vast chocolate cakes flanking the bride's cake, and Margaret had baked the gingerbread fairings, and left some plain among the gilded ones, and the others iced with delicate traceries of sugar frosting.

'There is only this venison to roast when I get up tomorrow,' Mistress Flora said, and when Barbara went out to see what all the fuss was in the corner by the kitchen wall, she found Margaret directing the men setting up the spit for the roasting of the lambs first thing in the morning. It had to be just so, straddling the empty space in the bricks, where tomorrow a fire would glow and the fat could spit in it and run down over the cobbles.

Mistress Grace's wedding day dawned cool and misty, a vaporous autumn day, with the promise of the sun, not the hot, white sun of summer, more golden now, hiding behind veils of gauze.

Barbara dressed quickly in the other new day-gown they had bought at the Dress Collection, which she had been saving for this day, cream silk muslin with blue and gold ribbons, and she perched a tiny straw hat on top of her curls, and tied it with blue and gold ribbons to match. She spent the last hour, before the whole procession wound its way to the church on foot, in entertaining her twin brothers, trying to preserve their black silk breeches and small embroidered coats.

But there was no sign of Jack when the ceremony began, and Mr Favenel read out the words of the marriage service. He had not arrived by the time it had ended, and the large company had walked back to Redayre behind Mr and Mistress James Aitken and taken their seats for the wedding breakfast, although why it should be called breakfast, Barbara could not say, since it was by this time four o'clock in the afternoon. John Reid took charge of the ceremonies in Jack's place. Margaret smiled proudly at him, flushed and triumphant.

'Mama looks so young again,' Barbara thought, and smiled at her.

She sat, serene and happy in her grey gown trimmed about with pink, beside James Aitken. Yes, her Mama had recovered well. Her grey hair was scraped back no longer, but curled softly about her face, and the dreadful scragginess of her figure had filled out to a delicate slenderness again.

'She has accepted what is past, without bitterness. She will have a different life, a far better life.'

Yet there was a trace of anxiety about her mother when she glanced in Barbara's direction, all through the long meal. When the last toasts were drunk, and the chairs scraped back, and everyone sat around or stood in groups before they should go into the Long Drawing-room and wait for the dancing to begin, James Aitken detached himself from the circle he stood in, and made his way across to Barbara.

'I must speak to you, my dear,' he said, 'as privately as possible.'

Barbara's heart gave a gigantic lurch, and almost stopped beating. 'We can go into the library,' she said, leading the way.

'You must understand, Barbara,' he said, 'that I would do anything under the sun for your Mama.'

'Yes,' she said. 'I understand that, James. I did, when I left Starlochy.'

'She was as low, then, as any human being ever could be, with her husband dead, and to be humiliated into feeling nothing but relief because of it, and then Sandy running away into the worst of company on the top of it.'

'Yes,' Barbara sighed.

'But she had high hopes of you, my dear. She wanted you to have the life she might have had, here at Redayre. And not a day has passed when she has not spoken of you.'

He sat down beside her on the couch. 'But she fears you are not happy here, that there is something wrong.'

'Did she send you to tell me, James?'

'No, she did not. She does not know I am speaking to you now. But,' he went on, his honest face anxious and grave, 'I have wondered so many times, myself, if you have ever thought of Sandy. Because she does, every day, too. She is his mother.'

'I try not to, James,' she shivered. 'But it is like a nightmare. Once, we played together. We were brother and sister.'

'He is draining the blood from your mother's heart, Barbara. I can see no end to it. She will not give it up, this eternal grieving. And I am here to tell you that her daughter cannot cause her any more worry. If it will make you happy to come back to Starlochy, it will make her happy, too. And if she is happy, so am I. We leave the day after tomorrow, and your old room is waiting, as it was before. Your Mama always said that it was only for a trial period, this time at Redayre. Think of it as a holiday, and come back home with us.'

'I will think about it,' she said, as they stood up. 'Of course I will think about it, and I will give you my answer in the morning.'

The moon was not blood-red now. It had burned itself out, it was fading, and hung limp and uncertainly, trembling yellow. Barbara stared out of the long windows of the library, at the clouds which chased across it, and then it seemed to burn again, as if it were not finished, and there was still some fire left in it, after all. She tapped her fingers on the pane impatiently and glanced around the room. The hands of the clock crept so slowly, and she began to pace up and down, unable to control her growing premonition of separation and of pain.

How could she leave him now? After all the adventures? Before anything had been resolved? In one brief summer she had lived out all her life, the years before at Starlochy had vanished into the past, the years ahead of her stretched out empty, without interest. She had never lived or felt alive except in these three short months, and before her eyes, like unbidden ghosts, the actors who had played their parts in them were assembling again, in ever-changing scenes.

There went the carriage, rumbling and lurching in the rough roads by the coast of Galloway, towards Redayre, the girl inside with her dark ringlets behind her ears, and the gentleman opposite, laughing and teasing right from the start—one glimpse and they were gone.

And where the trees crowded down almost to the water's edge, a brown fox slunk out upon the little clearing, sniffing the air to find a westerly wind, his red eyes greedy and malevolent, but scenting only his hunter close behind, vanished silently into the rustling leaves.

A house formed next, with something of grandeur about it, even in the moonlight, and from its dark walls a solitary figure ran, with her cloak about her shoulders, and her hair streaming out behind in a dark cloud, running over to the rocks, to stand there gazing in dismay at a three-masted ship, a phantom riding at anchor. And the little boat stole out towards it, and shuttled back and fore from it into the black hole of a cave, and the man standing in the bows was dressed all in black, with silver eyes.

Once more the picture changed to become a real stage, with real actors to strut and pose, a woman stretching out her hands to a man with a head like a lion, mocking emotions she did not really feel, yet charging them into all who watched and clapped, and clapped.

The clapping turned to drumming, and down in the Pit a man with an eye for the ladies whom his friends called

'Rab' was different now, without his pretty, plump companion, and shouting in anger. He would go drinking in the inn along the High Street with his hot-headed cronies, the inn where once the light streamed out and two strange figures scuttled past.

But inside it was a cheery place for men to meet, and pause a moment, ale in hand, at the sight of a slim figure with a three-cornered hat upon his head and ill-fitting shoes upon his feet, who spoke in the ear of the pretty, plump barmaid.

And there, over in another corner, sat a wild red-haired gipsy woman who cursed and mumbled in her drink, and ran outside to return again, as in a nightmare, in another setting, where the dark-haired girl was bound and gagged before her, to lift a cruel glittering knife above her head.

A log fell in the grate, suddenly crashing in a shower of sparks, and Barbara shivered uneasily, although the night was mild. Jack had been away so long. In a few hours the wedding would be over, and she must go now, and stop her dreaming, and join in the celebration, no matter how heavy her heart.

'Hang it, Miss Barbara, where have you been hiding yourself all evening?' Squire Marchbanks said, as she came out into the hall. 'I am determined to be the first to dance with the most beautiful little lady in all Redayre.'

He beamed down at her, tucked her hand into his arm, and smoothed down the lace at the wrists of his velvet coat, green and a little rusty. 'Let us go into the Ball, my dear. I shall be the envy of every other gentleman there.'

And so the evening wore on interminably, until once she went and stood at the window, a little ajar to let in the fresh air, and thought she heard a dog barking at the back. She stepped outside to investigate and heard the hoofbeats before she saw the rider. It was Jack, and behind his horse another of quite a different colour, pale in the moonlight—It was Snowy.

She picked up her skirts and ran out into the night, and round to the stables.

'Joe! Joe!' she heard him shout. 'Attend to the horses!' The boy ran out from the revellers in the smoke-filled noisy barn, a girl still holding his hand.

'Oh Jack!' Barbara said. 'You are safe back. Thank God for that!'

'You are pleased to see me, then, Barbara?'

'You know how pleased I am, to see you both, you and Snowy. Is he unharmed?'

'Without a scratch, by some miracle. The wedding is in full swing, I see, but I still have one bit of business to attend. Get a wrap, Barbara, and come back out with me. I must speak to you at once.'

There was a grave note in his voice, and she felt a little thrill of fear, along with her excitement, as she ran to do his bidding.

Once they were free of the house she was no longer afraid, the air was soft and warm, and the gravel crunched under their feet, while high in the sky the moon had turned a paler shade. Nobody would be interested in them now, not tonight, and soon the strains of the music were far behind. They walked swiftly through the trees, and back to the little clearing where they had had their midnight feast of fish and wine, and Jack flung off his cloak and laid it down on the ground for her to sit on. She looked up at his face and saw that his expression was almost sad; he seemed to be disinclined for the moment to speak, as though he were choosing his words first, with the utmost care.

This may be, she thought, the last time I shall ever sit here and look out at the sea, with him beside me. And even this is only momentary, a fragment in time that will never come again, like the sands slipping through an hourglass. She picked up a handful of the sand beside her, and ran it through her fingers absently, while she considered how fickle they were, these Solway sands, how deceitful and how cruel, like the fates who had brought her here to Redayre, so that she must fall in love, before they sent her away again as if it had never happened and none of it had ever been.

Jack sighed softly, and took her hand.

'What is it?' Barbara asked, and began to tremble. 'You have something to tell me, and you do not know how you can say it. Is that it?'

'I shall tell you the truth, Barbara. As I have always done. And you are a very brave girl, as well as a very lovely and innocent one. Do not be afraid.'

She wished she could smile back at him, but her lips were frozen with fear.

'When I left Dumfries today, Mistress Sharkey was imprisoned at the Midsteeple, and clapped in chains. She is charged with murder on two counts.'

'Two counts? Whom did she murder?' Barbara cried, visualising Kate with her knife up-raised.

'I am coming to that,' Jack said gently. 'She was found, still at the camp of a tribe of packmen.'

'The Lingtowmen,' she whispered. 'Whose tribe?'

'It was Sandy Powe's,' he said. 'And first they found one body, the body of Browne Faulks.'

Barbara looked up quickly at the note of hesitancy in his voice. His eyes were unreadable. 'I knew she would kill him, if she ever caught up with him. She said she would.' She was shuddering. 'So Browne Faulks is dead . . . Yet you look so sad. Are you not glad that the Fox is gone for ever?'

'Oh yes, I am glad,' Jack said, but there was no pleasure in his voice.

'And the other man, Jack? Who was the other?'

'It was Sandy Powe, Barbara.'

The night grew darker, as they sat in silence at the awful news, and Barbara told herself, 'He was my brother. He is dead. And yet I can feel no grief.'

She tried to remember the little boy who had played with her when they had been the only two children at Starlochy, what it had been like when they paddled in the Solway and looked for shells, and when he had climbed the old apple tree in the orchard and pushed her in the swing.

Perhaps some day it would all come flooding back to her, and she would remember, and weep for him. But not now. Now it was all blotted out by more recent, more bitter, memories of her brother, and the bitter legacy he had left her, to be the sister of a criminal, and worse still, one who had come to such a Godless end.

The gentle Jardine family would not wish to countenance such a woman as that. She should not have been allowed to stay on in Redayre, in any case. It was what she had dreaded for so long, what had been in her mind and her heart for so long, all the unhappy past from which she could never escape.

She lifted her head calmly and looked out over the gleaming waters of the Solway Firth, how they rippled so delicately now over the shining sands, those shifting, dangerous quicksands, which were like the quicksands of this life that mortals live, and must try to steer a course across in safety, or else founder.

'Yet, he was my brother,' Barbara said with a sob.

Jack did not answer her with words, but pulled her to her feet, and swept her into her arms. 'You were not his keeper,' he said, and showered kisses over her face and shoulders, so that her bones turned to water and her heart almost stopped beating. She dragged herself away, panting.

'No!' she cried. 'I was not his keeper, nor just another like him, nor any of his tribe, nor one of his sluts, that you should use me so!'

He drew away from her in bewilderment. 'What *are* you saying, Barbara?' he asked grimly. 'Have I ever used you like a slut?'

'No,' she sobbed. 'But you must think of me like one, to kiss me and make me want you to kiss me all the more, when you are to be married soon, to that lady.'

'What lady, Barbara?'

'That lady, the one you have chosen to be the mother of your sons!'

She wrenched herself away from the only haven she had ever hoped to find in this world, and stood panting before him, her breasts heaving palely in the moonlight.

'How you must have laughed at me, your little ward, while you and she were together in Dumfries! For that is where she is, is she not? You go so often to Dumfries!'

'Of course. So much of my business is in Dumfries.'

'Yes. That is where I saw you first, coming out of the Globe Inn with Robert Burns and his paramour.'

'I thought you liked Anna Park, Barbara?'

'I do like her! Of course I like her!' Barbara said indignantly. 'She helped me to speak to Kate Sharkey.'

'You were not in the company of Kate o' the Vennel when you were in Dumfries!' Jack looked scandalised, and stern. Too late Barbara realised the looseness of her tongue. But now, what did anything matter any more? She had lost it all anyway.

'And the love of your life, Louise Favenel, helped me as well,' she added recklessly. 'She joined in the conspiracy.'

'Conspiracy? What conspiracy?'

'She disguised me as a man, and I went into the Globe Inn by myself!'

'*Barbara!*'

She watched the emotions chasing across his face: shock, disbelief, outrage and finally hilarity. He threw back his head in a roar of laughter. But Barbara did not laugh.

'It wasn't easy,' she said.

'No?'

'No, not even with Louise helping me, before she went off with Courteney Carrington,' she added with a touch of airiness, to show him she did not care what had become of the love of his life—although her heart was breaking.

It seemed to have the desired effect, for his face was serious again, and he was not laughing now.

'And those five guineas for the bonnets, Barbara?'

'Ah. The bonnets . . .'

'Yes, the bonnets. You did not buy any new bonnets, did you? What did you do with all that money?'

Her eyes fell beneath his stern gaze. She had forgotten about the money, and the bonnets too, for that matter. She had also forgotten how Jack could tease.

'I may as well be hung for a sheep as a lamb,' she said. 'What does it matter now? I used the money to bribe

Kate Sharkey, when Anna brought her over to Mistress Flora's house at midnight. I never meant to buy any new bonnets from the very beginning.' She looked away, across the sea.

'Ah, then you told me a lie.'

'I thought everybody knew that is the one thing ladies are allowed to tell lies about, their bonnets,' Barbara said, with dignity.

'You must forgive me,' Jack said, and she thought there was a suspicious quirk of his lips. But his reply was as grave as her explanation had been. 'I had no idea that there had been such an important gap in my education. But it is never too late to learn, and that is one lesson I shall never forget, I promise you. I shall never question my future wife about the price of her new bonnets.'

And then Jack laughed and could not stop laughing, until at last he gasped, 'Oh, Barbie, Barbie, I knew I was right to choose a lady with so much spirit, truly a Jardine already. And in any case, Louise Favenel is not the love of my life, never was, and never will be.'

'No?' Barbara said doubtfully.

'No. Louise is an actress, and who could ever understand an actress, except perhaps another actor? She is well suited to her Courteney Carrington. He is older than she is, and let us hope he will prove to be an anchor for her, in such an unstable way of life.'

'Then you believe women should marry men older than themselves?'

'I believe one woman I know should do so.'

Barbara sighed, with a sob in her throat, and Jack's arms went round her again and cradled her, and he laughed softly in her ear.

'It does not matter now,' she said brokenly. 'Soon I shall be away from it all, away from here. James Aitken and Mama have asked me to go back with them to Starlochy.'

'And you will go, Barbara?'

'Yes, I suppose so. In the morning.'

'Without finding out about the lady, the one I would not, could not, speak of until now?'

She felt sure that her cheeks had turned pale, now that the time had come when he would finally put her out of her misery, and tell her the very last secret. But strangely, here in his arms, even that did not seem so important now, not when her trembling had nothing to do with fear or dread any longer, but much more to do with the way he was tilting back her head and kissing her with sudden possessive passion, to make her feel so weak.

'Until I had set my house in order, I could not speak of her, far less to her, Barbara, and ask her to marry me,' Jack said.

'Who is she? Why is she not here now, then, this lady?'

'But she *is* here, Barbie, or very nearly, I believe. The petals of the rose are unfolding. Kiss by kiss.'

'She is either here, or else she is not,' she said, leaning back in his embrace, and doing her best to hold on to her logic at least, since everything else was deserting her at the sight of his eyes, flooded silver with laughter and glowing with love.

'Certainly, it does not feel like a tomboy any longer that I am holding in my arms. She has arrived at last, my Lady Barbara.'

He searched in his pocket. 'I have been saving this for so long.'

'What is it?' she asked, with the little box in her hand.

'The last of the Redayre sapphires, the ring to match your eyes. I knew I would give it only to you from the beginning, from the first minute I saw you, leaning out of your window in the High Street.'

He took out the ring, and placed it on the third finger of her left hand.

'Will you marry me, Barbara? Will you be my Lady of Redayre? I have loved you for so long!'

'Oh Jack, I love you, too! I've loved you right from the start!'

'You did not really think I would let you go, did you, my darling?'

'I did not want to go. I have never wanted to go away from you, Jack! I love you so.'

It was some time later that she said in a small breath-less voice, 'I am finished with all my adventures now.'

Sir John Jardine, Lord of Redayre, laughed softly and triumphantly, and turned her round with him towards the great house, and there in the paling moonlight shining softly over the waters of the Solway Firth behind them, washing in shimmers over the shifting sands, he said, 'I promise you, Barbara, that they are only now beginning.'